BETWEEN SEPTEMBERS

BETWEEN SEPTEMBERS

KEITH BLACKBURN

The Book Guild Ltd
Sussex, England

This book is sold subject to the condition that it shall not, by way of trade or otherwise, be lent, re-sold, hired out, photocopied or held in any retrieval system or otherwise circulated without the publisher's prior consent in any form of binding or cover other than that in which this is published and without a similar condition including this condition being imposed on the subsequent purchaser.

The Book Guild Ltd.
25 High Street,
Lewes, Sussex

First published 1994
© Keith Blackburn 1994

Set in Baskerville

Typesetting by
Formaprint,
Worthing, Sussex.

Printed in Great Britain by
Antony Rowe Ltd.
Chippenham, Wiltshire.

A catalogue record for this book is available from the British Library.

ISBN 0 86332 915 2

PART

1

1

'Teeh! Look at it. Sleepin' Beauty. Come on, lad, come on. It's all right. You don't have to worry. Your mother's gone out to work for us. You can get up now.'

The voice bounced about his skull. Unintelligible at first, it forced a way into his sleeping retreat and dragged him from the timeless and illogical dimension in which he had been about to solve a whole series of totally unrelated and intangible problems.

'What?' he mumbled in response. It was the first thing he could think of.

' "What?" he asks. What! Get yourself up and out of it, that's what, idle sod.'

Sleeping Beauty fought for wakefulness, eyes wide, straining at the eyelids to keep them apart and wondering at his father's sarcasm.

'All right,' came his own voice from somewhere beyond him, and his glazed eyes fixed to the ceiling while he yawned and snorted through his half-doped state. He then became aware of his father hovering over him, not going away, waiting till he was out of bed.

'Come on. Get up!'

'All right, I'm up,' he murmured, making a token gesture of shifting his position. Here he remained for the moment like a moth emerging from a chrysalis in easy stages, waiting for the lifeblood to flow and fill his wings.

His father made a sudden grab for the blankets. 'Up, sithee, up. Get your bloody self up.'

'I'm comin', I'm comin',' came the wail of protest and twisting away in a sudden burst of energy, Steve managed to clutch tight hold and retain his grip.

'Well, get out or I'll tip you out. Nearly ten o'clock here and you're still stuck in bed.'

Steve hoisted himself onto one elbow as a token promise. The old fellah was definitely in a grumpy mood. You could tell by his aggrieved expression, and the way he stood there pouring out sarcasms, threats and condemnations, and tutting in disgust. He was already in his overalls too, blue bib-and-brace ones which he wore over a maroon pullover, and was also sporting a white collar and brown tie. It indicated the morning was well underway and he was ready for the off, ready for business and ready to condemn all idleness and sleeping in. The entire world beyond his bedroom seemed wide awake and he'd been caught red-handed, not active, not wide awake, but wallowing in the midst of sleep.

'Look,' he said, feeling guilty and irritated, 'Gi' us a minute, can't yer?'

'Give you a minute? Aye, a minute to go back to sleep in. Eeh, I don't know, what are you gonna do with yourself, right fair?' His father gave another disgruntled remark then turned to leave. 'Anyway, you can hurry up and shift yourself. Alec Watkins is meeting me down yonder at half ten and we'll be needing some help.'

Steve forced a loud yawn and grimaced. God! Alec Watkins! Work! So much for any painting today. The momentum, the flow of ideas would be stopped.

He lifted himself up a little further, reaching an arm to the curtains to view the active wide-awake world outside. As his bed was by the window he had only need to lift himself a little way. Nothing too strenuous for a start. Out there, in the back garden, his mother's roses, like those of the neighbours, were still a showpiece of brilliant colour. He had watched summer progress through the garden, seen the flowers in their various order bud and shine brief light, but now all that was lovely in the garden was fading fast. It was holidays over, back-to-school time, back-to-work time, back to the descending nights of winter and the old routine. The day was misty, coming up sunny for another warm Indian summer one, yet summer had passed like a dream.

Work! Oh Gawd! He let the curtain fall, then reached for his blue, crumpled shirt, retrieving it from where he'd slung it the night before, amongst the fluff and dust on his bedroom floor. Working for a living, getting up at a 'sensible hour', that was all anybody could think about round here, yet this was the last thing he wanted to worry about this morning. Thrusting the shirt over his head without first removing his pyjama jacket, he groaned as he thought and suddenly remembered.

He'd tried. God, he'd really tried. Even when she'd taken on the role of insanely jealous female on seeing the blue nude, and accused him of having another girl in the studio to pose for him, he'd tried. He had thrown himself into a rage as towering as any that Modigliani might have given vent to, hurling his palette and a jar of turps against the wall with such force the jar had smashed to smithereeens, scattering glass and muddy contents everywhere. But fool that he was, when Rachel had broken down, kneeling and sobbing before him, her mascara coursing down her cheeks in two black streams, he had rushed to her, hugging and kissing her to quench the tears. Worse than that, he had once again declared his love. Damn it all and blast it to hell! She was so lovely to hold sometimes.

He unfastened and took off his pyjama jacket, and recoiled as the unavoidable fingers of cool air played along his skin. Tugging on his shirt, he glanced around at the chaos of his bedroom; books, paper and the various items of clothing spread out in a jumbled heap amongst the dust.

His mother was refusing to do anything with his room until he'd made some effort to tidy up a little. I must do something about it sometime soon, he promised. It had become another of those many wince-inducing elements in his life but he felt immediately bored at the thought.

'It takes you half a day to stir yourself out o' that pit of yours,' his father went on at him as soon as he was downstairs. He wasn't letting go.

'Look, there's no need for you to be so self-righteous and victorious,' Steve told him, pushing by in the narrow aisle between table and kitchen sink. 'So sherrep rabbitin' on.'

He dodged as his father tried to land him with a quick smack on the head. 'Missed!'

'I'm tellin' yer,' his father offered as a perfunctory warning. 'I'll dot you one if you talk to me.'

'Yeah, who wants to talk to you?' Steve retorted, and slammed the bathroom door behind him on any possible further retaliation.

Positioning himself in the cramped space, he peered at his reflection in the mirror, studying it in his half-awake trance. The pale boyish face which stared back at him was whiskerless, apart from the few downy bristles which sprouted from the chin, and except for the myopic appearance of the slept-late morning had a fresh, almost girl-like complexion. The blond hair flopped in a thick untidy mop which hung in front of his eyes. His hair had always flopped. Even back in the days when he'd attempted to style it into an Elvis quiff, piling on masses of Brylcream. It had never held for more than a few minutes, no matter what the tonnage of grease. Nowadays, since he had left off using haircreams, his hair hung where it chose, and if he combed it down at the sides for fun it almost covered his ears.

He lifted his head slightly, proud and arrogant, trying

to decide if there really might be any similarity of feature between himself and Modigliani — or what he'd seen of him in those grainy black and white photos in the book Rachel had borrowed from the library. In certain ways he could fancy that there was; perhaps a suggestion in the line of the jaw or the level of the brow; but then the bathroom mirror, coated as it was with a fine layer of dust from his mother's dabbing her face-powder, had a tendency to soft-focus and flatter. Perhaps, after all, it might be as Rachel's best friend Gillian had said of him, he was 'rather pale and insipid'. Aye, that was more likely the reality, pale and insipid!

'Jesus Christ!' He groaned quietly as a fitting comment on his life in general and, turning his back on his reflection, braced himself for a cold wash before the washbasin.

His father was placing slices of a very dry looking cheese under the grill when Steve emerged from the bathroom drying his face. Clearly they weren't all that ready for the off but still at the stages of preparing 'snap'. It was to be one of those made-do snaptimes too by the looks of it, no fresh juicy pork pies or beefspread sandwiches to punctuate the day, just toasted cheese. He hated the sight and smell of toasted cheese.

'You must have a gut like a cast iron tank,' he commented to provoke his father when he saw the yellow puss-like mess beginning to bubble on the slices of toast. The dry remains of cheese and the last of an old loaf for toast seemed befitting of the mood, part of his father's 'that way outness', a sackcloth-and-ashes reappraisal of their lives, a sorting of the hives.

His father refused to be provoked but turned the gas flame full on, keeping a close check to make sure that nothing caught light.

'Cor, bloody hell!' Steve tried again, making a great to-do of wafting at the air with the towel he was using. The grill was sending up clouds of acrid blue smoke.

'Open the door if it offends your sensibilities that much, your lordship,' quipped his father, busy at his task. 'Anything as long as we don't have you suffering any discomfort.'

'Well yes, that's the trouble with you,' Steve told him, throwing down the towel and opening the back door. He fanned it rapidly back and forth, symbolic of clearing the air. 'As long as you can grill or fry up your ruddy concoctions everybody else can go to hell. Never give a thought to anybody who might have to share with you at all. Well, I'm not havin' any o' that muck for me snap, so don't think I am.'

'Who's askin' you to have any of it? Shurrup making your clever remarks — and stop waftin' that bloody door or you'll put the gas out. Come and get your breakfast, if you intend havin' any, 'cos I suppose it'll be left to either me or your mother to wash up and clear away after yer like a couple of idiots.'

He turned out the gas under the kettle which was now boiling, then lifted out the pan from under the grill.

'Bloody twenty years old, and you've no more sense now than when you were a kid. It's about time you were finding yourself a job and clearing off for good, I'm thinking. All we ever get is a load of cheek. Same goes for all three of yer, from t'youngest to t'eldest, nothing but a load of cheek. And I blame you. You should be able to set a better example. But do yer? You think you can just come and go as you please, say what you like and do what you like and none of it matters. You're pulling the wool over our eyes, lad, pulling the wool over my eyes and your mother's eyes. Or at least you think you are.'

'What d'yer mean, pulling the wool over your eyes?' They had descended once more to a very delicate level of argument.

'What do I mean?' His father gave a brief chuckle and spread the melted cheese over the slices of toast. Then he looked at him squarely. 'I mean acting on the way you do, pretending to daub about down yonder with paintbrushes, allowing your mother to go out and work and slave for you when it should be you stirring yourself and getting out to earn a bit o' summat.'

'Work and slave? What d'yer mean, work and slave?' Something had obviously pricked his father's conscience somewhere along the line and he was taking it out on him, laying the blame at his door. 'My mam goes out to work because she wants to. It has nothing to do with me. She likes working at the blinkin' cake shop. She says so herself.'

He watched as his father rinsed out the thermos flask before filling it with tea. Shaking out the drips of water, he filled it with tea which was already mashing in the pot, pouring it carefully over the sink and trying not to spill. The hot liquid made a hollow trickling which tightened and faded as it filled to the top.

'And how can you say I'm just daubing about with paint brushes?' he went on, 'when it was only yesterday you told me I was doing okay? One minute you're all for it and the next you're like this. Nobody knows where they are with you.'

It frustrated and outraged him that his father should accuse him like this. His interest, his belief in his aspirations down at the studio meant a great deal. He couldn't bear for there to be any doubt. 'I want to do something with my life,' he stressed. 'I want to paint, not pull the wool over your eyes.'

'You can't eat paint,' his father reminded him quietly.

'I know that,' wailed Steve. 'Chrissakes, I know you can't eat paint.'

'Then try and see some sense instead of refusing to. Eeh, I don't know, God knows how you'll manage when you haven't me or your mother to ride on anymore. A sad sorry day it'll be for you when that happens. Same goes for our Ralph and Ian. There's no shifting yer. None of yer.'

He was fraught with his concern for his sons, that all three of them should have proved themselves to be so impractical. Sometimes he expressed his disappointment in them in more basic terms: they hadn't enough brains between them to 'take 'em to the lav.'

*

The mood of discontent accompanied them as they left the house, Steve in his old grey corduroy jacket with the torn lining and his father in his donkey jacket, and carrying an old leather shopping bag which he used for carrying tools. The main complaint this morning — apart from the ones to be made about useless selfish sons — was transport, or the lack of it. It was the car, gliding down the avenue, its wheels crunching over the gravelled surface of the road as it came, which started him off. The horn pipped as the car passed by them and his father acknowledged the driver, who waved.

'Aye, they're all at it these days, riding around in cars,' he observed ruefully as the car, a blue and silver-grey Vauxhall Cresta, headed on down the avenue to turn out into the lane.

Steve kept his head lowered, shoulders hunched and hands thrust in pockets, watching his feet pace the cracks and nicks of the pavement. He was wearing a pair of worn out Chelsea boots, black ones, which he used now only for working in. They had holes in them which let in the wet when it rained, and like himself of late, they had seen better days.

'If you'd bucked your ideas up a bit,' his father went on, 'and taken some interest in mechanics and learning to drive, instead o' messing about like you have, we might have been running a nifty little van or summat by now. Instead of that I'm having to chase folk round if I need a lift with a stone, or a bit o' sand and cement, having to rely on Alec Watkins and such, like I am now, hoping they'll remember to turn up.'

Steve grimaced. Mechanic! He was an artist, for Chrissakes, not a mechanic. It was no use telling that to his father at present though. He was 'that way out' for definite, at odds with everything, allowing himself to be even more swamped and overruled by the fickle values of the 'consumer society'. He was caught up in a world where the ability to mend a car or a telly or a washing-machine was considered next to godliness, where you got down to it, kept your feet firmly planted and your nose to the grindstone, and hopefully succeeded in making the grade. No time for dreaming and messing about with paint on canvas in these parts, lad. His father had returned to the pressures and obligations such a world imposed, and become firmly entrenched.

'Aye, they're all at it,' he reiterated, sighing. 'Everybody's got four wheels — everybody that is except us.'

The fact was obvious on all sides, constantly reminding him: the progress and affluence of others, the neighbours coping far better than he was in this new age of plenty, climbing the bandwagon, making a success, carving a niche, getting on. And their offspring too, the bits of kids Stephen and Ralph had knocked around with, all doing 'right well' for themselves, or on the right road towards doing so, and where there had been only rusting bicycles to ride on there were spanking brand new motor cars for them to park and polish and show off in front of their homes. All the while he saw himself left behind, left high and dry, losing out on the race. The question of transport, the lack of it, remained as one amongst the many thorns in his side.

'Only chance I had of having me own,' he grumbled, 'and you had to mess it up for me.'

Steve gritted his teeth. How many more times were they to hear that, how many more bleeding perishing times? 'It wasn't my fault, Dad. I've told you till I'm sick of telling yer. That bloody van Jack Thwaite had the gall to sell yer was a load of scrap. The engine was past it, and so was the whole damned lot. It was clapped out. Anybody could see that just by looking at it.'

The van, a five hundredweight Ford Thames, had been stuck in the yard down yonder for months and all it had been any good for was making love in the back with Rachel. (It had had a nice spacious wooden floor for that if nothing else.) He'd tried to make an effort, of course, when the engine had been temporarily mended by a chap his father knew at a local garage. He had even gone as far as giving it a lick of paint before the chap from the garage had taken both him and his father out in it with 'L' plates. He hadn't done a bad job at driving either — far better than his father who had flapped like a nerve-wracked old maid at the wheel and performed abysmally on the hill starts. It was simply unfortunate that on the evening during summer, when he'd borrowed the van to convey a load of boozed-up art students to an all-night party, the big-end had chosen to shoot through the crankcase. ('It's only pinking,' someone had suggested when the knocking began.) That stupid van! It had a row of nines on the clock and that was the second or third time round.

His father still remained unconvinced. He still held Steve responsible for the vehicle's demise and it all added to this morning's disheartenment and dissatisfaction he felt with his lot.

'I bet the neighbours have a right laugh when they're

driving by and see me cloggin' it still and waiting for buses. "Look," they'll be saying, "silly owd bugger there wearing his shoe leather out when t'eldest has been at college all that time." '

' "They"! "They"! You're always on about "they". They'll be saying this, they'll be saying that. What the hell have "they" got to do with it? What have "they" got to do with anything your're doing, or what I'm doing, or what we might be doing? God, I'm tired of hearin' you go on. Why don't you just shurrup?'

'Oh, I ought to shurrup all right. As long as you're okay to go about dreamin' with your stupid attitudes and your daft long hair.' He nudged him as though suddenly remembering himself. 'Here, sithee,' he muttered affronted, and held out the bag, 'cop hold o' this. Don't expect me to lug it all the time like a bloody fool.'

Steve took the bag from him, sighing, irked by the pestering, the querulousness.

'Just where d'yer think it's leading to all this? Answer me that,' his father said.

Steve looked sideways at him. 'What d'yer mean?' he asked banally, stalling the necessity to answer.

'When are you gonna find yourself a job, man? Damn it, when are you gonna find yourself some work?'

'I don't know. Perhaps I'll look in the *Times*,' he gave out, feeling more tired-eyed and unwilling than ever to contemplate his future. Finding a job, going out to work, earning a living! He was sick to the back teeth with hearing it.

He glanced around him at the rows of semi-detached houses, each practically identical to their own, which made up Willow Avenue. His home environment! Some of the houses were familiar still, their single bay-windows and their lead-windowed front doors once the significant landmarks of his childhood. Their gardens had been grassless trampled playgrounds surrounded by the smells of washed clothes and cooking dinners, their front gates cowboys' horses or broken wickets for cricket matches. The avenue itself too had been a playground, a wide motor-free expanse for Wild West fantasies, hot-rice, hide-and-seek, touch-and-pass, macker-fights, and who-can-piss-the-furthest contests. The road had seemed much wider then, but the sycamores, spaced along the neat grass verges on either side, made it appear so much narrower now, as did the neat trimmed privet hedges which crowded in. As for the gardens, they were cultivated, well-kept, compartmental, their gates mended or replaced, but shut and private and residential, no longer welcoming since those friends had vanished to the world of earning livings in their separate ways. All of it, the avenue of childhood, the memories it might evoke, was another part of his life well and truly at an end, and he felt totally detached from it, out of contact, as though that remembered life had nothing to do with him.

2

'Ninety Four', as it was referred to, or 'down yonder' as it was more often known as back home, was a squat, dilapidated stonebuilt cottage situated a quarter of a mile or so further down the lane. Ninety Four, so called because of the number barely still legible on the solid paint blistered door, had once been the cosy habitation of an elderly couple until certain structural manifestations had made it unsafe and unfit for living in. It had then become a workshop, first for Jack Thwaite, local builder, ex-van owner and business friend of his father's, then for his father who had bought the place from Jack Thwaite and been the unproud owner of it over the past twelve years.

The cottage was in bad repair. The walls bellied outwards from the foundations at an alarming angle while the ancient cement rendering which covered them was cracked and crumbling away in large patches to reveal the decaying stonework underneath. A concreted yard in front of the cottage had provided a useful area for displaying finished headstones or kerb-sets, but too many times the 'scroundrels at the back' had tested the durability of edges and corners against half-bricks and other items of throwable debris they could lay their hands on. Likewise with the windows, and when the glass had been replaced, then broken again, they had been nailed up with pieces of board.

Ninety Four was in for the same condemnation as everything else this fine morning, his father tutting in disgust at the overall picture of dereliction which greeted them as they entered the yard.

'Teeh! Bloody eyesore. It ought to be pulled down, the

whole damned lot.'

Steve lifted his eyes to the weathered and faded signboard above the door, feeling somehow that his father held him responsible. On the sign was the legend:

P. Verity A.R.C.A.
MONUMENTAL SCULPTOR
Stone, Marble, Granite.
High class lettering
Renovations.

He wondered how many people bothered to read the sign, or could see the faint black lettering as they sped by in buses or cars. Obviously they must or he would never have had the steady trickle that brought in the work.

At one time the capital letters had been enhanced with goldleaf but since those days of optimism his father's enthusiasm for signboard presentation had waned.

He was now searching with the same air of defeat through his jacket and then his overalls' pockets.

' 'Ere,' he sighed as the thought occurred to him. 'You borrowed the key last night. Give us it, if you haven't gone and lost it. Watching me mess about like this!'

There then followed a series of manoeuvres which made entering the cottage a task in itself. First a sizeable block of stone had to be shoved to one side. This had been set in place to discourage any would-be housebreaker from removing the plank which in turn had been wedged against a rusty sheet of corrugated iron. The corrugated iron rested against the door which had been secured finally with a sturdy padlock. Anything to make it awkward for 'them varmints and young scallywags at the back'. He had a great fear of burglars, but, paradoxically, great faith in his own measures of security.

The workshop was cool and damp, and smelled of the years of emptiness, cement and mildew. Immediately behind the door, and half hidden amongst a jumble of wood, stone and other such pieces of debris, was Steve's metallic blue Triumph Tigress 175.

The scooter too came in for its fair share of criticism. 'There's another white elephant an' all. They saw me comin' when I bought that. Ninety-odd quid down t'Swanee and for what? Just summat to watch go rusty.'

The flamin' thing had broken down. It had always broken down. Right from that day just over a year ago when he'd let Steve talk him into buying it from that ruddy second-hand dealers in town. Ninety-odd quid and only 3,000 miles on the clock, and who amongst them was mechanically minded enough to mend it? The thing was flat-tyred, in dock for the duration, and as neglected as everything else in the place.

Blamed again, and feeling guilty and responsible again, Steve surveyed the interior of the workshop with the same despondency as his father. The whole place needed a good cleaning and clearing out, but neither he nor his father had the inclination or the notion of where to begin. The walls, peeling and blistered through the generations of wallpaper and mostly brown paint, were splashed liberally with dried cement and sandstone slurry, and the stone flagging of an uneven floor was carpeted with stone dust, stone chippings and flattened empty cigarette packets. There was a zinc bathtub over in one corner, lodged against a rusty black bicycle which had flat, rotted tyres and no chain. (The bicycle had been his only really reliable form of transport, apart from a wheelbarrow, and even this had given out on him.) The tub was surrounded with a conglomeration of empty bottles, jam jars, biscuit tins and baby-milk powder tins from the postwar years, and filled with newspapers and children's comics — Hotspurs, Dandies, Beanos, Suns and Comets — the residue of childhood years, damp and discarded and covered with a residue of dust.

The main trouble was his father was a hoarder. He

believed in keeping everything, no matter how apparently useless or rusty it might be. You never knew, he claimed. It might come in handy some day.

Steve glanced over at the broad iron fireplace with its range which had held simmering saucepans, and the oven with its thick iron door. All was rust-covered now, the range and the oven providing crevices for more of his father's junk. Along the dark brown mantlepiece he and Ralph had scorched their names in the paint, using a red hot poker. Underneath they had scribed the year: 1956.

'And Lord knows how we'll get this up yonder,' his father murmered, stroking his hand over the polished black granite headstone which awaited delivery, courtesy of Alec Watkins. 'Up yonder' in this instance meant the churchyard at the top of Lindlethorpe hill.

The headstone was supported on an upturned beer crate in the centre of the room, and leaning against a carpenter's work-trestle with a piece of folded sacking to cushion it at the back. The gold leaf in the sharp, clean-cut lettering gleamed against the metallic black hardness of the ebony granite. The bright cleanliness, its precision, looked incongruous amongst the clutter of rubbish and dust.

'We've only got to knock one of these 'ere corners,' he added, worrying prematurely at the thought of lifting and transportation, 'and that'll be nigh on a hundred and fifty smackers down t'Swanee an' all.'

Steve gave out a loud sigh. His father was for ever talking of possible monetary losses as money 'down t'Swanee', though he had no idea why he should choose his losses to float down that particular river.

His father noted the sigh.

'Oh aye, I know I shouldn't expect any sympathy from you. You're too busy goin' about with your head in the clouds to be bothered one way or t'other.' He pushed unceremoniously by, taking a couple of chisels to sharpen on the grindstone in the other room. 'Go on, shift outa the way.'

Steve listened to the whirring of the little hand-operated grinding wheel coming from the backroom, and the ring of steel against it. Having wondered whether to give some quip in retaliation, he had decided not to bother. This was obviously 'one of those mornings' where everything was designed as a conspiracy against his father and where everything that could go wrong would go wrong. He had to accept the fact, grouchy mood and all.

He idly picked up a joke postcard lying amongst the junk on a rickety table behind him. A cartoon showed a little girl with her mother observing a fat sow feeding her piglets. 'Oh, look mummy,' the caption read. 'The little ones have got the big one down and are biting the buttons off his waistcoat.'

He read again, as he had many times, the message written on the back: '. . . weather lovely, though it rained Tuesday. Been sunbathing today. Love, Aunt Hetty and Uncle Arthur.' The George VI stamp was franked, and almost obscured with black: Bridlington July 1951.

The postcard brought a silent memory of summer holidays long gone, the door of the workshop wide open and the sunlight blindingly bright in the yard, and he and Ralph making roads for Dinkies or sandcastles in the pile of builders' sand. How many years ago was that? He was twenty, would soon be twenty one. Thinking about it made him feel old.

He replaced the card carefully from where he'd picked it up, amongst the chisels, pop bottles and tins of rusty nails.

'Nipping upstairs a minute,' he called out towards the backroom above the whirring of the grindstone.

'Don't get carried away up there now,' his father told him, coming back and testing a sharpened chisel against his finger. "Alec Watkins'll be here any minute.'

Steve refused to wait and opened the staircase door which rattled and creaked noisily on its hinges.

Seeing the blue nude as soon as he came up the stairwell into his studio, and the broken jam jar and the turps splashed everywhere, made him cringe. The day before, when his father had been in a good mood and they had worked to the music on the wireless, the painting had rewarded him with a sense of achievement and satisfaction. The nude had emerged from the uncertainty of the struggle, its formalized figure glimmering against a background of burnt sienna and Prussian blue. His latest work! The first in a series of formalized female forms, he had decided. This morning the painting was drab, murky, nothing more than a series of unrelated shapes which depressed him. It was back to the beginning, back to the drawing board. He was getting nowhere. And the broken jar and the mess of splattered turps! He chewed with renewed despair over Rachel, last night's parting kisses, her lips searching, full of needing, clinging, wanting reassurance. Oh God! The problem was there with him. The situation was real and he was trapped within it. He must heave himself out, though when and how and where had had to be postponed for the time being.

He bent down to pick up some of the broken glass. Thankfully, most of the turps had landed on the floor with only a small portion forming a dark grey-green exploded pattern on the wall where the jar had struck. As he picked up the glass and dwelled on recent events, the self-promise as yet unfulfilled, he visualized again the night of his twentieth birthday party here in the studio, Rachel and he in each other's arms on the dusty floor, staying together the entire night when everyone else had gone. And the day after, how he had waltzed into college, full of braggardly bullshit about his conquest, how he had 'made it' with that bird from the Pre-dips. He hadn't dared confess that he was still a virgin after his night with the 'hottest chick' in college.

'Bloody fool!' he murmured out loud with a wince at his thoughts, and searched in the inside pocket of his jacket for a dog-end he knew he had there.

The dog-end was the remains of a cigarette he and Rachel had shared last night while she recovered from her weeping. He lit it, savouring the brief taste of tobacco and trying to ignore the slight perfumed aftertaste which tainted it whenever he smoked a docker Rachel had used. He regarded his latest painting with disappointment, blowing a mouthful of smoke towards it and watching the smoke rebound from the dull oil paint surface. The smoke curled and drifted about the room, rising and falling in slow motion gossamer-like waves. Leaning faced inward against one wall were his previous aspirations, pieces of hardboard and a couple of hessian canvases tacked over old picture frames.

His studio! He liked to call it that. At one time it had been the master bedroom — that was until the night the ceiling decided to drop in on the occupants as they slept. It had then been used as a storeroom, first by Jack Thwaite when he owned the property and next by his father who, when he took over, had packed it to the rafters with his junk. It was about a year ago that Steve had suggested using it for a studio, both for himself and his mate, Jim, from college. The 'in thing' amongst the students at the time had been to have studios. The upstairs room of Ninety Four had seemed an ideal place. So the lumber had been rearranged, or shifted to other parts of the cottage, and he and Jim had swept away the years of grime. Then they had painted over the walls with thin coats of white emulsion and, mainly under Jim's supervision, decorated them with various bits of 'studentish' bric-a-brac and newspaper collages. It had become their territory, their important little piece of space, and a reasonable spot to work in too, especially with the strip lighting his father fixed up for them. And at the beginning of the year, while Jim painted his Cézanne-inspired landscapes and Steve his heads after the style of Modigliani, his father had accommodated them further by knocking a hole in the back wall and fitting in a window.

He recalled that bitter early January afternoon, he and Jim at their respective easels while his father, in donkey jacket and wellies, stood on the raised plank amongst a rubble of stone and brick, marking and measuring the icy cavity and checking his measurements against a bulky old wooden window frame. It had been a relief to see him so busy. Winter was always an uncertain time of the year when snow or freezing conditions made it impossible to work.

With the window and the strip lighting they had the perfect studio. The only snag was that because there was no ceiling, only the gnarled beams and the stone tiling above those, grit and dust fell over everything at an alarming rate. Even more so in windy weather or when the sparrows fought and fluttered in the eaves. The roof had a tendency to leak too, and it wasn't unknown for the floor to be covered with an inch of snow when certain blizzard conditions prevailed. Yet he and Jim never concerned themselves with such details. They had no notion, at this early stage of their careers, of how time and dampness and dust might play havoc with their work. They had a studio, somewhere where they could be dedicated artists, and it had been fun.

Traces of the original wallpaper still remained here and there, hanging in map-shaped patches or torn washed-out strands. Amongst the collages Jim had pasted up there was the page from a newspaper dating back to the late 1940s which they'd discovered amongst the junk. He tried to make out a small headline which was partly covered with white emulsion and Jim's scrawled symbols in black paint. Russia was accusing America of aggravating towards another global war. Even then. So soon after the second lot. Molotov and Truman. Grim grey Russia and tooth-grinning America. He associated the threat of war between East and West with more recent years and the talk of megatons and hundreds of megatons, of spy planes and missiles, and Kruschev table-banging and MacMillan, ever typically British and unruffled, requesting a translation if he wouldn't mind. He associated it too with all the pamphlets that were kept circulating, telling you what to do in-case-of, and what effects a mere fifty megaton bomb would have if it dropped on your head.

It was almost a year ago already that they'd come to the brink, all the students and everyone you met waiting for the deadline, convinced that the whole of mankind was about to be vaporized in one last great nuclear firework display.

They'd been in Cragg's sculpture room that particular Wednesday afternoon, making outlandish plans and suggestions as to what they were going to do when the four-minute warning came. One wag amongst them had declared he was going to walk through the town centre with a fiver dangling from his flyhole. He and Jim, both having scooters, had made the offer to two of the girls to whisk them off to safety amongst the caves of the Ingleborough area that Jim knew about. Here, so he claimed, they could escape the effects of an atomic blast and fall-out.

Giving serious thought to the possibility, Steve had asked Doreen, the girl he was supposed to be partnering in the venture, whether she'd be willing to hightail it there and then into the hills without waiting for the deadline. But Doreen had not been so impressed with his knight-errant proposition, and neither had she been impressed with gleaming, polished metalic blue Triumph Tigresses. Nor did she feel desperate enough in those moments of uncertainty to escape the imminent holocaust. She had a fine body but too much common sense, and the common sense had prevailed against their heading off to continue the species in some post-atomic age — which is what he'd been thinking of doing long before they arrived in Ingleborough and Jim's cave.

They were all sitting during break in the new college canteen when the three o'clock deadline came. One of the students came rushing in.

'America's declared war on Russia!' he cried.

Steve had looked around him in disbelief, at the brand new fixtures and fittings of the canteen, at the gleaming newness of stainless steel and chrome, and the contemporary smartness of the plate-glass and pebble-dashed symmetry of reinforced concrete. He had breathed in the newness mingling with the aroma of coffee. Surely not war. Surely not the big one in these modern glass and concrete, pop song times. World wars belonged to those grainy black and white days of before you were born, those goose-step days of Hitler and Mussolini and Stalin, and grim black smoking chimney stacks, back-to-back slums with dry earth toilets, and underfed, rickety, barefoot children.

Of course, thankfully, it wasn't war. Kennedy stood firm by his resolve, caused the Russians to think twice about their projects for Cuba and called their bluff. It had been an opener for the sweat glands a little, but he seemed like a good bloke to have around as President of the United States, did Kennedy.

He took a last drag on the dog-end, stubbing it out against the stove and wondering where his next fag might be coming from. There were other remnants from his carefree student days besides the wall decor and the many beer bottles and glasses 'borrowed' from the pub opposite. There were the trophies collected throughout the year, the sign from a gents' toilet, a roadworks lamp, an enamel plaque advertising Robin cigarettes and a plastic gnome abducted from someone's ornamental garden and now grinning all the while at the dust and disorder which faced it. There were also the more utilitarian items, provided by those who desired a reasonable level of comfort at the studio parties, a couple of cushions, a sagging armchair and pieces of carpet. Draped over the front window, a length of chequered curtaining hung limply from two nails like a flayed skin.

Everything had once been nice and tidy. The chairs, the cushions, the pieces of carpet, all bathed in a red light from red tissue paper wrapped around the fluorescent tube, had made it feel like a real studio, almost like a small exclusive nightclub. But over the past months things had drifted and gone into the decline.

There was the steady courting. This more than anything had caused the drift. Jim had soon lost interest too when he became distracted by his own involvements, and weary also of having to make arrangements to be there only when it was convenient, having to rely as he did on Steve for the key. He had finally taken his hook, and his Cézanne-inspired landscapes, while Steve had devoted his energies to Rachel and allowed the dust to settle at will.

Yes, it had been fun while it lasted — as had the five years at college, or most of them. Five whole years! One of them in Post Secondary Art, two of them to pass one measly O level in Art and Craft, and a pass in Geography, and two more to sit and fail the Intermediate to a National Diploma in Design — or NDD as it was known. It had to be admitted that he was like the rest of the bunch in his year — idle and thick — and five years, hardly world-stunning in achievement, had vanished like a quick and idyllic dream.

Ah, but it had been good though, some of it, while it lasted. It had been good to play the fool, mark crafty dabs of paint on jeans or trousers in the hope that outsiders might recognize you as an art student. It had been good to walk proudly through the crowded town centre, especially during hometimes when all the shoppers and the working folk were gathered at the bus stops and staring after you, to feel as though you were a member of a separate élite group which could delight in the inquisitive stares of those trapped within their rush hour bus stop queues. It had been good as well to swagger into the dimly lit Flame — the coffee bar haunt of students and arty types which seemed to have been taken straight out of Chelsea, Soho or Hampstead, and deposited slap-bang in the centre of an unsuspecting, monochrome West Riding town. Here they had lounged with the in crowd of intelligentsia, paying 9d. for Russian tea or frothy coffee, and watching candles flicker in wax-covered Chianti bottles while they listened to blues from Big Bill Broonzy, or jazz from Barber, Bechet, Mezz Mezzro.

He yawned and stretched, wishing the yawn could flush him of all the trivia which engulfed him. He was left only with the memories, and the typed notification that he had failed his Intermediate. No going on further to other colleges, as he'd been hoping. That possibility had kept him ahead of the obligation to find work. But he had been given his chances, as his mother was fond of reminding him, and it was 'only right' that he should find himself a job. She wanted him to find a 'good one', one which might yet exploit whatever marginal benefits they could glean from his wasted time at college. His becoming a commercial artist in design or printing companies appealed to her as the most likely departure — if it wasn't already too late for him to be accepted into such a line of work. His father, on the other hand, had no such hopes or preferences. If a little bit of money was being earned he could work where he liked. But his mother wanted to retrieve what hopes remained in the ashes of her expectations, and was resolved to see him in a 'right and proper job'. After all, she argued, what would the neighbours say if they had to see him trudging about in mucky overalls after all this time at the art school? It didn't bear thinking about.

He yawned again. Parents! They didn't understand a damned thing. All they ever did was pester you about boring sensible things like money and housekeeping, and going out to work and paying bills. A dreary treadmill. He wanted to be an artist, bringing expression, reality to his dreams. 'Yes, we know all about it, Verity,' he could hear the sour laconic voice of Chalmers, the graphics tutor, telling him. 'You're going to be rich and famous, living with a wealthy lady in the South of France, and you're going to ride around in a brand new 'E type' Jag. In the meantime you're in my room to work, not fool and idle about.'

He stepped over to the back window which looked out over the blue misty morning landscape behind the cottage. Everything looked peaceful and still, the sunlight penetrating the mist and warming the damp land. There was a sizeable pond at the back of the cottage, surrounded by hawthorn bushes and banked with tall reeds which stood motionless in the quiet sun. The pond was the main attraction for the 'scallywags' and 'varmints', those gangs of youths and small boys who sneaked there ostensibly to catch roach and perch, or kill frogs and toads in the breeding season, but who, much to his father's chagrin, got themselves up to all kinds of mischief. Hence the plywood board nailed over the broken pane of this window, fitted only in January, which let in a draught.

When the place was deserted, as it was this morning,

he liked to imagine that it was a remote lake, or a Scottish loch, and Ninety Four was built on the banks where he watched dark waters lapping between the reeds. The vision pushed the trivia out of focus momentarily, all the workday dull normalities and non-expectancies, but the immediate non-expectancies returned relentlessly. The artist was essentially a man who needed food for his belly besides his thought, and this had become increasingly more obvious since his parents were reluctant to go on providing it. Artists were ten a penny, his mother would tell him, trying to make him see reason, and besides, she asked, how many of the hundreds and thousands of artists struggling for recognition were ever successful? It didn't bear thinking about.

He had to agree with her. He could easily feel lost and insignificant amongst those hundreds and thousands, inconsequential, in agonies of frustration and disappointment, a small voice in the big deaf world. Yet the alternative, that of not even trying, equally didn't bear thinking about.

He listened, thinking he heard the purring of an engine. Alec Watkins' van reversing into the yard! He went over to the front window, peering out through the flayed-skin curtain. There was the pub and the post office next door, and a couple of people chatting as they waited at the bus stop outside the pub. The noise of the engine increased, then a tractor came down the side road next to the post office, paused, then veered out into the lane, sending clumps of mud showering from its wheels into the road. Reprieved temporarily from returning downstairs, he wandered into the other, smaller upstairs room.

The first thing to catch the eye on entering this little back room was the oblong, black-framed glass case filled with a colourful display of stuffed birds. Set amongst a foliage of twigs, grasses and delicate ferns, kingfishers, blue tits and thrushes, together with a couple of magpies, a merlin, a kestrel and various finches, gazed out silently from behind the glass with bright full-of-life sightless eyes. The display had come into his father's possession as payment, in place of cash, for a gravestone which one of his clients, an elderly widow, had been unable to afford. ('Poor owd lass,' he had said compassionately and accepted the birds.)

There was some doubt as to what he intended doing with this veritable museum piece but one thing was clear: if he was to carry it home to his wife there'd be the devil to pay. Payment for a job? How d'yer mean, payment for a job? She'd be sure to raise the roof, regardless of how colourful the effect some long-dead taxidermist had achieved.

The case of birds, along with stacks of old picture frames, plaster figurines and mildewed books, remained in the meantime to gather dust with the rest of the stuff.

He sniffed at the faint mildew odour of old plaster and lack of use. The room was the dryest in the cottage, and the cleanest, still had a ceiling, and had been formerly used by Jack Thwaite as the office when he owned the place. (Jack had also been good enough to leave his sturdy office chair and a medieval typewriter that didn't work.) Over by the wall, next to the table on which the case of birds was propped, a large brown ungainly chest of drawers, the drawers of which were swollen with age and difficult to open, contained letters, notebooks, sketchbooks, postcards and photographs — the foisty documents of his father's early life.

He managed to prize open one of the drawers, just wide enough for him to reach in and pull out a couple of the items crammed inside. The first was a small etching, creased and looking slightly yellow. The etching had been done by a friend of his father's and was a portrait of him as a young man, lying face down, asleep, his head turned partially this way and buried in the pillows of an austere iron bed. Beneath the bed was a battered suitcase fastened with string. There was a sense of the makeshift, the temporary, the suitcase and a pair of brogues thrown hapazardly on the floor, and next to the bed, a single table on which there rested a cup and an open book. It was a picture of student life in a London bedsit during the 1930s, the period when his father had attended the Royal College of Art.

Amongst the many postcards in the drawers there were a number from Paris. The one he looked at now was a black and white study of the Notre Dame. It was from the time when his father had continued his studies in Paris, the year 1939 when he had won the travelling scholarship from the Royal College and visited the Netherlands, and even Germany, but spent most of the time in France.

It was his stay in Paris that impressed Steve the most. There had never been any need for him to rely solely on his imagination, pretending that a dingy backstreet in the West Riding was in Montmatre or Montparnasse, or that a grimy local pub was one of the cafés on the Left Bank. He had lived it for real, had lived and breathed Paris of the 1930s, visited the famous galleries and museums, worked at his sculpture in a studio which had been Brancusi's, rubbed shoulders with now recognized contemporary artists and writers, and spent the evenings drinking wine and vodka on café terraces like the Dôme.

Browsing through the memorabillia of his father's past, as he often did during idle moments when he was here at Ninety Four, Steve could feel a certain ache of regret that his father should have lived through such an eventful experience, one that must have held so much promise, only to find himself in the end firmly entrenched in the confines of the present. Paris and promise, yet there he was, returned to the common ground of his upbringing, tethered to the commitments which had befallen him, rummaging about in the workshop for sponges, chisels or carborundum stones, and more than likely fretting that Alec Watkins might not turn up.

The choice had been his, though the war had had a great deal to do with his making the choice, but he had committed himself to marriage, opted for domestic and family security, something onto which he could anchor belief when war made the future so uncertain. He had married and reared a family rather than choose the uncertainty and insecurity of freedom. And he had stuck by his commitments, by the beliefs and codes of his forefathers, those codes which had kept strength through generation after generation. You made your bed and you lay on it. You didn't shirk your responsibilities and go 'gaddin' off' — not in these parts anyway. Despite personal disappointment, regret, the suffocation of identity and the general differences of opinion, he had maintained those commitments for the past twenty three years.

Steve pushed the postcard and the etching back in the drawer. Sometimes of late he could see himself becoming dragged towards a suffocation of his identity. Aware of his father's near successes, those promising but lost-opportunity years to which the drawers of memorabillia bore testimony, he could see himself eventually giving way, giving himself up in meek submission because there'd be no other way, no escape from his own deep-rooted instincts. Married to Rachel! Tethered like his father, forfeiting freedom, the sense of his own destiny, for fatherhood, for the one function expected of him, becoming merely another breadwinner, going out day after day in the monotonous rotation of earning money and sacrificing himself for the sake of acceptable living standards and kids.

Married to Rachel. Married and tethered till his soul and his hair turned grey. He shrank from the vision, crying 'No!' from his depths.

3

'Your lad left art school for good now, Percy?' Alec Watkins the undertaker enquired in his light anxious voice. Without waiting for a reply or acknowledging that Steve was there, he opened the back doors of the runabout, almost clapped-out van meant for collecting bodies.

The van had been carelessly repainted in black over the chipped and dinted original paintwork, and one of the front mudguards looked about ready to fall off. He cleared a few odds and ends aside in the back, including the starting-handle, then spread a purple dustsheet to cushion the stone.

'I should've been here sooner,' he explained, his movements quick, pent-up, as if business was brisk and he was in a constant hurry to attend to it. 'But I had to make a couple of calls. I'd've liked to have stopped and given you a hand to fix it as well, but there's that funeral this aft' to get ready for.'

He was tall and thin, stooping even, in his mid-forties, with a small, sharp, pointed nose and sharp cleft chin. His face didn't so much look cleanshaven as scraped several layers of skin down. It glowed raw and pink, as if battered by a strong cold breeze. He was wearing a black tie and a shabby black blazer, and the white shirt was starched and ironed, yet appeared grubby round the oversized collar. The uniform was provisional but casual. He was not exactly dressed for funerals but sufficiently attired should he suddenly be called upon to negotiate one.

He avoided eye contact with Steve, as though he considered the sons of business associates — especially weird long-haired ones — should be seen and not heard.

Steve fumed silently, sensitive about his own adulthood and resenting being treated like a fledgling in the nest.

Once everything was ready the headstone was carefully lifted off its supports in the workshop, then lowered slowly, gingerly, onto a couple of wooden rollers, about six inches in diameter, which were a necessary part of the equipment when moving heavy stones. Once firmly set on the rollers, the headstone was then manoeuvred easily out of the cottage, struggled with a little as they negotiated the doorstep, then brought out into the yard.

'Nice "deskhead" job, this, Percy,' the undertaker gasped, pushing shoulder to shoulder.

The headstone moved slowly, gracefully, advancing steadily towards the opened doors of the van like a great monument from the days of the Pharaohs. The two 'grown-ups' heaved and pushed together, the rollers bumping and grinding over bits of pebbles, stone and broken glass which littered the yard, while their untutored apprentice seized up each roller as it emerged from behind to re-insert it at the front.

'Shift it this way to the doors,' said Alec, talking his way through the strain. 'Now, Percy, if we can push it edge on here your lad can steady it while we lift it in.'

'Nay, Alec,' said the other. 'don't strain yourself for my sake. You can soon put your back out in this game if you're not careful, you know. Stephen! Don't just stand there gawpin'. Get them two pieces of planking and slot 'em in here then all three of us can lift.'

'What pieces of planking? Slot 'em in where?'

'Them, lad! Staring you in the face. Bring 'em over here and slot 'em in there.'

Steve grabbed one of the pieces of planking and thrust it roughly at his father. He detested being relegated to this inconsequential backdrop role, and being treated like a half-wit and yelled at in front of Alec Watkins. But his father was getting himself into a flap, concerned for the safety of the stone and worried that Alec, on a tight schedule, wanted to be finished and gone. The lengths of wood were wedged hurriedly between the unpolished back of the headstone and the edge of the van's doorway, providing a pivot as they lifted together and pushed.

The van sagged, the springs creaked as they took the weight. There! Thank God it was in without mishap or injury, or strained backs. His father brought out the flower vase and the metal container that accompanied the headstone, then Alec and he carried between them the sandstone plinth on which the job would rest. Finally, having made sure the two rollers were in the van, he fetched the shopping bag, which was bulkier and heavier now with all the equipment it contained.

The door of Ninety Four needed a hefty slam to shut it properly; so much force was needed to shut it the entire front of the building, bulging outwards so precariously, seemed about to come toppling down on them. Steve thought of the scene in the Buster Keaton movie every time his father shut the door: the house side falling and they remaining safe as the apertures of a door or window sailed over their heads.

'Rogues and idiots, today's youth,' his father remarked tersely as the padlock was secured and all the extra precautions of security returned in their correct order.

Aware that he was keeping Alec waiting, he made only a cursory check on everything instead of the usual more elaborate one, then pinned a torn-open empty cigarette packet to the door. On it was written 'Working in Lindlethorpe churchyard' for the benefit of any visiting rep or possible customer.

'A right rum shop,' he gave as a parting derogatory comment and they were on their way.

*

Lindlethorpe church could be seen as a grey square-towered landmark in the misty warm sunlight above the village. Also dominating the scene was the tall dark grey pencil of Ralstones' chimney stack. This towered above the rooftops and the surrounding farmland, indicating the way as the lane wound towards the village, passing rows of terraced houses on one side and open fields on the other. The road continued under a red-bricked railway bridge, then came out immediately by Ralstones' mill where squalid grey stone buildings with their zigzagged black roofs crowded in on either side.

As Alec's van motored on between the mill buildings the roar of machinery could be heard above the grinding of its engine. Along with the noise came the greasy tang of boiling wool which seeped in through the van's open windows. Steve knew what lay behind the high mill walls and the heaped-up, sack-covered bails of shoddy. Ralstones was a brief encounter with that other world of industry which he and his best mate Maurice, or Mozz as he was nicknamed, had experienced during the summer vacation a couple of years back.

And never again, he promised, watching as the mill's dark windows careered past his view. That had been like a return to the industrial revolution: the heat, the fluff clinging to the sweating skin, and the looms with their constant roar, day in, day out, locked from the bright days of summer. 'Despair and die, despair and die, despair and die, I don't know why, I don't know why, despair and die . . .!' Their chant had drowned him.

After the mill the road climbed to meet the village and they turned left into the high street, heading for the steep climb up the hill to the church. His father asked if they might stop off a moment at the butchers to 'pick a bit o' summat up' for their snap.

Steve watched him go, wondering what he could say to

Alec to make conversation. Seeing how he drummed on the steering wheel, making no effort to communicate himself, he thought, why bother? He took note instead of the meats, the sausages, the pies on display in the butcher's shop window, the way the sunlight penetrated the open doorway, illuminating the few customers, and how the butcher in his blue-striped apron stood behind the counter, exchanging friendly banter.

A tiny spark began to glow within him as new ideas stirred. He observed the activity of the high street, a couple of ladies with shopping baskets chatting outside the greengrocers, and nearby, where a blue Morris Minor was parked, a pensioner sitting on a bench, reading his newspaper in the clear stillness of the morning.

'Spot on, man!' he could hear Mozz telling him, and could see the composition already, painted on the rectangle of hardboard he had primed and ready at the studio. Not a series of formalized nudes but a series of the West Riding scene, complete with corner shops, parked cars, housetops with their chimneys smoking lazily, luxuriously in the early autumn sun. He would make a start as soon as he could — if he could afford the paint.

'Right, we'll get off then, Alec,' said his father, returning with paper bags containing the things he'd bought. He seemed slightly more cheerful. The narky mood was definitely thawing and had begun to do so as soon as they'd left the cottage. The fates, he'd realized, weren't set against them after all. It wasn't going to rain, they hadn't been struck by earthquake or lightning, and Alec's tinshack van had not lost a wheel or broken down, although it was to steam from the radiator when it took the heavy load up the steep incline of the church hill.

*

'Looks like you're ready to boil over there, Alec,' the gravedigger called out as they came round the side of the church and halted on the open ground near his hut.

He was a small, stockily built individual with a round weatherbeaten face and eyes that twinkled mockingly when he smiled. 'What's wrong wi' it? No water in your radiator?'

'It always does that, Harold,' Alec told him with an embarrassed clearing of the throat. He glanced at his watch, in a rush, having no time for idle chatter with the gravedigger or for discussing the conditions of his van. ('That Harold Hutchinson,' he had said on the way to the churchyard. 'He's a rogue is that one, Percy. Always on the pop and full of cheek.')

'Well, it looks like it's had it, that van o' thine,' Harold grinned, wanting to taunt him. 'It's worse than 'one Percy had. What's it held together wi'? String?'

He gave a hoot of laughter which didn't amuse Alec in the least, then turned his attention on Steve climbing out of the back of the van.

'Now then, Percy, I see you've brought some help wi' yer. Your lad is it, or is it a lass?'

'It's t'lad,' answered Steve's father apologetically, adding, 'He could do with his hair cuttin', I know.'

'Bring him over here to t'shed,' suggested Harold. 'We can put a basin over his nut an' use 'grass shears. Eeh, youth today, eh, Alec?' he grinned, wanting to draw Alec and bring a reaction from him. 'When you were his age you'd've had yer head shaved wi' a one inch fringe, I bet.'

Alec made a sound of reply, preoccupied, anxious for the sake of business. He gave a quick glance at Steve's untidy mop, regarding it with distaste. 'If we'd had hair like that we'd've been called cissies.'

Harold lifted the grubby flat cap he was wearing, showing off his bald head. It looked stark and white against the ruddiness of his face. 'Think you could lend me some to put on here?'

Steve gave a laugh and accepted a cigarette from the packet his father offered round. Harold provided the lights and he inhaled expansively on the first drag. A whole fag! He looked at Alec, the way his dark hair, turning grey, was slicked back and greased flat against his scalp. The back and sides were cropped short, almost shaven. It was the accolade of smartness, the mode of the sensible man.

Forgetting for the moment he was in a hurry, as he paused to light his cigarette, Alec enlarged on his opinions about hairstyles and present day youth, all the advantages they had which he hadn't had. 'All these beatniks and these pop groups with their hair over their collars.' They should never have stopped conscription, he opined. That was the worse thing they did. 'And it'll show in years to come, you mark my words. The world's turning upside down, Percy. Turning upside down. A stint in the army 'ud do 'em all a world o' good.'

Steve looked away. He'd heard all this before from all sides. It seemed to have become standard conversation amongst the 'elders and the betters'. He focused his attention on Harold's little green hut. Through the open door could be seen the equipment for cutting grass: a motor mower, a scythe, a couple of rakes. Hanging from hooks were several spades and coffin-shaped templates of varying sizes made from strips of boxwood. There was Harold's snap-bag and his flask on a bench.

'They don't seem to want to dress smart like we did,' Alec was saying. 'Same goes for the lasses. They're just as scruffy as the lads.'

Steve turned away from the hut to the expanse of headstones, obelisks, angels, cherubs and white marble crosses stretching through the churchyard. They formed a chequered landscape of greys, ochres, whites and blacks amongst the grass, their epitaphs bearing the names of those who no longer cared about youth's advantages, or whether a bloke grew his hair too long within the brevity of his lifespan.

'Are they keeping you busy Harold?' his father wanted to know, bringing conversation from the topic of present-day youth.

The gravedigger spat, hung his cigarette from the corner of his mouth and leaned on the spade he'd been cleaning with a piece of wood.

'Aye, by heck, I'll say they are. Ah'm havin' to work like a silly bugger since they sent that time-and-motion study chap round all 'parks and cemeteries. Some'dy in a white collar who don't know a shovel from a spade, tryin' to work out how much can be done in t'shortest possible time. Accordin' to his reckonin' I'm supposed to dig a two-coffin grave, and cut an acre of grass, in less time than it takes to dig a single. It's like tryin' to dig your way through solid rock an' all in some parts o' this 'ere churchyard, Percy.'

'It'll keep you on your toes though,' put in Alec with a gleam of triumph. 'No sittin' with yer feet up in the shed now.'

Harold ignored the remark. 'Since yon' town council took over from t'local parish everything's at sixes and sevens.' He pointed towards the new lawn cemetery which lay behind the shed. 'Look at that lot for a start. What do we need that up here for?'

The lawn cemetery extended the new boundaries of the church. The council had introduced it with the idea of streamlining, keeping up with modern trends. The graves on lawn cemeteries were to be allowed no kerbs, only a single headstone mainly of a uniform 'deskhead' design. The idea might restrict the inventive skills of the monumental trade but would certainly improve the efficiency and general upkeep of the place. At present it was a flat turfed area which looked more like a bowling green, having only recently been claimed from a number of allotments, the tenants of which had stuck up posters proclaiming, 'Life not Death', but to no avail. The land had been cleared of carrots, turnips and cabbages, levelled, set with grass, then blessed and surrounded by a tarmac path.

So far there was only one headstone, a sandstone deskhead blank standing at one corner and serving as an example of the new style of grave. The one they'd brought this morning was for the first 'customer', the start of the first row.

'It's all right for Alec,' Harold was saying, half joking but half serious, complaining about the measurements for a grave Alec had given him the previous week. 'All he has to do is make t'boxes, it's me has to dig out t'muck and get rid of 'em.'

'Oh, that's not all I have to do,' Alec corrected, barely hiding his annoyance. 'It's not as simple as that, not by a long chalk.'

Gazing over at the bowling-green plot, Steve thought about all the 'punters' who at some future date would help to fill its ranks. They were all out there at present, beyond the confines of the churchyard, and unaware of this green 'modern' acre as they carried on with their daily lives. But one day soon they'd be lying beneath the deskhead rows, part of the clean, streamlined order rotting in the good old-fashioned way beneath the turf.

Alec nipped his cigarette and pushed it behind his ear. He looked quickly at his watch. There was the funeral at two; it was time to return to immediate concerns.

Harold spat on his palms.

'Out o' the way, young glass-back,' he said heartily, but protective, pushing his way in front of Steve. 'Keep your hands nice and soft for thy lass, eh Percy?' he suggested with a grin.

'Aye, and let him make sure it's them rollers he gets underneath, not his feet,' echoed his father, worried that Harold was joining them, and worried that the art of gradual manoeuvre was about to be superseded by the philosophy of sheer brute strength.

'Be careful . . . don't . . . if we can just . . .!'

'Tha's right, Percy. I've shifted many a stone in this 'ere churchyard by meself.'

'Is it okay?' Steve asked when, after the strain against weight and concern for corners, the headstone was finally on site. His father began checking every angle, every edge, as soon as Harold and Alec had gone.

'Hundred and fifty quid down t'Swanee if there's any damage,' he muttered, scrutinizing the face, the back and all the edges. Things had moved just that little bit too fast and too easily for his liking, and he was suspicious of his own good fortune.

'It'll do,' he admitted grudgingly, which meant that thankfully all was well. He took the spade they'd borrowed from Harold and dug out a shallow section at the head of the coffin outline discernable in the turf, wide enough to take the plinth. The soil beneath the turf was soft, rich and dark.

The plinth was next carried over from where it had been lifted out of the van.

'You're always on about cuttin' capers,' Steve remarked as he stepped backwards cautiously with his end of the plinth. 'I reckon I've cut some capers with you as well.'

His father showed amusement at his uncertainty as they went over an uneven part of ground. 'It shows you're not used to heavy liftin'. Wait till you're handling six-be-seven red granite kerbs in freezing weather. This 'ere's chicken feed, man.'

Steve noticed his amusement. His father had become much brighter now that he was working and things had turned out right. You could see it in his eyes and in his expression, which had ceased to be so hangdog. He was more ready to smile and be amused, whatever regrets and self-division might rest beneath the surface.

'Spirit level,' he requested when the plinth was lowered into the trench and he stamped his foot over it to make sure it was firmly bedded.

Steve searched amongst the chisels, sponges, carborundum stones and various other pieces of equipment in the shopping bag for this well-used and vital item. The spirit level was placed at the middle of the plinth, but when the bubble in the phial of silvery green liquid refused to hover dead centre his father requested the spade.

'Spirit level,' he demanded like a surgeon requesting a scalpel.

'Spirit level,' repeated Steve like an assistant in an operating theatre. They had played this game before.

'Slate,' requested his father, having removed a sliver of earth too much from one end of the trench, and replacing some of the topsoil he'd taken away.

In the bottom of the bag, underneath everything, were small pieces of roofing slate which came in for use as packing when too many slivers of earth had been removed. Along with the pieces of slate were one or two pieces of an old 78 rpm gramaphone record which drew a nice soft line on stone when he was marking out the lettering. Steve recognized the pieces from a fragment of turquoise blue label: the bones of Elvis's *Hound Dog* which had met with a sad end under the weight of his mother's backside.

'Spirit level.'
'Spirit level.'
The bubble hovered doubtfully at centre then drifted off slowly, changing its mind.

'Slate.'

'Slate.'

'I don't know why you make such a fuss,' Steve told him, becoming impatient with their game. 'It's not as if anybody's gonna come along with their own spirit level and test what you've done.'

'Listen, if a job's worth doing then it's worth doing right,' was his father's reply as he continued with a struggle for perfection, his finger ends with their hard cracked skin probing the black topsoil, spreading it evenly as he balanced the plinth and inserted another wafer of slate. 'There's too much shilly-shallying goes off in this world as it is without me joining in,' he added, stamping down on the plinth once more to make sure it was firmly seated. 'Folk always trying to get as much reward as they can for as little effort as possible. It isn't work people want nowadays. Just money so they can show off. If I'm going to do a job I believe in doing it properly, ne'er mind all this slapdash attitude and doing things in half measures.'

He believed in the work. That was the important issue rather than the rewards, and he insisted on precision throughout its completion, whether there be wind, rain, hail, sleet or freezing temperatures. Only the extremes of winter ever defeated him.

It was at this juncture that he frowned on his son's attitude to work. Aside from all arguments for leisure, for the need for free time to develop as an artist, he could never condone such opposition to his principles.

'It doesn't matter in the least what a fellow does for a living,' he stressed. 'As long as he is doing something and can arrive home at the end of the day knowing that it hasn't been wasted, choose how much or how little he's done.'

For him each new job was like a new adventure. The monumental trade he'd chosen might seem after all to be a 'dying trade in the back of beyond' but it sometimes seemed to him to be a challenge. 'Rather like life itself is a challenge,' he said, giving the levelled plinth one last gentle tap with his foot.

He pushed two pieces of steel rod used for dowelling in the two dowel holes which had been cut in the top of the plinth. The two holes corresponded with two that were drilled in the headstone's base. 'You say you're searching for something more in life, but we're all of us searching around for something in life, some goal or other. It's what gives us the necessary urge to make life worthwhile. It's what makes life worth living. To achieve and do a good job,' he concluded as they bent to the task of pushing the headstone the last few feet from where it had been left on the rollers. 'That's the thing. It's a service to yourself, but it's a service to others about you as well.'

He spoke with a smile of revelation. He was always at his best when he could immerse himself like this in his work.

Now he took a small bag of cement they'd brought with them and poured a heap of it onto the plinth.

'Lovely grub,' he murmured as he poured water from a borrowed jam-jar onto it and whipped the mixture into a paste with his trowel. He spread the mixture like runny icing sugar over the plinth, working it mostly into the holes and around the dowelling.

'You come on with this 'ere, you see,' he continued, giving commentary to his actions, 'then the idea is to get the dowels lined up so you can come on with the headstone and plonk it straight on top.'

The next stage was a little trickier. They had to work fast before the cement could set — which it did in seconds when it was mixed neat without sand. Watching fingers and toes, they had to rely on innovation and improvisation, begging or borrowing whatever lay at hand and transforming it into a useful tool. On this occasion his father chose a plank and a couple of bricks near where Harold had been earlier digging a grave, and pushing one end of the plank beneath the base of the headstone and the bricks behind for leverage, he prized up one end of the stone, using the plank as a crowbar. As he balanced the weight on the plank Steve lifted out the first of the rollers; then the plank was lowered gently, allowing that end of the stone to settle gradually onto the plinth.

He repeated the procedure for removing the second roller but lining up the job so that the dowels aligned immediately, first try, was not always possible.

'Never stick fast, lad, that's the idea,' said his father when the dowelling grated against the hard base of the headstone like an irritating pebble of obstruction, refusing to let the job lie secure and flat.

He levered up with the plank once more, inching the stone over slightly to adjust its position, and when this failed, wedged in pieces of scrap wood for packing, making a gap wide enough for him to insert his hand and realign the dowels.

'All this for the dear departed,' he gasped, mocking his own tenacity while he groped and searched for the dowels. God help him if the stone should fall! It was a tense moment when he chose to take such risks, seeing the goal so near. But at last he had it, and as they levered the stone up and over the dowels together it slid and settled with a last gentle but heavy bump that splattered the surplus cement.

'There, one more accomplished,' he remarked as they wiped away the residue of cement and wiped the joint with sponges and clean water. The black granite with its gilded inscription gleamed in the sunlight against grass and earth. It stood as first in the line, ready for the day when it would take its place amongst the ranks.

His father nodded in approval, standing back to appraise the work as if it were a piece of sculpture he'd just completed. Then he gave the whole a final wipe for luck before picking up the bag and wandering leisurely away towards a seat at the pathside.

'Where d'yer think you're going?' Steve called after him. He knew very well and was glad.

4

'Snaptime', dining alfresco and sharing tea from a thermos flask, that was definitely the most enjoyable thing about working away at cemeteries or churchyards.

'Your favourite part of the day,' his father would joke when it came time for their midday break, and certainly this had been the highlight whenever he'd tagged along as a child.

Those were amongst some of the best days — the long school holiday during summer, he on his blue and white Raleigh and his father on the black roadster with the white flash painted on the back mudguard (the same bike which now resided in the workshop as a rusting emblem of his more mobile days). They would cycle together to wherever his father happened to be working and he would be full of enthusiasm, carrying the bag of tools over to the job-in-hand when they arrived and exploring amongst the grass mounds and sunken graves for jam jars or flower containers to fill with water for the stone cleaning. Sometimes he would try his hand at the cleaning, though when he was little he'd never been able to apply enough pressure on the carborundum to produce a thick build-up of sludgy residue like his father could. But always there were the fresh morning sounds and smells of summer in those churchyards and cemeteries of his memory, the scent of grass and flowers, the noises of insects and birds.

Churchyards on mornings like those had never been the places of death. The gravestones and tombstones had been simply structures that existed in their own right and the churchyards hidden retreats which filled him with a joyful sense of being in anticipation of the picnic he and his father would share. Only afterwards, when the picnic goodies had been scoffed and the afternoon stretched out in the long anticlimax before him, would enthusiasm wane.

They sat now on the seat by the tarmac path, Steve watching in amusement while his father fumbled with the bag. He seemed to be savouring the moment of the imminent feasting, unable to decide whether to share out the grub first or take a 'wet' from the flask.

'Take the money,' Steve suggested at his indecision. His father, deciding at last on one of the paper bags, produced it like a conjuror performing a trick and presented two pork pies.

'Here, sithee, get one o' these in your fist,' he said with a pretended coarse indifference, knowing that the lunchtime menu for today would please.

They bit into their pies, his father accompanying his with the earlier toasted cheese creation (waste-not-want-not) and taking large bites which he chewed with a fully absorbed enjoyment.

His false teeth rattled as he bit and chewed. It was a homely, familiar, even if sometimes annoying sound.

Savouring the crispness of the freshly baked crust, the meat and the jelly melting over the tongue, they gazed out over a panorama of fields and housing estates from the vantage of the church hill. From here the whole area could be seen spreading to the warm haze of the distance. Below them was the village itself, huddled round the mill, and beyond the village was the patchwork pattern of the cabbage fields, rhubarb fields, and recently ploughed fields, all invaded by the pylons which marched over the landscape like H. G. Wells' alien machines advancing in their determined line. The fields gave way to the council housing estates and beyond these was the townscape of Calderton with its town hall clock tower, once a proud central landmark, lost amongst the new high-rise flats and office blocks. The town with its busy lunchtime streets, the factories and quietly smoking chimneys, hummed and pulsed in the distance with its life.

From where they were sitting they could also see the lane which had conveyed them in Alec Watkins' van winding in a snaking mile back towards Ninety Four and on past their own estate and Willow Avenue. A cortège run, the route along which many funerals ran. There was the silvery glint of the pond behind the cottage, and behind the pond the glint of the greenhouses of Askey's market garden. To the right of Askey's there was Thompson's farm, the haystacks and barns providing a backdrop to scenes of childhood for Steve — the red-faced irate figures of Askey and 'owd Beetroot-neck' Thompson giving chase when he and the rest of the mob were caught mischieving or pinching peas or carrots. Thompson's farm rose towards the sweep of the golf links and was cut by the branchline which came in over Lindlethorpe, curving its way past Ralstones and the golf links towards the sunsets over Halifax, Huddersfield and Bradford.

Although his train-spotting days were behind him, Steve still liked to see the steam trains chugging their way up the incline. They were mostly squat little tankers pulling the coal wagons to and from the colliery, the winding gear and pit-top structures of which stood in a distant silence on the horizon beyond the golf links. Sometimes a 'Wardog' would heave a consignment of dirty coal-laden trucks, and more rarely nowadays a B-oner might be seen pulling freight vans or a complement of a two or three coach suburban train headed for Bradford, but mostly it was the diesels, which were less spectacular. Diesels were too much a part of the changing times, of things being updated, modernized, and he found that boring. More boring was the fact that the line was soon to be closed anyway, according to local reports.

His father, busy chewing, reached for the flask and unscrewed the cap which served as a beaker. The inside of the beaker was stained darkly with tanin while on the outside pieces of Elastoplast had been stuck over where it was cracked. He poured a small measure of tea as though pouring the finest brandy, handing it to Steve.

'Why don't you just pour it?' Steve asked and chuckled at the meagre contents steaming in the bottom of the beaker. It soon went cold if you did that, was the explanation, and together they shared the measure, taking it in turns to sip.

After the pork pies there were small egg custards which had also been included. 'Here, you're like a chick in t'nest wi' your beak always open,' his father joked with the same indifference, adding, 'Eeh, I don't half look after you.'

'So you should,' Steve retorted with a laugh, sniffing at the aroma of nutmeg from the custard. 'You bred me, so you should look after me. I didn't ask to be born.'

His father smiled, shaking his head in face of all the issues that were between them. 'Teehee! You're a cheeky sod and no mistake.'

Steve grinned, perceiving the brightness of his smile, the way his eyes, almond-shaped, had an oriental look about them now that they were no longer under the duress of his earlier grumpy mood. He considered the portrait he might paint of him: the dark hair flecked with grey, receding from the high tanned noble forehead, brushed straight back without a parting, and cropped short so that it exaggerated the prominence of his large ears. There were his cheeks, high, ruddy, tanned by working outdoors, and his nose, small but somewhat bulbous, bucolic like a Clausen peasant, like a clown's nose, or so would be the self-deprecating claim when attention was drawn to it. His father was rather self-conscious of his nose, though the bushy moustache he wore didn't help matters, and he would dab the end with face powder when his wife wasn't looking, hoping to tone down the redness and camouflage it a little. But the face was handsome and gentle when he was bright and smiling, and with his slender build he still appeared youthful and energetic for his fifty three years. The hands too were energetic, large and powerful, the wrists thick and muscular from the wielding of mallet and chisel, and the lifting of heavy stone.

He now reached for the flask and poured out more of the tea, leaving enough for a 'wet' during the afternoon. Then he pushed the flask back into the bag and took out his cigs. Smoking, they stretched expansively, basking in the Indian summer warmth. Down below, in the village, the bell at the infants' school rang, summoning the children back to their classrooms, back to the afternoon shift, back to the filling of skeps and supplying the looms with bobbins of weft. Steve inspected the hole in his boot, scraped together a small heap of dead leaves between his feet and made desultory conversation with his father. The early afternoon was glorious, one that made you wish for time to stay its hand, for the summer and its weather and the moment to last forever. There seemed a permanence, as though there could never be anything beyond it. This was the minute, the very second to which all history had been leading and they were at the apex, the conclusion, smoking and basking in its sun.

*

The job for the afternoon was a cleaner and re-fixer, a headstone with set of kerbs somewhere down at the bottom end yonder, amongst old graves and tall grass.

'Nar then, Percy, ready for the off again, are yer?' asked Harold, wandering down from his hut to join them briefly for a smoke and a natter. He had kept out of the way while they were eating, respecting privacy, but they would have been welcome to join him in the hut had they wished it. He remarked about the deskhead, saying it looked well now that it was fixed. 'So what's on for this aft?' he enquired.

He immediately recognized the name and knew the whereabouts of the grave as soon as he was told.

'Owd Hubert Armitage's, eh? It must be well over two years since I took that one off. A re-opener for his missis, that wa'.'

'Things get done sooner or later, I suppose,' answered Steve's father, non-commital.

Harold lifted his cap to scratch his white bald head. 'Well, tha can't miss it. It's on row F. F thirty six,' he asserted, familiar with his territory and the location of all his 'patrons'. 'Next to that one o' Jessops — one wi' 'white marble cross.'

They decided to start on the long kerbs first, pulling them out from the tangle of grass and weeds which had overgrown them where they'd been left. Sudden life erupted in the flattened wormhole gulleys left by the stones, long-legged spiders and shiny centipedes scurrying over woodlice and seeking shelter from the inflicted light. Steve and his father carried the kerbs over to the flat area of grass between the Jessops' white marble cross and a Portland stone tablet of a soldier who had been killed in action at the age of twenty one.

Steve searched in the bag for sponges and carborundum stones, then went to fetch water from the ornate Victorian hydrant over by the church. He regarded the grey stone walls of the church, listened to the silence behind the leaded windows, read the 'here lyeths' on blackened tombs and slabs while he held a borrowed metal flower vase under the lion's mouth. The hydrant, the tombstones of ancient dead and a red granite memorial which had what appeared to be a Greek urn carved on top of its tall column, and was nearest to the church, were the first things which had always caught his eye as he came into the churchyard as long as he could remember. And the hydrant, solid and cast in iron, had fascinated him as a child, the way twisting the knob caused the lion to spew clear water from its mouth. He carried the contents of the lion's endless stomach back to the job and swilled the first of it over one of the kerbs. The water scattered like globules of wobbling mercury over the black time-patined surface of the stone.

'Not too much,' his father cautioned, 'or you'll soon find yourself workin' in a swamp.'

He pushed the carborundum in a long sweeping movement, following the length of the kerb, squeezed out more water, sparingly this time, then went to it more lively, allowing himself to merge with the automaton rhythm of the cleaning, working back and forth over each manageable section like a shuttle on a loom. A dirty grey, sludgelike sediment began to build up and cling to the blunt nose of the carborundum. The cleaning absorbed him. Patterns, designs were formed in the slip-trails of stone-sludge and water, surrealistic images of landscapes, seascapes and mythological caves, the 'slow light across the Stygian tide', the grey and ochre scenes of Dante's Purgatory. Thoughts drifted lazily in unison, mostly those which had been a constant murmur in the background of consciousness since he awoke — thoughts of Rachel and all the problems which attended nowadays when he thought about Rachel.

His mind alternated between making plans on how to end his relationship with her and enacting, complete with dialogue, the little dramas which might accompany the ending of their relationship. Then the dramas faded gradually, almost unnoticed, before the wishful thoughts and imagined scenarios of his own success. 'An exciting young artist emerges from the West Riding of Yorkshire!'

He saw himself posing studiously in a double-page spread of the *Sunday Times* colour supplement, visualized the article about him, similar to the one they'd done recently on Modigliani, with reproductions of his work: rooftops, chimneys, billboards, corner shops, the essence of the North.

His father, busy on one of the other kerbs, came over to check how he was doing. He wiped and dabbed his sponge over the worked area. The rubbing had brought the stone up clean, though there were one or two areas of black speckling, hardly noticeable, which were deeply pitted like pockmarks in the wet buff surface.

'Champion,' he said. 'Keep it going like that.'

Steve swilled more water, continued again with the short rhythmic movement, listened to the swish-swishing of the carborundum scouring the grime. His eyes went to the soldier's grave, the white military tablet with its carved regimental badge. Killed in action at the age of twenty one. He wondered what he would do if he were told that he would die at the age of twenty one. Less than a year to live! He would paint as many works as he could in the few months remaining to him, he decided. He would work like fury, live life to the full, stagger drunkenly from pub to pub while Rachel, clinging desperately to his weakened, drooping form, would try in her frantic love to hug him back to life. But he would shrug her away from him in one last heroic and single-minded act of determination to leave his mark on the history of art. He would carry on to the end, artist and lover, and on the day of his funeral, when they were about to deliver him to this very churchyard, perhaps to the new lawn cemetery, she would throw herself over his open coffin, pouring tears and kisses onto his youthful, calm dead face. He wanted to be the tragic hero of his dreams, a Keats, a Rupert Brooke, a Mozart, a Modigliani, creating the great works of his life in one short, brilliant, dynamic burst of energy. That was part of his romantic notion about art and about life (and where were mending cars and tellies, or making money in all of that?) The possibility of achieving all and dying before the age of thirty seemed acceptable when youth was raw, untried, and time expanded leisurely towards a next decade which as yet seemed as distant as the moon.

So the afternoon wore on, he and his father working side by side, sometimes pausing to make conversation but for the most part remaining silent, each engaged in his own thoughts and private dreams. Sometimes his father whistled a few brief notes of some tune going through his mind, or made light-hearted comments at the way things were progressing, chuckling at his own witticisms because they were progressing. The pessimism of the morning had evaporated, was totally forgotten. This up here in the churchyard, the work, the fresh air were the real stuff of his life, and the obligations, the disappointment and frustrations belonged to a different existence somewhere out there beyond the immediate horizons.

Eventually the sun moved out across the golf links, descending behind a line of yews by the churchyard gates. There was a coldness about the light which increased the sense of weariness which Steve had felt creeping over him during the past hour. The church and trees were silhouetted now, and Harold's hut, locked and shuttered against vandals, became lost in their shadow. Harold had knocked off around half four and that seemed ages since.

His father appeared unaffected by weariness or hunger. He was still preoccupied, giving the thing a final rinse and finishing off now that the framework of plinths had been re-set. The area was clear and the grave neatly defined.

'Won't be a minute,' he promised, noticing the peeved had-enough expression of Steve's face. He gave the cemented corners of the plinths another rinsing, dabbing the joints dry with the sponge.

'There, it'll be as good as new when we've done,' he said, slinging the contents of milky water into the grass. He gave the rusty flower vase they'd been using a careful wiping then handed it to Steve. 'Here you are, son, take it back to where you found it and don't forget, put them few flower stalks that were in it back as well. The idea is to leave things as you find 'em. That way you can borrow 'em again.'

He smiled at his own philosophizing and at the unamused sidelong glance Steve gave him.

Was the bag packed, he asked then, when the vase had been returned to its proper place. Yes, the bag had been packed, Steve assured him, knowing how packing up to leave could be a real drag — especially when the weather happened to be bad. His father followed through with the predictable checking and re-checking, making sure that nothing had been left out: had both carborundums and the sponges been put away? What about the collapsible ruler? Well yes, of course they'd been put away, where did he think they were? Well, just make sure everything else is away, and what about these pieces of slate? They might come in handy for another job. Then there were a couple of bent nails which might come in for . . . well, pop 'em in anyway. You never knew, they might come in handy one day.

Steve waited for the off, sighing impatience while his father fussed. It was the remainder of the cement he'd brought which now distracted him. There wasn't enough to warrant carrying it home but there was too much to throw away. He pondered a while, then wrapped it in several well-used polythene bags, searching the vicinity for a suitable hiding place.

'Why the hell don't you just sling it?' Steve said, irritated to the limits. But no! His father persisted until he found a shallow hole, then pushed the little parcel in, covering it with a couple of grass sods and stamping them firmly into place.

'Waste not, want not,' he offered as his maxim, then stood once more in admiration of the afternoon's work. He nodded absently. That should suit 'em. A thorough job had been done and he was satisfied it was now 'something like'. There was the headstone to be re-fixed as yet, of course, but the inscription would have to be cut first. He would come tomorrow to finish off if the weather held out. He pulled out a scrap of paper on which the inscription was written from his overalls pocket. 'Also the above named Amelia Armitage.' He counted the number of letters, pricing the total at the rate he charged for plain black laquered. Steve picked up the bag.

'Are we off now?' he asked, muttering, 'Christ!' under his breath.

'Oh, come on, then,' his father responded, pushing the paper back in his pocket. 'I know how interested you are in what's got to be done and what hasn't. Eat, sleep! That's about all you can do, i'n' it?' he suggested, good-humoured. 'As long as you can draw up to the table you're happy.'

'Get lost! I worked me guts out for you today,' Steve told him.

'You've done a bit, I suppose. How much do you reckon you've earned?'

'Ten quid!' Steve said tersely, unwilling to share his father's good humour.

His father laughed, coughing with his laughter. 'Ten quid? Teehee!' He sorted through his loose change as they made their way up the central path of the churchyard. 'Here, sithee.'

'A dollar?' cried Steve aghast, looking at the two half crowns and then at his father. 'Cor, that's a cheap rate you pay your labourers. It's five and threepence ha' penny an hour is labourer's rate, not five bob a day.'

'Eeh, come here, then, you're badly done to I'm sure.' He took back the two half crowns and pushed a crumpled ten shilling note into his hand.

5

'Over the road' meant the taproom of the Fleece. His father had said, 'Over the road'll be open,' as they stopped off at the workshop with most of the gear, and suggested a 'quick 'un' before they headed home.

'Your dad havin' to cough up for thee again?' the landlady asked with her brusque familiarity as she pulled two pints.

She was a heavily built, middle-aged peroxide blond with pinched, corsetted waistline and a large bosom. Steve found his eyes attracted by the full swell of her bosom even though she was knocking on the door of fifty and had a face that sagged beneath its generous make-up. In addition to the large figure she also had a large mouth which offered raucous laughter to the men she fancied, but short change to would-be fresh customers she didn't find appealing and 'slips of lads' like him.

His father laughed unnecessarily loud at her quip, trying to accommodate her familiarity and, as always, not quite succeeding. He floundered, overwhelmed by her presence, lacking ready answers and the sharp rapartee from a quick tongue.

'It's been a nice day today,' he ventured clumsily. 'A bit better than the rain we've been havin'.'

She eyed him through her smoke, coughed through a lipstick-stained cigarette that was pincered between brightly painted lips. 'Oh, aye.'

'September and October can be nice months,' he struggled. 'Nearly always anyway.'

'Aye,' she said again, not helping him. He too was one

amongst the many who admired her bosom.

They sat at one of the round iron tables near the dartboard. Beyond the bar, at the other side, was the lounge, unlit as yet and empty of those jovial souls who fed the landlady all the jokes and double entendres she thrived on. She leaned on the counter, smoking and fingering a cluster of bracelets, wanting someone to talk to, someone to chat her up. As it was 'early doors' and there was no one in she was quite willing to make do with these unlikely lads.

'When's tha gettin' thy hair cut?' she wanted to know, having decided to focus her attention on Steve. 'I bet tha'll be able to stuff a bloody cushion wi' that lot when tha does.'

Steve sniggered briefly and shyly, surprised by her and the fact that she admitted her awareness of him in the first place. Whenever he called in at the Fleece without his father she ignored him, except for the slight grimace which constituted a smile. There were times when she'd pull him a short-measure pint, confident that he wouldn't dare complain. It all depended on her moods.

The beer went down well, if not the conversation, and as he'd had nothing to eat since lunchtime the pleasant effects soon made themselves felt around his eyes and over the bridge of his nose. From somewhere out back, in the living quarters, came the sound of a radio. Billy J. Kramer and the Dakotas were singing, *Do you Want to Know a Secret?* It was a song from summer, bringing memories of soft light and tender falling-in-love kisses. He accepted a cigarette from his father and leaned back in his chair, studying the red and blue squares of linoleum on the floor, noticing how they were worn through in one spot where the darts-players stood. The dartboard, set above a small tiled fireplace, had been pinholed so much that the fibre bunched out behind the wire, mostly at double-top. Next to the dartboard and pinned on the yellowed wall an advert for stout showed a young woman with a pearly smile. The advert too was yellowed and its caption read: 'A Jubilee for me.'

'Where's that black-haired bird o' thine?' the landlady suddenly came at him again.

'Which one's that?' he asked, attempting a loud bravado but hearing his voice issuing ineffectually as his ears and his cheeks burned.

The landlady guffawed, then broke into a barking cough which jolted the ash off her cigarette and scattered it over the bar. 'Which one's that? Tha knows which one, cock! Or tha soon will when she comes wailin' 'tale that tha's pu' her in t'family way. I've seen thee. Climbin' into 'back o' that van you used to have over there. It's a wonder t'bloody springs didn't give out before t'engine.'

She gave another raucous laugh and broke into another fit of coughing. His father answered with a mild chuckle.

'He'll soon have to pull his socks up if he does that.'

'It wain't be his socks he'll be pullin' up, luv,' she said knowingly, adding with a shake of her permed peroxide head, 'By bloody hell, yon's t'black wider hersen!'

Steve lifted his pint and heard the sound of his own gulping. He worried that the landlady might hear it as clearly as him. A wave of depression washed over him in spite of the embarrassment. During the afternoon he had been able to distance himself, temporarily at least. The landlady's banter reminded him that he would be with her again in about two hours' time.

He took another drink. It would have to be done, he told himself while his father offered the opinion that 'the lad' couldn't afford to court. He would have to hurt her, though he dreaded having to. At the moment it was mere speculation, something that had to be faced, and she'd be sure to do something crazy if he really were to lay the cards on the line. He could recall only too well the time she'd tried to throw herself under a lorry. All because they'd quarrelled over some meaningless little thing. Perhaps for a minute he'd not paid her enough attention, or he'd said something she didn't find flattering, but she'd stormed off along the middle of the road, saying she was going to kill herself. And she'd carried on when the big lorry came, and it was a puzzled, bewildered, then angry driver who'd had to slam on his brakes. Failing to kill herself by traffic, she'd then run off into a field full of sheep, sobbing and declaring that even the sheep were ignoring her.

The episode belonged to those frequent ones where she was ready to accuse the whole world of ignoring her, and she hated to feel she was being ignored, did Rachel.

'I think I'll get my sketchbook,' he said to his father. He would take it along with him tonight, draw the inside of a pub, draw her portrait, anything which would save him from having to talk. He would pretend to work while he blew the ten bob.

His father, being as polite and attentive as a suitor, was now attempting to stimulate the landlady's interest in the problems he encountered with transport and delivering finished jobs. The van had served no help, he was telling her.

'Give us the key,' Steve said quietly, not wanting to interrupt, nor wanting the landlady to know his business. He knew she'd be all ears and ready to jibe him at every opportunity.

His father searched absently in his overalls pockets, not really comprehending in his preoccupation with the landlady, and pulled out a grey handkerchief, bits of stone, matchsticks and the odd peanut set amongst brown flakes of peanut chaff.

'What you wantin'?' he queried, resenting the intrusion.

'The key to Ninety Four,' Steve repeated slowly, as though talking to someone hard of hearing. 'I want my sketchbook and I've left it over there. I need the key.' His father got on his nerves sometimes, pratting the way he did.

'Why couldn't you make sure you had your sketchbook with yer when we were over there?' It was his turn to be annoyed. 'Here, take it, and make sure you give it back this time.' He turned to the landlady. 'Kids!' he sighed, but she remained deadpan, the short exchange thankfully beyond her interest or understanding.

*

He waited at the kerb for a couple of cars to pass and was about to cross when he heard the familiar voice yelling to him.

'Are you deaf or what? I've called you about half a dozen times.'

'Didn't hear you for the cars. Where were you?' he asked as his mother marched up to him out of the twilight.

She indicated the post office next door. She had just popped down from home to post a letter. 'Where's your dad?' she asked.

He nodded towards the bright yellow light of the pub doorway. 'We've just nipped in for a quick 'un,' he said.

'I'll give you "quick 'un",' she adominished dryly but not without humour.

She was small, sturdily built with wide hips which made her look pear-shaped, and though she'd never possessed any of the qualities which might have marked her as an attractive woman she had a pleasant face and smooth complexion that showed a minimum of wrinkles for her fifty years. Her brown hair, turning a mousey grey, had been recently set in fashionably tight 'bubble' curls.

'I'm off over here to get my sketchbook,' he told her and asked if she would like to see his studio while she was there. 'You're always on about wanting to see my masterpieces. Now's your chance.'

She scoffed, smiling, but condescended to follow. 'I bet

they'll be masterpieces all right.'

She stepped carefully over the cluttered floor when they were in the workshop, avoiding the many obstacles and sharp corners which threatened to mark the light grey coat she was wearing or ladder her stockings. He noticed how he towered above her now, how small she was, yet assertive in her clean tidiness as she stood amongst the dust and disorder, unfamiliar with all that he found familiar. He opened the staircase door, expecting her to follow, but a headstone, carved in white marble in the shape of an opened book, had attracted her eye.

'Is he still working on this?' she exclaimed with a note of annoyance, and patted her hand on the smooth unlettered surface. 'I thought he'd finished it and sent it out ages ago. Eeh, if I'm not there to pester him . . .'

'I thought you wanted to see paintings, not do a time-and-motion study on me dad.'

'Well, what he thinks he's playin' at I don't know.'

He held the door, waiting for her. She sighed, resolved, under obligation.

'Oh, go on, then. Let's go and see all these great works of art you're supposed to have done.'

Her first comment as they came up the stairwell into the room was, 'Don't you ever think you could keep it a bit tidier? It looks like your bedroom. A damned tip.'

He brushed the remark aside. 'I work better when it's like this.'

'I think it's more a case of being bone idle more like.' Her eyes went to the blue nude.

'Never mind tidiness,' he said, pushing the nude quickly to one side and presenting one of his abstracts. 'What d'yer think to this?'

'Who's that supposed to be of?' she enquired, more interested in the nude.

'What d'yer mean, who's it of?'

'It's not Rachel, is it?' she suggested with a chuckle, though there was a hint of suspicion in her voice.

'Is it heck as Rachel,' he said, rearing in embarrassment. 'It's just a nude. It doesn't have to be of anybody, does it?'

Her eyes smiled, mocking him. She was noncommital. 'It wouldn't surprise me. Who knows what you two get up to while you're here.'

He groaned. 'It's not Rachel. All right? It's just something I painted off the top of my head yesterday afternoon.' He pushed the nude out of sight, forcing it demonstratively behind the small pile of his other work which was leaned against the wall.

She eyed him knowingly. She needed only to be told half the tale and she could guess the rest.

'It's not Rachel,' he gave as a final assertion.

She 'hmmned' without conviction, her thin lips tightening as she assessed the abstract he'd been trying to hold up in front of her.

'Not bad. A bit dark,' she said at length.

'A bit dark? That's the way I paint.' He set another painting on the easel, a formalized landscape with trees. He was proud of this one.

'You paint a bit too dark, if you want my opinion,' she insisted. 'You ought to have more colour. What about some nice orange or red? There's too much black and brown.'

'No, no, I don't want things to be too technicolour,' he argued. He was searching for suggestion of colour in the brown and black, suggested colours that weren't really there.

'But surely a painting's all about colour,' she answered, her voice beginning to rise. 'That's what painting's all about. Colours! Nice fresh colours, not all this muddiness that you've managed here.'

'Of course it's not. Painting doesn't always have to be about nice fresh colours.'

'Oh well, you carry on. But you won't sell any like that. People won't want such drab stuff hanging on their walls.'

'So what? I don't paint to suit people's walls,' he said, annoyed by the shallowness of her criticism. 'I'm not bothered if they want 'em or not. I paint to please myself.'

'What the dickens is the use of wastin' your time up here like this, then, if you're not gonna be bothered about selling any?'

'I'm still at the experimental stages.'

'I'll say you're still at the experimental stages. And how long d'yer think that's gonna go on for, being at the "experimental stages"?'

He pretended not to be aware but knew quite well the direction their argument was leading them. 'Till I've found my way, I suppose.'

'And just what do you think you're goin' to live on until you've found your way, as you call it?'

He sighed, feeling cornered as always. She was seizing hold of the issue, like a hound with a rat, needing to worry it. No matter what the topic they somehow had to return to the question of his working for a living.

'It's all right sighing,' she said. 'It's about time you faced facts, m'lad, and realized you can't just live on fresh air.'

'Okay, I know. You don't have to keep goin' on about it. What with me dad an' all. Jobs, jobs, jobs! Work, work, work! I'm fed up to the back teeth of hearing it.'

'You can be as fed up as you like, but you'll have to put your mind to something, and the sooner the better, if you ask me.'

'I should've been born amongst the upper crust,' he reflected bitterly. 'Not this lowly measly existence.'

'Well you haven't,' she said, going to the stairs. There was no point in saying anything more. Their argument was taking them nowhere except to the point of falling out. 'Come on, let's go and pull your dad out of that pub, 'cos it's like floggin' a dead horse, tryin' to make you see any sense, and that's a fact.'

He was surprised when she actually accompanied him into the taproom instead of waiting outside. His mother didn't care much for pubs. The smell of the beer was enough to turn her stomach, so she would claim.

His father was equally as surprised. 'Well, well, what brings you in here?'

He was still making vain attempts at conversation with the landlady and popping peanuts, his favourite nibble, one at a time into his mouth. A slight blush, a caught-in-the-act guilt spread and glowed momentarily through his suntan. She frequently teased him and accused him of fancying the 'painted piece of mutton dressed as lamb'. He asked her if she'd like a drink.

The landlady smiled a forced but polite smile, one woman to another, when she asked for a bitter lemon, then, having poured the drink, retired to the lounge, pausing only to adjust a few of the trinkets adorning the glass shelves behind the bar. Men she could handle, but men with their wives was a different kettle of fish.

His mother took a sip of the bitter lemon, inspecting the rim of the glass as though expecting to find something which might contaminate her. The action was derisive, implying her criticism of the pub and its decor, and her doubts about the landlady's efficiency as regards upkeep and cleanliness.

Steve handed the key back to his father, slapped the retrieved sketchbook on the table and returned to his pint. He was enjoying the novelty of his mother having joined them. It was the first time he'd been with both his parents in a pub like this. It was the first time he'd known them sit together in a pub — except for weddings, and even then his mother had joined the women and children while the menfolk stayed at the bar.

'I came down to post a letter,' she was saying. 'I had

to post it off as soon as possible. It's that agreement I had to sign to have the operation.'

'You've had the results of your check-up, then?' replied his father.

'Aye, this afternoon. It's women's complaint, just as I expected.'

'What's women's complaint?' put in Steve naively, having a vague idea that it had to do with secret internals and 'tubes' and things. 'I thought women always complained.'

His father ignored him. 'It'll mean a well-earned rest for you anyway,' he told her, 'and this lad here'll have to shift himself whether he likes it or not.'

'Whether I like it or not,' Steve mimicked and slouched in his seat, scraping a fingernail at the dog-eared corners of his sketchbook.

'It doesn't matter, Stephen,' his mother tried to reason for the umpteenth time. 'You'll have to pull your weight while I'm laid up. Besides, there's our Ralph and Ian see you staying in bed on a morning and they want to do the same. Why should Ralph have to go out to work while we let you stay at home? It's not fair to him above everything else.'

He flicked a rolled-up fragment of his sketchbook cover into the ashtray. 'Oh, I'll look for a blinkin' job. Tomorrow! When you going into hospital?'

'Beginning of December, I think. Nothing's been arranged for definite yet.'

'How many weeks will you be going in for?'

She shifted in her chair, impatient with him and the questions. 'Nay, I don't know. It'll all depend.'

'On what?'

'Hey, now you've no need to worry yourself,' his father interrupted, cheerful and sarcastic. 'You won't have to do without her cookin' and washin' your clobber for long.'

6

Oh Christ, did he have to? Was there no way out? Couldn't he simply turn back, keep out of her life, never call on her again, just hope that she might forget all about him as much as he wanted to forget about her? But how could you tell a girl who was absolutely besotted that you wanted nothing more to do with her? How could you say, 'We're through, we're finished, it's over, kaput!' and how did you say such a thing? Just close your eyes and let the words tumble out?

His feet crunched the black cinders as he went along the narrow path. He always felt ill at ease walking down here behind the disused greyhound stadium. It was lonely and creepy in the dark, especially where the path approached the railway viaduct. There was a broken corrugated iron fence and beyond it an overgrown wasteland of twisted bike frames, pushchairs, tyres and other dumpables which had been thrown there for good measure. The only source of light came from dim gas lamps which were spaced yards apart. It seemed the perfect hunting ground for footpads, murderers and teds.

He pushed his sketchbook under his arm for reassurance, then felt a momentary shock that shot to his knees and ankles when he mistook a fence post for the hunched shoulders and greased cockatoo 'Curtis' of Dougie Fleg. 'Phew!' he breathed in deep, coughed to clear his throat and regain composure. Anybody but Dougie Fleg!

He appreciated the fence post, grateful for its dumb, wooden inertness, and plunged on once more in gloomy introspection. The uneasiness of the place and the uncertainty which faced him churned in a nerve-racked cocktail inside his guts, but this evening had to be the evening. He had made up his mind about that. How could you go on telling a girl that you loved her the many many times she needed to hear you say it when all you really wanted to do was get the hell out of her company? You had to be frank about it. 'Look here, Rachel, it's no use pretending and beating about the bush. We're through!' There still remained, however, that part of him which was slightly less adament, and it was this which kept reminding him how good it had been, how flattering and boosting to the ego it was to have a young lady so attractive and sought after declaring her undying love. This part offered also the memories, filling him with the sense of regret and longing for the magic of their times together.

He remembered the first time he'd seen her as a shop assistant working in Woolworths. He had wandered in with a rowdy bunch of fellow students one lunch-time and they'd spied her at the sweet counter. She was wearing a light green overall like the other girls but she was strikingly attractive. She had stood out, charismatic with her dark, heavily made-up Cleopatra eyes and jet black hair piled high and sweeping down her back in an abundant pony tail.

'That's Rachel Brewer,' one of the students had informed him, adding as a character reference, 'Screws for nuts and comes back for shells.'

The next time he saw her she had lost the pony tail, or rather the attached hairpiece which formed the pony tail, but was still as striking as ever. And she was now a student at the art college.

It was nearing the end of the autumn term when she arrived. She had joined the year-long Pre-Dip course in the belief that destiny had a far worthier role for her than that of mere shop assistant, and convinced it might be achieved through her 'flair for art'. Immediately she arrived she was surrounded by admirers — mostly an eager, slow-timing, chatting-up mob of youths who crowded round her in the canteen during breaks. She adored the attention, posed before them like a mannequin, like a ballet dancer about to launch herself into the dance of the dying swan. She posed like a pampered movie star for their benefit, like some disorientated princess of the silent screen, confident she was and always would be the focus of their hungering eyes, and unwilling to accept life on any of its dull, dreary, everyday terms. Rachel was innocent, naive, her act contrived, affected, but there was no denying that she was a corking little piece.

She was seventeen and he celebrating his twentieth birthday with a studio party when they were really introduced for the first time. He wanted to be like his hero, Modigliani, proud, handsome, a prince amongst bohemians, strutting arrogantly before her and reciting fragments of poetry: a line of Rimbaud, of Dylan Thomas, a hint of Rupert Brooke.

'Ah, so beautiful, so wonderful,' she sighed, her arms extended dreamily towards him in a delightful imitation of her silent-screen princess.

That first night they had spent together in the bonemarrow-chilling studio was traumatic, or for him it was at least. Rachel appeared to take it in her stride. With the party over and the last of his guests departed they had remained in each other's arms on the hard floor. She had been passionate with an open, trusting innocence. He was an artist, a romantic poet, someone she had only ever dreamed of meeting, and she was his, responding, accepting.

He had feigned passion, dreading to fail her as she began to move beneath his trembling inexperienced body, dreading as she probed his mouth with her warm searching tongue that she would outpace him and he lose control over her. He lost his nerve, back-pedalled, tried to dilute her intensity with tender little kisses. It was the first time he'd spent the entire night with a girl.

He was full of disappointment and despair. He believed he had failed her, failed the expectations of friends and fellow students, and also failed himself. If the truth should emerge! If anyone should ever know how his shivering virginal body, wrapped in a piece of grubby carpeting for warmth, had longed for the dawn, that cold grey hopelessness filtering the empty beer bottle dregs of their night. How they'd have laughed, those who had been so sure of him, winking knowingly, taking it for granted when they left that he was 'onto a winner there, the lucky swine'.

But Rachel, much to his surprise, had been more than suitably impressed, had taken his sexual novice's hesitancy as a sign of respect and consequently fallen for him. This fact she had revealed a couple of evenings later at the college's Easter Ball, clinging to him in the dim red light of the dance hall. She had wept, fainted for attention, then, lifted by a gathering of girl students who had flocked to her assistance, had murmured with a fluttering of eyelids, 'I love you, darling.'

From then on their love affair had borne them aloft on its wonders and ecstacies, absorbed all his time and attention, brought scorn and rollockings from Telfor, Craggs and Chalmers, and glances of quiet contempt from the principal of the art department, dreary Dearden. More than anything it had helped in bringing about his failure in the Intermediate, but how could anyone think about college, about life drawing or pottery, or painting and sculpture, or put their minds to mounting work for assessment when their whole being was consumed by this aching agony of joy known rather more commonly as 'being in love'? Rachel had glowed in her youth and beauty. They had glowed for each other with a need and desire that went far beyond mere sexual gratification, loving with a longing to be more close, more tender than seemed physically possible as they strolled in their embrace along summer evening streets.

So what had caused the breach? What had made him start to question and reason logically at last in all this exquisite insanity? Was it something trivial, Rachel accidently farting as they sat holding hands one bright sunshine morning on the college steps? Or was it that she claimed from the every beginning that she was a virgin? ('If you want to know something,' she had informed him on one early instance of tension between them, 'I'm still a virgin.') Yet, if so, he asked, how come so many blokes knew about her — not only in the college but also out and about in town? 'Hear you're knockin' off Rachel Brewer, jammy sod,' or 'Rachel Brewer, eh?' followed by a nudge and a chorus of sexually deprived groans and gutteral 'Waughh's'. She had a reputation which seemed to stretch far and wide, and this had tended to gnaw at the soul.

Then there was that evil, scrawny individual, little Dougie Fleg, who, according to the usual unreliable sources through the grapevine, had been threatening to 'smack that milksop art-student git' daring to take the credit for her deflowerment. The message was: 'Dougie Fleg's after yer 'cos you've pinched his bird!'

To use the astronomical term, Dougie Fleg could be compared in stature to a white dwarf. It was as though his head, the size of a football, had condensed to one the size of a cricket ball. Dougie was as hard as granite and had a penchant for beating the shit out of any unfortunate youth he happened to meet and didn't know. What exacerbated the situation was that Dougie had been 'courtin' steady' with Rachel, so rumour had it, and they'd been saving for the bottom drawer.

Confronted with the question of Dougie Fleg, Rachel had denied everything vehemently. God, Dougie Fleg?

She'd only been out with him a couple of times and couldn't abide him, she said, recoiling in horror. But even this reassurance went to complicate the matter and the question of her virginity, or who had taken it, remained disputable.

But then of course there was the question of his mother. Her attitude had certainly helped in gnawing at the frayed edges. Yet you couldn't pull the wool over her eyes, as she was fond of declaring amongst all the other things she was fond of declaring, and according to her reckoning Rachel fell short of the ideal he had tried to bestow on her. Perhaps, though, it wasn't Rachel as much as the heavy mascara and the tight knee-high skirts which had encouraged his mother to label her 'common as muck' and inform him, 'You'll likely end up havin' more children than you beget with her.'

Yet he had so much wanted his mother to take to Rachel the Sunday afternoon he brought her home to tea. Sitting there in the front room that Sunday in May, best china on the new drop-leaf oak dining table and the clean white cloth. There was Ralph and Ian being shy and well-behaved, and Rachel taking to the youngest, Ian, because he was the baby in the family. She had attempted to conduct herself with absolute charm while his mother, taken aback by this dark-eyed siren with the pale pink lips, had remained for the most part reserved, answering with polite sounds and forming impressions.

Maybe there was nothing which particularly cooled his ardour towards Rachel in the final analysis, neither the rumours nor the threats from suitors, or the fact that she conducted herself like a 1920s 'flapper', was generally pig-thick and made a complete mess of everything she tried to cook, including warming baked beans in a frying pan and producing soggy chips. Perhaps too it was nothing to do with those wince-inducing moments — Rachel's mother questioning, 'Would you know by any chance what this stain is on her new dress, Stephen?' or his father's wry comment: 'It's your mother who has to wash your underpants.'

Nor was it to do with the time his mother, deciding to include his corduroy jacket with the weekly wash, left the contents of the pockets in a neat unannounced heap on the kitchen table, including the 'top shelf Woodbine' he'd bought from one of the lads at college for a bob.

Perhaps the responsibility lay with himself. He had allowed the break in the magic and now, because it was broken, he was ready to pay more attention to her faults. Things were different in their varying degrees. At times he might have drifted, full of acceptance when she talked of weddings or wedding rings, but the vision had changed. While she talked of love he saw himself in pubs. He saw himself as sole achiever, as serious artist, and as serious artist he would never achieve anything sitting with his one and only woman, holding hands and swearing undying love to her every blinking night. Serious artists didn't do that. They went out into the world, made love to many women, met with fellow artists, discussed life, got drunk together. They didn't allow themselves to be dragged into dreary arguments of female logic or suffer pangs of remorse because they happened to forget to say, 'I love you too, darling.'

'Oh God,' he breathed. If ever he managed to free himself of this involved mess he'd damn well make sure not to step into it so lively again.

Her house was one at the back of a small row of back-to-back terraced houses where there was a communal red-bricked yard complete with wash houses, clothes posts and shared outdoor toilets. The yard with its clutter reminded him of Utrillo scenes: picturesque but lived-in courtyards tucked away amongst the imaginary thoroughfares of Montmartre. He had thought of it like that the evening, or rather the dawn, he'd insisted on knowing just exactly whereabouts it was Rachel lived. Until then he'd left her at the end of an entirely different street, a 'nice' suburban one, having no cause to disbelieve her when she claimed to live in one of the large semi-detacheds which stood in an imposing line. She would apologize as they kissed their prolonged farewells. She couldn't ask him in. There was an uncle, an explorer returned from his travels, who was staying with them and he was convalescing after being dangerously ill.

Of course he believed her. It seemed natural that a girl like her should live in a house like that — and come from such an unusual and exciting family background. He would drive away on his scooter, leaving her to wave and blow kisses after him from 'her' garden gate. Until the night his scooter, in one of its regular cantankerous moods, conked out and refused to start. He had to leave it then till morning, parked outside the house.

'I never felt so embarrassed in my life,' he ranted and raved afterwards at her, having called for her at the house when he returned next day. 'Calling the bloke Mr Brewer, and asking if you were in!'

She admitted her guilt. She was ashamed of where she lived. 'I had to tell you a little white lie, darling. I just couldn't bear to let you see our squalid little house.'

They returned to her actual home in the grey early hours after the college's midsummer night ball, sneaking in and up the narrow staircase to her cramped little attic room. He winced as he recalled how he had virtually diced with death, passing the open door of her parents' bedroom and he filled with all the dreadful stories he'd been told by fellow students about a drunken, violent, over-possessive father. But he'd been impressed with her room. It had appeared at first sight like the perfect artist's garret with skylight, the stairs, like the stairs to his studio, leading in directly through the stairwell. Frank Bramley, the Newlyn School — though no door to hide behind if her father should come. Incredibly, unbelievably (he shook his head at his own audacity) they'd immediately made love on her creaking, chunky Van Gogh bed. Then, while Rachel had dozed peacefully beside him, he had lain awake for the rest of that hopeless dawn, like a fugitive, like a trespasser on her parents' private lives. He had watched the grey light growing brighter through the skylight, observed the magazine cut-outs of pop stars and film stars gracing nearly every inch of wallspace, so many of them, a silent gallery of smouldering eyes and pearly teeth, their bright clean-shaven faces smiling vacuously at him with lopsided Elvis grins, and all of them free and uninvolved in the dicey position he'd inadvertently landed himself in. It had puzzled him why there should be so many when Rachel had declared she had no time for such shallowness, only poetry and art.

Oh, then the arrival of morning with the alarm clock ringing and the sounds of voiceless awakening, so homely, so familiar, yet so alien and fraught with danger. He had shrunk like a frightened animal into the mattress, Rachel wrapping herself and the eiderdown over him in the hope of giving the impression she was alone in bed.

Fortunately no cause arose to put her camouflage to the test. Rigid, not breathing, heart thumping, he had listened to that unknown, unseen quantity that was her father moving beneath the floorboards, heard the creaking stairs and the heavy tread. Whether the steps were ascending or descending, for a long second it had been hard to tell. It was relief, sheer relief, when her mother had finally called from the bottom of the stairs, 'We're going now, Rachel, love. Are you awake? I've left you two shillings for a packet of cigs.'

Rachel had replied with just the right amount of sleepy

casualness and an undertone of irritability at being disturbed.

He glanced round the yard as he came down the passage. Muffled patches of light shone behind some of the closed-curtain windows and were reflected in the trickles of water that remained in the gutter. He could pick out the low boundary wall, the white salt on its bricks luminous in the dark, and also the clothes posts and the outbuildings, their detail indistinguishable in the black, moonless, end-of-summer night. In sunlight summer it had been the courtyard in Montmartre, the only element to destroy this illusion being the scrapyard over at the other side of the wall where the bulged and dinted corpses of heaped cars stretched like a massive road disaster to the tall arches of the viaduct beyond. At that moment, as he came into the yard, an express train bound for London thundered out slowly, hesitantly over the viaduct, making its way over and away from the town. It waited to build momentum, the lights of the coaches moving like a long taut string of giant light bulbs suspended in the night sky. The locomotive gushed power with its initial exertion, the big driving wheels slipping then gripping, then slipping again.

He sniffed at the damp oily warmth of steam and smoke which drifted out over the housetops and across the scrapyard. The locomotive waited for clearance, then gained speed gradually as it headed out onto the main London line.

He watched the train depart, wishing he was on it, sitting inside one of those light bulbs suspended above the brick ramparts of the viaduct. He had never been to London. It remained as yet an uncharted land full of his own fascinated but uncertain images of it. One of these days soon he was determined he would live in London.

7

She was strikingly attractive. You couldn't deny that. She was wearing a pink woollen sweater which showed the gentle curve of her breasts and went so well against the tight-fitting black skirt. And those dark nylons! Ah, for a girl not quite yet eighteen didn't she have the most marvellous pair of legs. Control yourself, young man, he told himself. You are an artist and should stand firm by your own convictions, not be weakened by shallow appearances.

'I see you have your sketchbook,' she noted, all smiles as she let him in. 'Is it to do my portrait like you promised?'

'I thought it might be a good idea,' he told her as he followed her into the single downstairs room that served both as living room and kitchen. Saying his hullos to her parents, he sat on a stool by a table still littered with the dishes from their evening meal. No words of upset for the moment, he thought. Especially when her parents were there — especially when her father was there. Better that he never get to cross purposes with that gentleman. Dougie Fleg had already made that mistake, or so rumour had it, and ended with a fractured jaw for his troubles. Mr Brewer was broad and muscular, running slightly to fat but standing well over six feet.

At that moment Mr Brewer was slumped in one of the frayed armchairs in front of the fire, the evening paper held before him as if he were hiding behind it. He was deeply suntanned, had short, tousled, greying hair and still looked boyishly youthful even though he was forty five. Rachel thought he looked like her favourite film star, Paul

Newman, but as far as his unpredictable moods were concerned he reminded her of the sea. Steve could appreciate the similarity — the still calm and the raging storm — though thankfully he had only learned of these storms through weather reports issued frequently by Rachel and her mother.

Rachel said, 'If we're going out I'll get ready.'

She had boasted when they first met that her father was a member of a scientific research team, but this story belonged with the one about the explorer uncle and the early in-love days when she lived in the large semi-detached house. In reality he drove a bulldozer, levelling land for building sites.

He watched as she went over to a mirror above the sink. The sink, over in the corner to one side of the chimney breast, was the kitchen area, surrounded by the paraphernalia of gas cooker, draining board and cupboards and shelves for utensils — rather like a bedsitter. She stood poised for action with her long-handled steel comb.

'I thought you were ready,' he said.

'Oh, no, not quite,' she answered quickly. 'I don't want to go out with my hair in a mess like this.'

He laughed to hide his irritation, wondering how a single hair in that great black puff-ball could be out of place. The hard, lacquered, toffee-like, skeletal structure surrounded her smooth blemishless face like the busby of a palace guard. As with all the girls flaunting this popular hairstyle she appeared, from behind, to have an enormously oversized beachball head. 'Your hair's okay,' he told her.

'Oh, but I want it to look right,' she insisted, tapping at the unyielding ball with her comb.

'We're not going to a dance,' he said, rather more irritated but forcing another chuckle.

'Been nice today,' her mother interrupted to break the silence and the tension threatening to mount within it as

Rachel attacked her hair. She was in the other armchair, busy with her knitting and counting the stitches.

'Lovely,' he agreed, nodding and smiling at her. Rachel had also boasted that her mother was the daughter of an Italian count and that they visited Italy frequently. Believing her, Steve concluded that Rachel must have inherited her dark Mediterranean beauty on her mother's side of the family. True, Rachel did have a certain amount of the Latin beauty about her but as for her mother, she appeared to have as much of the Mediterranean blood in her as his mother, and she'd been born and bred in Castleford.

He always found it easier to talk and respond to her mother. She was mild-mannered, easy-going, and he could joke with her, act the clown, leaving both mother and daughter joyously laughing together. But when her father was there, established as king of the roost with his two females, he soaked up all effort and attention, dominating the scene with his uncompromising strength and silence. Conversation with him usually centred on man-to-man stifled discussions — the weather or the best beers, and perhaps a derogatory comment about current affairs or the government. It was a gesture of his friendliness, of showing his acceptance of the daughter's young man. Otherwise he was reserved, drawn deep into his quietness, generally polite but not given to many words.

Steve glanced at him. It was difficult to tell if he was in a good mood or a bad one. The face remained impassive, like a polar bear's giving no indication of whatever might rage below the surface. Perhaps it might be a bad mood, otherwise he might have exchanged at least a couple of words in greeting instead of the brief nod he'd given above his newspaper. But he looked done-in, his grey work-shirt open to reveal a hairy chest and grubby string vest. A pair of wellies, mud-caked and the mud drying on them, stood in the hearth.

Rachel squirted a jet of lacquer onto her already well-cemented hair, turning her head this way, then another before the mirror before continuing with more of the frantic back-combing.

'How long are you gonna be?' Steve asked casually, failing to keep the edge out of his voice.

There came no answer but the spring of the steel comb as it encountered obstacles in its path.

He watched her for a moment in her obstinate single-minded concern for her vanity. When roused it pushed aside all other considerations. He hated it then, her beauty and her concern for her beauty which fed tritely on itself and became enmeshed with all the many exquisitely feminine mass-produced glass bottles and jars littering the sideboard. Her beauty. Her vanity! So many varying shades of eye-shadow, like pans of watercolour in plastic paintboxes, then the long black fluttering eyelashes looking like joke bluebottles, and the sootcakes of mascara and the pale pink lipsticks for the final touch. Even her hair was dyed. The gleaming blue-black smothered completely any natural colour which, so her mother had informed him, was more of a dark brown.

So often had he tried to talk her out of applying all this make-up. He wanted to see the natural Rachel, he would appeal to her. He wanted to know how she really looked, not how she appeared to look.

'You wouldn't like me then if you saw me, darling,' she would say, pushing his entreaties aside. Her vanity was major fault number one. It had come between their love so many times.

He sighed quietly in the uncomfortable heat of the room and studied the staircase door facing opposite. A large full-length painting of Rachel, done by herself on a hardboard panel, still disguised the hole her father had kicked in the door. It was one of about half a dozen self portraits she'd produced in glossy housepaint, and as with the others her face was long and oval, the neck long and swanlike and set on a quick suggestion of sloping shoulders, the eyes dark and pupilless and staring dreamily ahead. Rachel, like himself, wanted to devote her life to painting — or some of it. The rest she wanted to devote to him.

She squirted another jet of lacquer, filling the air with a sickly acetone and perfume smell. She went on prodding and tugging, using the comb handle to prize up and tease out the interior of the dome, clearly disregarding the grapevine tale of the girl who was supposed to have been found dead with a nest of cockroaches inside her bouffant hair. Rachel had been horrified by the story of how the girl complained of a headache, then died, and how the autopsy revealed that the cockroaches had been eating into her brain. But not horrified enough! She went on prodding her hair.

'I see there's a new pop group who say they're gonna grow their hair longer than the Beatles,' he said to her father, cynical, man-of-the-world to humour him. 'Call 'emselves the Rolling Stones, I think. Gathering moss. Summat like that.'

Mr Brewer glanced slowly over his paper, gave a nod in response. 'Soon have it as long as yours in that case,' he murmured without humour.

Steve looked over to the fireplace as Mr Brewer went back to his paper. He must definitely be in a bad mood. Mrs Brewer went on clicking her knitting needles, pulling at the ball of black wool she was using and clicking and knitting. She muttered under her breath when she dropped a stitch. He focused his eyes on the chimney breast, at the wallpaper printed in a crude design of a stone wall. The old contradiction! They plastered over the brickwork, then covered the plaster with wallpaper designed as brickwork.

The wallpaper made him think of barns and farmyard walls, the cool wind and rain of outdoors which he longed for, sweating and waiting for Rachel before a roaring fire. He picked up that morning's paper, lying folded and discarded amongst the debris of breadcrumbs and dishes on the table, and took a closer look at the photo which had caught his attention and prompted him to try conversation with Mr Brewer. It was of the 'fab four', head and shoulders, facing the camera. The photo was grainy, contrasted artily, making their fringed white faces seem flawless like alabaster.

'Are you ready yet, Rachel?' her mother put in quietly, ineffectually. 'Don't keep Steve waiting.'

'Give us a minute,' Rachel answered her snappily, giving her hair yet another squirt of lacquer.

Her father gave a sudden snort and glared over at her, a frowning yet puzzled expression on his depthless, suntanned face.

'Get yourself away from the mirror,' he commanded, though he made it sound more like a gentle request.

'W-what, Dad?' Rachel forced the stutter, as if she held him in dread. Steve cringed with embarrassment.

'Get away from the mirror,' her father suggested, not looking at her but settling behind his paper, his stocking feet with holes in the toes spreading towards the fire.

Rachel flinched as though about to be struck. The reaction was overdone, too obvious, the poor misunderstood child suffering at the hand of a domineering brute of a father. Even then she attacked her hair once more, lunging at it with even more determination. Suddenly she threw the comb at the mirror, flopping sulkily onto the nearest chair.

'Damn rotten lousy hair! I'm not going out.'

Steve looked nervously over at her father who kept on reading the paper. 'Crumbs! What's wrong with your hair,

Rachel? Leave it. It's okay. Let's go.'

'Yes, come on, love,' her mother coaxed, lowering her knitting. 'Your hair's all right.'

'No, it's not all right,' Rachel muttered and forced a sob for the sake of it.

Her father now lowered his paper for the second time, eyeing her steadily as something powerful inside him simmered ready to erupt. He screwed up his eyes against her as if dazzled by the sun.

Mrs Brewer said plaintively, aware of her husband, 'You're always looking in the mirror. Do as your dad tells you and put your coat on. Put the new one on we bought you.'

Rachel turned on her sharply. 'Oh, shut up, Mum! It's not you who has to go out with your hair in a mess.'

'But it's not in a mess,' Steve cried, wanting to reassure her, wanting more than anything to take sides with her father who at the moment looked as though he was about to froth at the mouth.

Rachel tried another sob. 'You won't like me if my hair's in a mess.'

He tried a laugh through mounting anxiety, spreading his palms towards her father, helplessly appealing. 'As if it should make any difference to me. I take her out, not her hair.'

Her father looked at him without seeing him. The next moment he zoomed in on his daughter. In one swift movement he flung the newspaper aside, seized one of the wellies up out of the hearth and threw it at her. The welly bounced harmlessly against the wall behind her, then fell amongst the crockery on the table. There was the clatter of a whole dinner service breaking but only one cup was knocked to the floor and didn't break. Steve sank, feeling his guts about to exit from his backside. He studied the muddy wellington where it had landed like a crazy centrepiece gracing a dinner-party table.

'I've heard all I want to hear from you, miss,' her father followed through with his action. 'Now clear out before I throw you out,' he warned, his voice strangely light yet tightening in its fury.

'Y-y-yes, Dad! I'm going. I'm going.'

Rachel gushed wide-eyed, full of terror but somehow stupidly provoking. Steve looked away, his head shaking nervously, sure that the man would run amok. She stayed rigid, not making a move until her father had retrieved his newspaper. Then she went to the table, making an exaggerated genteel effort of lifting the boot and replacing it alongside the other in the hearth.

'Rachel,' her father cautioned softly, heedless of the chewable tension he'd left in his wake, 'just go, eh? Just get out.'

Steve made certain to keep his distance as they left the house. The prospect of having to hold her hand after all that was positively unappealing. He needed to remain withdrawn from her, smarting in his annoyance and humiliation, and fear. Rachel, unashamed, struggled playfully against him as he held himself aloof.

'Oh, darling, it's so lovely to be with you again,' she said, light heartedly sarcastic at his reticence. All the trouble in the house was forgotten, an incident she had left behind her.

'It must be all of eight hours since we last saw each other,' he mumbled, hunching his shoulders and gripping his hands in his pockets.

'What's that you say, darling?'

'Bloody hell, Rachel, I could swing for you,' he told her. 'Carrying on like that with your dad! Are you tired of living, or something. If you are don't take me with yer.'

She gave a dismissing wave. 'Oh, don't worry about him. What is he to us? Just an ignorant peasant.'

'Oh, you reckon, do yer? Well, if he is he's a dangerous one as well.'

She laughed. 'Don't worry about him,' she urged and hugged her arms around his neck, pulling him to her and giving him a warm soft kiss on the cheek. She was happy. They were together again. 'He'd never do anything to harm you. I wouldn't let him. Besides, he likes you.'

'God help me if he didn't. That's all I can say.'

She made a little gurgling sound in her throat, amused by what he said, and held out her hand to him, waiting. 'You look a little tired, darling', she observed.

'I feel okay,' he said, allowing her to take his hand. 'Perhaps a little tired,' he added, remembering to address her as 'darling'.

She smiled, then squeezed his hand, kissing it as she walked beside him, head held proud, towards the town.

8

She was cool, elegant, didn't have thin ankles, didn't totter unbalanced on her high stilettos, nor did she throw her feet about or waddle like a duck, but carried herself with such sophisticated grace. She knew how to dress to the best effect too, whether it was her knee-high tight corduroy skirts or the Little Lord Fauntleroy velvet outfits that she sometimes liked to wear with silk blouses. This evening she was wearing a three-quarter length brown suede coat, the long buckleless belt tied in a loose single knot and the collar turned up so stylishly against the coolness of the evening.

He gave her a sidelong glance, watching her as she admired herself surruptitiously in the mirror of a furniture shop window that they passed. Aye, she was a smart piece all right, outstandingly attractive, and against all his resolve and better judgement he couldn't help but gaze with pleasure at what he saw, that she was looking so good.

But no. Oh no! He didn't want her like she wanted him, didn't look to her for his future wife like she looked to him for her husband. Yet they were supposed to be engaged, damn it! Unofficially, of course. She still wore the cheap Woolworths ring which he'd bought for threepence off one of the Pre-dip girls. He'd been drunk at the time, and everyone had thought what a splendid idea it would be to announce an engagement before the end of the college year. The ring was still there, alongside another Christmas cracker ring that the explorer uncle was supposed to have brought back from the Himalayas.

'I sold a painting today,' she suddenly informed him, squeezing his arm with glee. 'Five pounds, darling. Five whole pounds.'

He was sceptical, wondering if this was to be a repeat of an earlier sale-of-work episode when she'd helped herself to a fiver out of her mother's wage packet. She had only borrowed the money for a couple of hours as back-up proof of a fictional sale. She had wanted to impress.

'Who did you sell it to?' he asked.

She gave a vague sweep of her arm, unwilling to go into detail. 'Just a friend of my father's. They landed home at tea-time a little intoxicated, I think.'

'Ah, I thought your dad was looking a bit off.'

'Oh, him! He'd just got up. He had a bit of a head, that's all.' She continued to enthuse about the sale of the painting, how she'd been in the yard working on it when they landed and how the friend had offered to buy it right away. She had taken her painting equipment, the tins of gloss she used, and turning deaf ears to all the banging and clattering that went on daily in the scrapyard, and ignoring the calls and whistles of the workmen, she had set out her stall.

'I painted it because I felt moved by the beautiful day,' she went on in a loud modulated voice. 'I painted it just as it came to me, just as you advised me to do.' It was, she believed, her most successful painting to date. 'I called it Ve Girl in Blue.'

He cringed at the loudness of her voice, her words delivered theatrically rather than spoken in the grim street. God! Why couldn't she ever behave normally and straightforwardly instead of in a way that made people think she was mad? But Rachel never paid any heed to the glances of the curious, nor their behind-the-hand smirks. She knew no half measures on that score but took her role-acting to extremes before her two-tone unsuspecting public. Yet she did it so naively, so obviously and somehow so clumsily. But what were those people to her, those insiduous mockers, those scorning females with their own beehive hairstyles and their uninspiring fashions, or the roughnecks calling out to her like howling randy dogs from passing lorries or building sites? They were all part of the drab normality, the uniformity of an essentially grey conformist society, and she felt herself above it, had no wish to be part of it, even fractionally. Their grey uniformity, the greyness of their lives, tainted her like grime.

'You called it Ve Girl in Blue?' he asked. 'You mean The Girl in Blue.' He thrust his tongue between his teeth demonstratively. 'Th, th, th! The, not Ve!'

How many more times had she to be told? She was forever saying 've' instead of 'the', and 'frough' instead of 'through', and he couldn't bear to hear her.

He stopped himself. He was forgetting. It should no longer concern him how she sounded her tee-aiches, but, oh God! Why couldn't she act normally instead of constantly doing and saying things which made him want to curl up foetally? But now she was on the defence against his fault-finding, refusing to accept that she was regressing to old habits both he and her mother had taken great pains to break her from. She added for the sake of it, 'Ve Girl in Blue, like I said.'

'Suit yourself,' he retorted, thinking that this was simply another minus to add to the long list he already had against her. She could be just as stubborn about her spelling, refusing to accept that she'd spelt a word wrongly even when it was so obvious. 'I spell it that way,' was the answer so, like it or lump it, he'd had to accept in the love letters that she'd written him that their love made her 'cry grate tears of hapiness' and that he had 'brort' her into a world in which she could 'tresure' every moment they were together.

He allowed her to lean against him, tightening his arm around her more in gesture than as a need. 'So, you got a fiver for the painting?'

'Yes, darling, a fiver — though I had to give mum the pound back I owed her. That leaves me with four.'

'And you say your dad's friend bought it while it was still wet?' He suspected benevolence borne on a few lunchtime pints. Or perhaps the friend might have been fancying her. He hitched his sketchbook further under his arm. Perhaps her dad had been trying to fix him up for a date with her . . . 'Our savings?' he asked in alarm, suddenly hearing the subject mentioned.

'Yes, our savings. I said we don't have to worry what we spend tonight, as long as it's no more than a pound, and the rest we can put towards our savings.'

He held himself tense. She was making bold advances, touching on sensitive issues. Nevertheless he managed to smile. 'We don't have to worry about that now, surely. Spend as much as you like. It's yours. Put some of it towards a new dress or a new pair of shoes.'

Rachel looked at him. 'I bet you say that because you don't want us to be married,' she accused, making a vague attempt to pull herself free of him. 'I really think you're just a playboy at heart.'

'No, no, it's not that,' he said, searching frantically for the right words and trying to hold onto her in spite of himself. Rachel could be surprisingly quick on the uptake at times. 'I just don't think now's the time to worry about it. I just don't think it's . . . it's fair on you.'

'Why not? Why do you say that?'

'Because . . . look, let's discuss our savings when I'm earning some money — which should be soon. And if you get a job as well,' he assured her, tongue-in-cheek, 'then we'll be able to start saving together.'

God, he thought. Why couldn't she forget about his Christmas cracker ring?

Rachel moved in closer to him again, placated, full of understanding. 'You're right, as always, darling. I'm sorry.

I know what a worry it must be for you, not earning anything. So, we'll not think about it. We'll live for the moment. Enjoy what we can while we can, as you say. We can go to the Horse, if you like. You can draw my portrait in your sketchbook.'

'Or Helena and Mozz might be there.'

'Yes,' she said. 'I want to see Helena and Maurice and buy them both a drink.'

'The Horse it is, then,' he agreed brightly but mentally kicking himself.

*

The Horse was down a narrow cobbled alley known as Pottersgate, near the town centre, and was said to be one of the oldest pubs in town.

There was a certain charm about Pottersgate, an old-world charm of Dickensian shop fronts with dusty bottle glass windows and unevenly lumped-together buildings. He liked to imagine that this was how the backstreets of Montmartre might appear, narrow, picturesque and steeped in quiet antiquity. Walking down it, he could pretend he was an artist living in Paris. Pottersgate and the Horse were a sanctuary, especially at the weekends, hidden away from the general bustle and charmlessness of a ted-infested town, though the pub did attract a small portion of the rougher element which might happen to stray from the main thoroughfare. But they were soon off, back to the bright lights and the jukeboxes. The 'Hoss' was a dead-hole for them, full of old men and arty-farty puffs.

The inside of the pub consisted of a single narrow saloon with the brass railed bar running the length of it and about two centuries of black dust covering everything. Gnarled black beams were suspended overhead while over the floor was a liberal spreading of sawdust which became polluted with cig-ash, spilt beer and tab-ends. The sawdust was swept up and changed regularly once a week. A hard wooden bench-seat ran along the back wall and there were round, cast iron tables, their brown linoleum tops cig-scorched and beerstained. Wooden stools served for those who could do without the comforts of a wooden backrest pressing into their spine. At one end of the room there was a large fireplace which made the place Christmassy on dark winter nights when the fire glowed (and made it overpowering too when the coals were banked too high). Complete with the mirrors which bore adverts for Scotch whisky and cigarettes, and a pendulum clock which ticked loudly and lazily on when the pub was empty, the Horse was like a tableau reconstruction from a museum. This evening was one of those when there was quite an unexpected crowd so that they had to ease and meander their way to the bar in easy stages.

It became like that from time to time. Midweeks there were usually just a few of the regulars lounging about or propping up the bar, but sometimes it was as if word had spread to distant parts that the Horse was worth a visit and for no apparent reason the world and its dog would suddenly descend.

Steve pushed his way in, making sure that Rachel kept up with him as a matter of course. He didn't like it when it was too packed. He felt lost within the throng, insignificant, inconsequential, wondering if he'd ever reach the bar and whether, if he managed to force a way through, he'd have become invisible on the way. 'What d'yer know,' he'd say to Rachel whenever he remained unserved and ignored, 'it looks like I've forgotten to put the bandages on tonight.'

He noticed how one or two of the blokes eyed up Rachel, how they stepped politely though pointedly aside for her while remaining an almost impregnable barrier for him.

A bad move, coming in here, he thought, and asked Rachel if she wanted her usual lager and lime or a short.

'But darling, I'm buying,' she insisted, reaching into her bag for her purse.

'No, I'll get 'em first,' he said, relieved for once from the weekday waiting for gratuities, the scraping together of here-and-there pennies and ha'pennies for a packet of five Woodies and a couple of halves of mild. He shuffled his way in between two tall duffle-coated bods, waiting, trying to let his impatience ebb. The bar with its beer pumps and shelves full of glasses and bottles made him think of Manet's bar at the Folies Bergère. But here there was no beautiful but sad-eyed barmaid to serve him, only Paddy the unrushed landlord, and Maud, his equally unrushed wife.

He waited, feeling invisible, exasperated by the lack of urgency shown by Paddy and Maud, and hating the tall bods who pressed in on either side of him with their drained froth-clinging glasses. Everyone seemed determined, at least on this side of the bar, like pigs at the trough. He was a little runt piglet putting up a useless fight for a teat. He caught his reflection in the mirror behind the bar, saw no photogenic impressions of Modigliani but his own pale, insipid and insigificant little face lost amongst the many big significant faces surrounding it.

Christ! he thought and wished that Paddy or his wife would realize there was more than half a dozen in the room and get a move on.

It was the landlady who eventually caught his desperate, almost demonical stare and thankful, relieved, he slithered away from the trough with the half of lager with a dash of lime for Rachel and a pint of bitter for himself.

'Excuse me. Could I just get by? Thank you.' He smiled in spite of his tension. A tall attractive girl with long blond hair, very arty, very deb, returned his smile.

Wonder if she's fancying me, he thought, taken by surprise. It was the question he immediately asked if he managed more than a few seconds' glance from any attractive girl.

'Over here, darling. They're over here,' Rachel called to him as he forged his way after her, the two drinks held carefully away from jostling elbows and his sketchbook clamped precariously under one arm. The arty deb glanced at Rachel, heard the affectionate way she addressed him and lost all interest. At least that was how the brief drama unfolded itself before him. Rachel and her 'darlings'! Damn her and blast her to hell.

They were all sitting around one of the tables at the bottom end of the room — Mozz and Helena, Sarah with Humph and some of the last year's leavers, Ponch and Stan, and there was Bev and Tony and Denty! A couple of others hung on the periphery, first years he'd known only by sight, now moved up in the wake of last year's lot as fully fledged art students themselves. And blimey! There was Frank Bassen, or Baz, one of the creams-of-success from previous years and now on his second year at one of the big art colleges in London.

Steve waved at Baz but Baz, with his thick curly black hair and his beard making him look like an El Greco Christ, didn't wave to people, or shake hands and all that social custom crap. He just sat there in his black polo-necked sweater and brown leather trenchcoat looking distinguished, important, his gestures predetermined, his mannerisms cool. He eyed Steve blankly, giving no indication that he'd seen him or recognized him, or gave a damn.

Helena was the first one to acknowledge him. She wiggled her fingers in hullo, then told Mozz to squeeze up along the seat and let Rachel sit down. Steve grabbed a vacant stool, thankful to be out of the mêlée round the bar and with people that he knew. He took a swig of beer, looking round at the others and exchanging nods of acknowledgement. Here they were again, the bright sparks who had been the bane of their tutors — all except Baz and Ponch. Ponch was amongst the tiny few who'd managed to pass the Intermediate on the year just gone and was now on the NDD at Leeds.

'Now then, Stan. How goes it?' Steve asked.

Stan yawned, then laughed. 'Me? I'm a full-time failure, after an honours degree in it, I am. Failing.'

'I'm a failure as well,' put in Denty and picked up Steve's sketchbook without permission, flicking through the pages. He made a growling sound at the back of his throat as though he was about to spit.

'What about you, Tony? You pass?'

Tony sniggered. Him pass? What a giggle. What did a lousy intermediate in art mean anyway? Blokes were hosing out toilets and sweeping roads with their degrees and NDDs.

'Aye, too many bleedin' artists,' put in Bev, eyeing the two new hopefuls with their new college scarves self-consciously draped round their necks. He pushed one of them roughly aside from him. 'Come on, settle down now.'

The others laughed, echoing, 'Yeah, come on, settle down now' in a mutual take-off of the dreary Dearden. They were all familiar with that ineffectual cliché: Dearden, doodling and daydreaming, lost in his own little world until the students became too noisy and unruly, when he would give the standard reproach, 'Come on, settle down now.'

Steve heard the voice as he'd heard it on his last day at college, standing like a naughty pupil in Dearden's stale tobacco smoke-filled office, Dearden chain-smoking, doodling designs on the corner of a drawing board: 'You'll just have to face facts, Verity. Forget about art. Get a job. You're no good. Just no good at all.' All part of the memories, all part of the 'do you remember's' and the 'what about when's'.

'Do you remember that old Austin Ruby of Arthur's?' he asked. 'Eight of us squeezed in the back?'

'And the door dropped off as we shot down the road?'

'Bleeding' crazy, Arthur was.'

'Yeah, used to drive that thing when he was pissed and could hardly stand.'

'What about Jim? Has anybody seen him?''

'Ah, Jim's had his chips. He's almost married.'

'What about when Jim had that party, and Verity borrowed his dad's van?'

'Fourteen of us in the back o' that one and all pissed.'

'It was off the road for good after that, wa'n't it, Verity?'

Steve smiled, indulgent.

'I'm a constant disappointment to me dad.'

'What about the party at Jim's, though?'

Ah, yes, and what about the party at Jim's — women galore running about the house dressed only in their nighties. The party had been an all-nighter back in June, when Jim's parents were away, and there'd been Debbie Ingham from the Dip AD, blond, doll-faced Debbie with the most marvellous figure and wearing a flimsy pale pink 'baby-doll'. Cor! It was the night he and Rachel got engaged, for Chrissake, when he'd given her the ring, and they'd made love, as though to 'seal the deal', in the back of the van, parked where it was in the street. And afterwards they'd had one of their tiffs, over something or nothing, and Rachel had stormed off into the house, locking herself in the bathroom. Then, as he followed her, there was Debbie, doll-faced Debbie with the 'baby-doll', asking him if he'd a light for her fag and looking at him with that leg-weakening expectancy in her eyes. It was at that point Rachel had decided to go dramatically berserk in the bathroom, declaring she had overdosed with whisky and tablets and was about to die, and everyone had rushed to drag him away from Debbie, telling him that it was his responsibility to be there at Rachel's passing.

Bloody Rachel! Only too soon had there been some other bloke to offer Debbie her light while he'd been left holding the limp rag-doll drunken Rachel to sob out her heart, and the contents of her stomach, down the front of his shirt.

Debbie was a memory, another of those unavoidable lost opportunities receding to the distance like a stopping-place he'd paused at briefly along his journey. Likewise with his years at college, he could see those in the perspectives of a journey, a station at which he'd halted now disappearing further into the distance from where he'd come. It was the same for all of them — for Denty, Tony, Stan, Bev and the others — all of them on their way, moving on again, though for the moment sitting like this and swapping anecdotes before time should make them part and go their separate ways.

'And how's Mozz, then?' Steve asked him and indicated the guitar in its worn leather case propped against the table. 'What should we give 'em tonight? A bit of Leadbelly or Broonzy?'

Mozz tapped his chest with the flat of his hand and gave a little nervous cough. 'Don't know yet, meself, man. Tell you when I've sunk a few more pints.'

He was slenderly built, quiet and shy, with a pale thin face which peered out myopically from beneath a thick fringe of dark unkempt hair. He was wearing his usual shabby black duffle-coat which had half the pegs missing and a faded college scarf which looked as if it hadn't been washed for the past four years.

'We could let rip with Midnight Special if you like,' Steve suggested jokingly, feeling as reticent himself to wail his head off in the crowded pub. A few more beers perhaps, then they'd be off; Mozz, encouraged by the vociferous Humph, casting caution, or his shyness, to the wind.

Mozz's guitar, or 'guit' as he called it, was as much a part of him as Helena his 'gal'.

Rachel, busily talking to Helena, reached out without looking to take Steve's hand. He allowed her to lace her fingers round his but wished she wouldn't hold his hand in the pub like this. It made him feel tethered, like a Siamese twin, cramping his freedom of movement. Besides that, it made his arm ache.

He smiled and nodded at Helena. She was a friendly and pretty girl, nineteen, nearly twenty, with a small elfin face and brown eyes that were almond-shaped and large like a Persian cat's. A long tangle of auburn hair, which she never bothered to comb or brush, hung down her back, almost reaching her waist. She wore scruffy dark polo-necked sweaters most of the time, together with jeans that were faded and patched. Sometimes she wore a grey skirt which showed off her thin schoolgirl's legs, and with the skirt she'd wear the thick black wool stockings which had seemed the popular attire amongst the art college girls. Helena's stockings made her legs look even thinner and more schoolgirlish, and they always had round 'potatoes' in them which revealed her white skin beneath.

She was the exact opposite to Rachel, never bothering with any of the feminine niceties which might enhance her appearance, yet he'd always found her somehow more appealing, more fascinating. Rachel, chatting happily away, looked synthetic. Helena, patient, tolerant, diplomatic and intelligent, looked real.

Sarah caught his eye then and he exchanged a smile with her, still unsure after all this time whether he ought to speak. Sarah was another of his past hoped-fors, a dark-haired, petite and very attractive girl who was gentle and mouse-like quiet until she felt strongly about some topic; then she would air her views with surprising force. He'd taken her out a few times in the days before he met Rachel, careering through town with her on the back of his scooter. Sarah had fancied him. The grapevine had informed him of that, and on their first date he'd headed off with her along a straight, reaching nearly eighty miles an hour — an amazing feat for his Tigress, which crackled like a chip-pan full of burning fat whenever it touched anything over forty five miles per hour. 'We did over a ton there,' he'd lied to her proudly.

Then Trevor Humphries had fancied her, long, tall, angular Humph with his long pale face, sunken cheeks and fine goatee beard. Humph had charisma, was quick-witted, popular, highly entertaining, people gravitated towards him. He was boisterous, brow-beating and insulting and boss-of-the-show, but played excellent guitar. One evening when they were in the Flame Humph had manoeuvred himself with the skill of an adept chess-player (or a jackal) and called checkmate on a beautiful and blossoming relationship. Clearly he had the personality she'd wanted. Sarah had turned her back on scooters and arrogant, self-opinionated would-be artists, and gone off with an arrogant self-opinionated guitarist instead.

Sarah and Humph were an accepted 'couple' now, as were Helena and Mozz, or Rachel and himself, and all those weeks of torture and hurt pride, and the dread of meeting face-to-face were behind him. He took it for granted that Sarah and Humph were together, constantly quarrelling in public, more so when Humph was canned and practically incapable, but as a couple he still thought they were weird.

Humph noticed his smile at Sarah and broke off from a conversation he was having with Baz and Ponch.

'Hullo, Verity. Brought your sketchbook, I see. Is that to show off you're an art student?'

Steve struggled for a quick answer but couldn't think of one. Humph had him stitched up before he could take a breath to speak. He preferred to keep his distance with Humph. He could be a sod when he wanted, taunting people and trying to belittle them, especially if he had an audience. It had been like that throughout college and Steve always found himself left with a sense of helpless rage whenever he was at the brunt of Humph's wit. He thought vaguely of telling Humph to piss off but feared he might receive a punch on the nose if he did. He looked across instead to Baz, forcing eye contact and, when he got it, made sure not to smile this time, or say hullo, or anything corny like that.

Baz nodded ever so slightly. He was big, heroic, elemental in the little backstreet pub, on one of his quick visits north, a big fish floating a while in a little pond, not roped in with the grim shallowness of life or possessive girls.

'How's life then, Baz?'

Baz shrugged, puzzling over the question. Steve cringed at his own stupidity in asking anything so banal. What did he mean? What was the implication in 'How's life'? He was certain that was how Baz would be weighing the question.

'How's London?' he rushed in, equally as banal.

'Big!' replied Baz at last, never using half a dozen words where one would do. But Steve knew and appreciated his worth. Even Humph did, although he'd often made scathing criticism against Baz and his 'intellectualism'. When you managed to penetrate that cool exterior you made contact with a lively, intelligent mind.

'Are you up just for the weekend?' Steve asked, leaning towards him, wanting to draw out conversation. He became aware of Rachel holding tightly onto his hand. It distracted him, held him in check. He wanted her to let go. Didn't she ever get tired of holding hands all the time? Baz eyed her lazily, smirking with his eyes at Steve. Was he still with that crazy bird of his? he seemed to half want to know.

Steve felt stupid, holding hands in front of Baz like a ruddy smitten teenager. 'Whereabouts are you living in London? Still in the bathroom?'

Baz frowned. 'Bathroom?'

'Yes, you remember. You told me you had a room no bigger than a bathroom in Earl's Court last time we met.'

'Oh, that?' Now he remembered. 'That's history.'

'So, now where you living? Still Earl's Court?'

'Notting Hill.'

Steve wracked his brain for intelligent questions but his brain wouldn't budge. He asked if he was living in a flat. Baz nodded slowly, seeing all, knowing such a lot but worldweary with his knowledge.

'Yeah, a flat.' He never liked to say too much when he was out in a crowd, never liked to let his left hand know what his right one was doing, as he'd often put it himself.

'What's it like? Big, or pokey like your bathroom?'

'Pretty big,' he said, allowing himself to volunteer a little more information. He spoke with the slight London accent he'd adopted during his days at the art college in Calderton, having made every conscious effort to drop the Yorkshire one. 'I share with two guys who go to the Royal College. It's costing me a bit more though. A fiver a week.'

Steve gasped. 'A fiver a week?' That was about as much as he could expect to earn in a week if he took one of his mother's 'proper jobs'. He visualized London as an exotic place filled with architectural grandeur and peopled by wealthy, sophisticated ladies and gentlemen driving around in vulgar expensive cars. Everything about the place would be massive and important. Notting Hill, Earls Court, Shepherd's Bush, the West End, they were simply names to him, and all juxtaposed in his mind's eye in an area around Buckingham Palace, Big Ben and the River Thames. He wanted to live in London. He must go to London. It was where anyone worth their salt went to live.

The rest was paltry shit.

'What's London like, Baz? What's it really like?'

He became aware of Rachel sighing restlessly beside him. It was her way of showing that she wasn't altogether happy with the amount of attention she was being given.

'Darling,' she whispered pointedly, 'I think I shall have to go away and talk to someone else if you don't want anything more to do with me.'

She laughed, but he knew by the tone of her voice that she wasn't making jokes. Baz turned away to rejoin Humph and Ponch and to speak to someone else who'd joined the group. He didn't hang around, definitely not if it meant inconveniencing the privacy of a loving couple like Steve and his crazy bird.

'You haven't spoken two words to me since we came in here,' Rachel complained, her voice edged but low so no one would hear.

He took a drink, looking into the enclosed personal world of his glass. It cut him off for a few brief seconds from Rachel and her silent demands. He wanted to flare up at the way she had imposed herself on his and Baz's serious communication.

'You were talking to Helena, weren't you?' he said, his voice also taking on an edge but low.

'But I don't just want to talk to her all night,' Rachel whispered between her teeth. 'I'd like to be able to talk to you some of the time.'

He exhaled through his nose, cast eyes to the beams above him. 'Well, so you can talk to me. What the hell's the matter?'

'I want to know that you're with me. That you're there. I want you to talk to me — and look as if you're with me and want to be with me. Not somewhere else.'

'I am with you, aren't I? I am sat here, aren't I?' He knew what she meant but hated this usual sense of obligation he felt towards her to keep her entertained. He sighed within. God, what more did there remain for them to say to each other after all these nights, after all these weeks?

'I mustn't be feeling very talkative for the minute,' he told her, smiling for the sake of peace.

Rachel refused to accept the explanation. 'Yes, I know. You mean you don't feel talkative as far as I'm concerned. I can see you'd rather be talking to your friend Baz. Don't think I didn't notice how your little eyes lit up as soon as you saw him.'

'Oh, Jeez! Dearie me. I've told you. I'm not talking 'cos I don't feel like being talkative.'

'And I know why,' she cried, her voice up now, no longer whispering. There were tears in her eyes.

She was right, of course, she did know why though he couldn't bring himself to admit it.

'You always have to exaggerate, don't you,' he said. 'It's always got to be extremes, never half measures with you. You always have to twist things round and bring 'em round to yourself. Just because I don't speak to you for a couple of minutes, just because I'm not there to shower you with all love and attention you become like this.'

She shook her head, on the brink of tears. 'It's because you don't love me any more. I can tell, you don't. But if that's the way you feel . . .' She got to her feet, determined, as if on some errand of self-destruction. 'I shall have to find someone else, someone who'll be willing to show more interest in me than you do.'

He noticed one or two people were looking. 'Go on then,' he challenged angrily, yet nervous all of a sudden at his own uncertainty. 'Find who the hell you like.'

They glared at each other, both of them acting out the need to hurt. He saw the black-lacquered, backcombed hair, the way it enshrouded her pale, smooth, round teenage cheeks, and her eyes dark and glistening behind their false eyelashes. She was a young girl, a young slip of a lass masquerading as a woman. But she looked beautiful, tragically beautiful and pale like a corpse.

His heart thumped. This was the opening, the opportunity he'd been planning for and waiting for. She was going, either to hurl herself under another lorry or at another man, and he would be free of her, no more hassle, no longer tethered, no more precious time wasted on sweet nothings. Then why did he rush after her to catch hold of her? Why did the jealousy, the need to keep her, surge through him suddenly, so real and overpowering?

It came like a conditioned reflex, the strength to make the final break replaced by weakness and a real need for her. Faced with the ultimatum of separation he couldn't let go. He feared being without her, of life being empty, completely and utterly drab and empty. It was a profound, choking, lonely fear, though he couldn't believe the fear was real or that he was subject to it. He was caught up, heart, body and soul, in the relationship, in spite of all his discontentment and yearning for release, dependent on it and dependent on Rachel as if it depended on his very life. That was how it was in that instant. He visualized life without her. He would never find a girl to love him as much as she had done, or one as beautiful ever again. As for freedom, or Baz and living in London, these counted for nothing. Without her life would be dire.

Rachel knew his fear and played on it, as much as she had done throughout their time together. She was the offended one, the hurt one, took umbrage at the least provocation and achieved the response she wanted. Walk away in a huff and the man would follow, wretched, bewildered, desperate to please. She knew too, as he knew himself, that for as long as she held that power over him she had him bought and sold.

Helena, having noticed their short exchange, enquired, 'You two aren't falling out again, are you?' She sighed, wearily but amuzed. She and Mozz were for ever having to talk the one or the other of them out of their moods.

Steve put his arm round Rachel. 'No, it's nothing. We'll sort it out between us sooner or later,' he assured her.

Rachel snuggled up to him and laughed, though there were still tears in her eyes.

PART 2

9

He discarded formalized nudes, abandoned the idea of the series on Northern Streets and began on the works which, he told himself, would be noted by future art historians as the turning point in his career.

He worked on canvas now instead of the pieces of hardboard Rachel had given him to work on. The hardboard pieces were in fact the total output of Rachel's painting endeavours — apart from the one she'd sold and the one nailed to the staircase door — but she had decided to give up painting. She had met the latest boyfriend of her friend Gillian, a drama student whose name was Justin. Justin had told her she possessed a natural ability for acting so now she found herself attracted more and more towards the dramatic arts. This, she believed, was where her true destiny lay.

Having no wish to stand in the way of destiny, Steve had accepted her sacrifice to painting, and the hardboard, and happily painted over her paintings. When the supply was exhausted he took the pieces of old bed linen his mother had sorted out from her rag basket for him, tacking them onto old picture frames. Unfortunately, once primed with size, the material lost all tension and sagged miserably. Yet he persevered and with canvases reasonably stretched, and primed, stood back to contemplate his theme. He needed something less complicated than street scenes, something more immediate and quick.

Inspiration came one afternoon when he was with Rachel and they were on their way to meet with Helena and Mozz. Heading towards the housing estate where Mozz lived, they had to walk by the maingates of Roundhill Colliery. Rachel was busy telling him about Gillian's new boyfriend, how he was hoping to get onto a drama course in London and eventually take up acting as a profession. He would make such a splendid actor, she said, and with his looks would be sure to make it into films.

Steve nodded, gazing over at the superstructure of the pithead. The winding-gear appeared like a giant modern sculpture with its arrangement of black struts standing proudly above the noise and activity within the busy blackgrimed pityard.

He noticed the tangle of grey, rust-splashed steel girders, the black pitch-covered hot water pipes hissing steam from their leaking joints. Between the dark interiors of the hoppers there came the thundering of coal falling into lorries and railway wagons waiting to receive their loads. The noise, the banging and clattering, the roar of the dynamo and the eddying of the black dust, this was the essence, the very spirit of the pithead, as were the men in their hard protective helmets as they gathered at the lamp-house before the changeover for the afternoon shift. The skeletal structures of the towers with their taut cables and revolving twin-spoked wheels were its totem. He knew he had found his theme.

Work began with the preliminary drawings which he took from sketches done in his sparsely filled college sketchbook. Then he returned to the colliery, accompanied by Mozz who also wanted to 'keep an eye on this drawing and painting lark' now that he, like Steve, was out of college. Mozz was happy to make a couple of sketches of the pithead but he much preferred landscape and country scenes — a plough by a barn door with a couple of chickens in the foreground. He'd never had much time for the 'slick' exploratory stuff which had surrounded them at the art college, but wanted to mirror a childhood ideal of some bygone rustic age. He was an excellent draughtsman, observant of his subject matter. As they sketched at the pityard gates he was able to criticize Steve's efforts, accusing him of not looking closely enough at what he was drawing.

'See how you've stuck that mass of black there,' he said, pointing to a lot of scribble Steve had done beneath the outline of his winding-gear. 'There's no patches of black like that, lad.'

'Of course there is,' said Steve, arguing for fun, as he often did with Mozz when they went sketching together.

Mozz shook his head. 'Of course there isn't.'

'There is if I see it like that.'

'But it's a very intricate pattern of girders in deep shadow,' Mozz insisted. 'There's not even a sign of any girders in what you've got there. It looks more like a pile of wire netting. See how that girder meets up with this one, and see how they crisscross behind that heap of slag or whatever it is.'

Steve sighed, annoyed because he knew Mozz was right. He could almost see Humph and the rest of the mob looking over their shoulder, agreeing, loud and derogatory. 'It's not all that necessary and important to get every detail. I want to break free of all that.'

'Why isn't it necessary and important?' asked Mozz, willing to pursue argument for argument's sake. 'You've got to know what you're working from, choose what you might do with it afterwards in the studio. Look how you've got the winding-gear for a start.' He forced a loud derisive laugh. 'PSA level, is that. It looks like it's stuck on top of the roof, not sitting behind it. If you took the trouble to look you'd see how it does. That corner there's great, man. Spot on.'

'Ah, sherrep, Mozz,' Steve told him, admitting defeat. 'Get back to your pretty pictures, hosses pulling ploughs in nice ploughed fields.'

'Nothing wrong with hosses in ploughed fields,' Mozz replied patiently. 'I like paintings of horses pulling ploughs. I like 'em leaning over stable doors as well, next to nice country cottages.'

'Yeah, with ivy growing up the walls. Twee crap!' said Steve, making sounds of choking and vomiting. Yet he took heed of Mozz's criticism.

'Draw what you see, not what you think you see,' Mozz reminded him.

Back at the studio he worked more freely, using lengths of wallpaper which his mother had also rooted out for him. Pinning the lengths of wallpaper to the wall, and ignoring her earlier advice about using more colour, he applied black on black, allowing washes of Indian ink to course down the surface of the paper and over areas of candlewax resist. Then he suggested the structures of the winding-gear with charcoal and black chalk.

The days of drawing and painting followed in quick succession, interspersed with those when he helped his father, either in the workshop or at churchyards and cemeteries. Sometimes they were interspersed too with mornings in Rachel's bed while her parents were out at work. He would feel that strong urge to be with her, knowing she was alone in the house, knowing she'd be still in bed and wearing her light, flimsy cotton nightie. He would follow impulse, to hell with painting, convinced that his love for her was as strong as it had ever been. Afterwards he would lie there spent, deflated, overfaced by her nearness and her unquenchable need for him. He would long to get away, back to his pitheads, back to his own reality outside her bedroom. Yet he would stay, knowing of the upset it would cause if he didn't spend some part of the day with her. Always there was this obligation.

In addition to these weekday distractions the days of working at the studio were interrupted by several fruitless journeys to prospective interviews at commercial design studios. With a portfolio of his college work wedged beneath his arm he took buses to Leeds and Bradford, seeking out addresses amongst the tall black edifices of offices and shops, climbed dim narrow stairways to top floors, then descended, out of luck. There were also visits to design sections in carpet factories, textile mills and printing firms, and each time he would return home weary, still penniless and without a hope in hell. It grated on his soul.

Then came the nagging. His mother refused to let him settle. Had he tried such and such a firm? Had he thought of such and such a job? What about this one they were advertising in the evening paper? Had he thought of applying for that?

'Oh, for cryin' out loud!' he groaned at her, sick of the whole issue.

His mother glared at him, holding out the paper towards him then throwing it down. 'Eeh, you're just an idle so-and-so. You're not even trying to get a job. You're just shirkin' so you can spend your time down yonder in that studio of yours. You've no responsibilities and you refuse to have any.'

'Of course I'm tryin' to get a job,' he yelled at her. 'What the hell do you think I'm doin'? I'm trying the best I can.'

'Then you can't be trying hard enough, as far as I can see. You should be making some effort now instead of sittin' on your backside. What about writing letters to more firms and getting your stuff together? You're bone idle, that's your trouble, m'lad.'

It was at this low ebb that he discovered Rachel was seeing someone else. The jealousy rankled. It hurt more than he'd ever imagined. She'd been acting strange all week, laughing at him at times with a laugh that seemed curiously hard and cynical. He put it down to her periods. Then she told him she wouldn't be seeing him on Thursday night because she was visiting one of Gillian's cousins who had recently had a baby. She was full of apology. She had promised to go with Gillian, she said. She couldn't let her down.

He didn't mind. He looked forward to an evening's freedom, but the following evening, as they sat in the Horse waiting for Mozz and Helena, he asked her casually about the visit to Gillian's cousin. He wasn't really that interested, simply making conversation.

'How d'yer mean you took the Bradford bus to Hamsley? I thought Hamsley was more towards Doncaster.'

'Well, this bus didn't. It went the Bradford way.'

'The Bradford way? How can it've gone the Bradford way when you're going the other way?'

'I don't know, darling. It just did, that's all.'

'That's funny. It must've gone round in a circle. And you say Gillian's cousin lives near the Fox and Grapes in Hamsley?'

'Yes.'

Curiosity turned to the sudden thrill of sensing her deceit. He knew the Fox and Grapes at Hamsley, and the Saturday night dances in the Subs' hall further up the road; the talent, the teddy boys and the fights. There was a crossroads near the pub and on one corner there was a fish shop.

'There's a church next to the pub, isn't there?' he asked conversationally. 'And the junior school's opposite on the corner?'

'Yes, that's right,' she replied, full of certainty. 'Gillian's cousin lives just up from there.'

'But how can the church be next to the pub when there's a cricket ground there?'

'Oh, I don't know.'

'And it isn't a school that's opposite. It's a bloody fish shop.'

'Goodness me, darling,' she said, exasperated, mere

detail interrupting her flow. 'I don't take all that much notice of where things are.'

He sensed the tension in her voice. 'You didn't go to Hamsley last night, and I bet you didn't visit Gillian's cousin either.'

'Yes I did. Ask Gilian if you don't believe me.'

'Ask Gillian? I wouldn't ask Gillian owt. She'd tell me the moon's made of green cheese to cover up for you, she would. Tell me. Where were you last night?'

'I've told you. Visiting Gillian's cousin.'

His insides churned with the cold excitement of discovery. 'Where were you last night?' he asked her again slowly and meaningfully.

There came a slight flush on her cheeks. She was flustered, wanting to make an end to the conversation. 'Mozz and Helena should be here soon. Did they say they'd be in?'

'Tell me. I won't be angry or anything like that,' he repeated calmly, seething with a sudden panic of jealousy, needing to know everything.

'But I've told you,' she said. 'I was with Gillian, visiting her cousin.'

He fought to keep the calm in his voice. 'No, you haven't told me. You know you haven't. Please, Rachel. Don't lie to me. Just tell me where you were, that's all.'

She lowered her head, ashamed like a young girl caught out, blushing.

'Look, it'll only make things worse if you don't tell me. I'll brood over it till things are out of all proportion if you don't tell me. You know I will.'

She didn't answer.

'Tell me. You weren't visiting Gillian's cousin, were you?'

She kept her head lowered, like a child needing to be coaxed for answers. He felt he wanted to slap her, he was that desperate to know.

'You weren't visiting Gillian's cousin and you weren't in Hamsley either, were you?'

She shook her head, keeping her face hidden from him. He delved further from the hollowness expanding in the pit of his stomach.

'You weren't with Gillian either.'

She bit her lip.

'You weren't with Gillian?'

She shook her head again, cornered.

'So you weren't with Gillian. Who were you with?'

'Oh . . .!' She shook herself and lifted herself up, weary of hiding, knowing there was no way out and that she must confess. 'If you must know, darling, I went out for a drink with a friend.'

'A friend? Which friend?'

She tutted, sighed and took hold of his hand, stroking it in her concern, wanting to spare him. 'I went for a drink with Gillian's friend Justin, that's all. Just a drink.'

'Justin?' Ah, God, the pain, the pain! It smacked into him and bruised him somewhere behind the ribs. 'What about Gillian? What did she say? Didn't she mind?'

'No, darling. Of course not. It was just a drink.'

'Where did you go with him for a drink?'

'Just a drink. We just went for a drink.'

'Yes, but where?' He needed to know. Everything.

'Oh, to this pub he knows somewhere out of town. In the country. The Plough, or something like that. It was only a friendly drink, honestly. He wanted to talk to me about drama and how I can go about applying for a drama course at his college. That's all there was to it. Honest, darling.' She shrugged and smiled.

He smiled in return, accepting her explanation though he was wounded, flayed, outraged, broken inside. 'Oh well, if it was only a drink and a natter with him . . .'

'That's all it was,' she assured him, oblivious of his pain. She believed his jovial acceptance and confessed all, opening her heart to him. She'd accepted Justin's offer of an evening out only because Steve had been so off-hand with her of late, saying he was stagnating and mentioning living in London, even travelling off somewhere without her. And what about the other morning, she reminded him, when he'd called at the house, made love to her, then walked out on her afterwards in that foul mood? Well! Justin had asked her out quite a number of times and she'd always refused, but this time she had decided to accept. The whole episode had been a one-off innocent drink together and had meant nothing more. She had simply gone with Justin to a couple of pubs in his Austin Healey sports car.

'An Austin Healey?' He has one of them?'

Oh, yes. She confessed everything down to the last detail. The sports car was coloured metallic blue, was Justin's pride and joy, and had raced at Le Mans.

'Did he drive you in it up to your house?'

'He dropped me off at the end of the street.'

'He didn't get out to see you to the door?'

'No, darling. He just dropped me off at the end of the street.'

He paused. He knew what he had to ask her next. 'Did he kiss you?'

There followed the tension of an unanswerable moment.

'Did he kiss you?'

'Just a quick peck.'

'Where? On the lips?'

'Just a quick peck, that's all.'

'On the lips?'

'It was nothing.'

'He kissed you on the lips.'

'Just a quick peck as I got out of his car, darling. And

look. Take this. I don't want it.'

She had opened her heart to him and now she handed over a small black and white photo which Justin had given her. She felt totally cleansed.

He took the photo and looked at it. It was of a dark-eyed handsome man with black tousled hair who posed arrogant and confident, like a ballet dancer. Steve wilted in his jealousy and helpless sense of betrayal. Justin was tall, athletic, drove an Austin Healey sports car which had raced at Le Mans, and in the photograph he looked far more like Modigliani than he ever could, the bastard!

Ah, the pain, the pain! He couldn't believe it. He didn't sleep. Not for two nights. It was unreal. Everything was unreal. Jealousy replayed the scene of her confession on a never-ending loop inside his head. He who had been so full of his self-esteem with Rachel had been swabbed out by another guy. It was as serious as that. He saw the two of them, Rachel, his Rachel with the dark-haired, dark-eyed handsome Justin, the beautiful couple out together with the evening intimately woven round them both. He was staked out with his jealousy. How could she? How dare she? Lying to him, keeping the truth hidden from him, going behind his back. His guts churned to his thoughts. His mouth became dry and tasted vile. He felt pogged with his nerves, washed out, tense with his grief. He moaned his troubles and misfortunes to friends like a whipped dog. Women were subtle, devious, he said, they mellowed you, softened you till you couldn't tell whether you were on your arse or you head, then they tore you apart.

Ah, the pain, the pain! He still yearned for Rachel in spite of everything. It must be love. Real love. He still wanted her totally for himself. She belonged to him, had to belong to him, exclusively. He was crazy about her, crazed in his jealousy over her. She had gone off with someone else and he felt betrayed. And what if she should sleep with him? God! What if she should sleep with him? The thought was too horrible to contemplate, like a nuclear holocaust, like the outbreak of World War Three.

Rachel, all innocence and unaware of his torment, carried on as normal, loving him, kissing him tenderly as if he were a sick child, reaching out to him as though to make amends. But she had the advantage over him and was strong in that knowledge. While he floundered like this her position was strong.

His mother was also unaware of his torment, or chose to be unaware. She came at him again with the evening paper.

'Ne'er mind girlfriends. It's a job you should be concerned with, not girlfriends. Let her go if she's found somebody else and thank your lucky stars.'

There was 'this 'ere job' being advertized, a big textile works in Calderton and they were seeking for an assistant in their publicity department, preferably someone art-trained. 'It sounds just up your street.'

'Christ!' he sighed at her in his jilted lover's misery. 'Is that all you can think about? Bloody jobs. Going out to look for bloody jobs.'

'You can just get yourself up off your backside,' she answered him sharply, impervious to his suffering, 'and apply for it. It's in Calderton. You wouldn't have to travel so far to work.'

He did as he was told, made the effort, described himself in his letter of application as experienced in layout and design through his time spent at Calderton art college. He was summoned by the company a few days later to attend an interview.

The interview was an ordeal which he was obliged to undergo like having a tooth out. Scrubbed and cleaned, wearing clean white shirt, his slim-jim tie and best charcoal grey suit, he waited watery with nerves in the reception.

He couldn't stop himself from blushing when a group of office girls giggled amongst themselves as they passed. Their giggling made him feel vulnerable, semi-dressed and he wanted to check the buttons on his fly. He flicked absently through glossy brochures to do with an alien boring world of textiles and industry, and waited to be called like a prisoner condemned to Madame Guillotine.

'Do you usually walk into interviews with your hands in your pockets?' was the first gentle enquiry as he entered the publicity manager's office, one hand thrust into trouser pocket for the sake of poise.

The publicity manager was a distinguished-looking gentleman with silvery hair, red face and wearing an immaculate light grey suit. He sat upright at a large desk, observing the applicant with a lazy eye. Then he glanced dispassionately at the folder of drawings that were handed to him.

'Sit down,' he said, clearly no sufferer of fools.

Steve felt starched and tethered, as he always did when wearing his suit. The trousers with their sixteen inch turn-up bottoms were prickly and uncomfortable, and the jacket made him sweat. The heat in the office was dry and stifling. He longed to breathe.

The manager skimmed through the work and nodded grudgingly. Some of the drawings showed promise, he admitted, but could have been presented more neatly. Tidiness was important, he said.

'And a word in your ear about that,' he added, 'It's not a good idea to attend an interview for a job with your hair so long. It doesn't give a good impression, hanging over the collar.'

He returned to the drawings. Yes, he certainly had some talent but there'd be little opportunity for him to put it to use at Calderton Textiles.

'I'll be frank with you. You'll be on a very low salary

— just over five pounds a week — and you'll be expected to do the most menial jobs and work hard. When you reach twenty one, of course, your salary will increase, but it's not a matter of that. We're a growing concern. The prospects for the right man are boundless. It's not what you'll be doing at present, or how much you'll be earning, but what you'll be doing in twenty or thirty years' time. We're looking for a young man who is willing to work hard and willing to put in long hours of extra work, when it's called for, without expecting extra money.'

Steve nodded understandingly, unable to comprehend such a vast time scale as twenty or thirty years. They might as well be talking of 1984, or even 1990, it was as futuristic as that. He looked down at his hands, at the white cuffs of his shirt. In the bright fluorescent light of the office they looked grubby. He struggled for something enthusiastic and convincing to say, but the manager didn't wait.

'All that out there,' he said, turning on his swivel chair to face the window and indicate the wasteland beyond, 'is going to be developed by the company. We are going to expand, and the publicity department is going to expand. Our department at the moment is tiny compared with what it'll become.' He turned back to face Steve, flicking again through one or two of the drawings. 'The young man we employ could find himself in charge of a department of his own in a few more years. And when I retire, which I will be doing in another ten years, he might find himself in charge of the whole caboodle. As I say, the prospects of the job are boundless.'

Ten, twenty, thirty years' time! Steve was torn from the present to this vast distant promised land.

'The young man we're looking for has to have that kind of ambition. He must be keen and willing, and not frightened of long hours and hard work.'

'Oh, yes, I agree, that's the way you have to look at

it, definitely,' Steve declared, energetically interested and stifling the desire to yawn. Yet he must have given a good account of himself, in spite of hair-too-long and hands-in-pockets. The publicity manager looked him up and down approvingly, like a dealer buying a horse.

'We'll be in touch,' he said.

*

Rachel went out with Justin again the following week. Still doing her best to be honest, she went to the trouble of telling Steve, saying she'd promised to meet Justin and didn't like to let him down.

'It's only for a drink, darling. Justin is interested in my acting ability and wants to help me, if he can. But if you'd rather I didn't meet him just say so. I'll tell him I can't make it.'

'No, you go,' he said, fascinated by the developing involvement. He had suffered his extremes of pain and jealousy and become toughened by it.

The evening following her date he asked if she'd had a nice time. She underplayed it.

'Hmmn, it was all right, I suppose. Nothing much. We went to the pub he knows, the Plough, and the four of us just sat there talking for most of the night about acting.'

'Four of you?' he asked, generally enquiring.

'Oh, yes, there was Gillian with her boyfriend, Harry. He's on the same drama course as Justin.'

'Gillian? I thought Justin was supposed to be with Gillian.'

'No, darling,' she corrected him. 'Gillian's going out with Harry.'

'But I thought Justin was supposed to be Gillian's new boyfriend.'

'No. Justin is Harry's friend. They're both at the same

college, studying drama together.' She sounded rather flustered, going pink round the cheeks. 'They talked all the time about this play by Ibsen they're busy rehearsing at college,' she went on quickly, hoping to avoid any more questions, 'and Harry was going on about something called "method acting" and said I'd be good at that. So did Justin,' she added, skipping over the name because of the delicacy of the issue.

He nodded casually with feigned interest, fighting against the urge to tremble as the jealousy surged up like blood from a re-opened wound. The picture came clear in his mind, the foursome sitting cosily together in some plush, oak-beamed, countrified pub, Gillian and her Harry opposite Rachel and her Justin. Everyone in the pub would have seen Rachel and Justin together and idly taken it for granted that they were lovers. And Gillian! He thought of Gillian, happy that she'd separated him from Rachel.

'What time did you land back home, then?'

Rachel shrugged. 'Oh, early. Half past ten. I'd heard enough about Ibsen by then.'

He smiled, nodding again while the rage of jealousy mounted in his chest. When the shaking came he tried to counteract it with yawning.

'Not long out, then?' he managed. He didn't trust himself to speak.

'No, darling. Not long out.'

But he knew different. He'd called round at the house after the pubs had closed. Having then been informed by her unsuspecting mother that she wasn't 'home from Gillian's yet', he'd lurked in the shadows of the street, jealousy and a perverse desire to catch them together giving him that desperate edge. He had waited for nearly an hour until gone midnight and still she hadn't returned.

It was the embarrassingly messy process he'd dreaded, ending his relationship with Rachel. It was the old thing, the old pitfall, the old pattern, the same struggle against the urge to return. But though remorse gripped him, though he saw the emptiness before him, it no longer had to matter. He neither had to believe nor disbelieve her. It no longer had to matter. He left her, covering his ears against her heartwrenching cries.

10

Summer disappeared forever, the days turning grim and dark grey as they shifted into winter. Over Askey's and Thompson's the fields became a wet stark patchwork of dark ploughed earth, serenaded by the death-croaks of black crows circling overhead.

During the second week in November a letter arrived from Calderton Textiles, telling him to report to Mr Major, the publicity manager, at nine o'clock on the following Monday morning.

'Mozz, save me,' he begged as the last weekend of his freedom dwindled away.

He was doomed to the drab dull-brick environment of Calderton Textiles, to the factories and mills along the dismal river banks where coal barges bellied the river's black polluted waters. He was to be swallowed up, drawn into its black hole like a piece of outerspace flotsam, no longer an artist but a forty-hours-a-week assistant to the publicity manager. He would be married to industry, tethered to a fruitful and expanding textile company; muck, short haircuts and commerce. The prospects were boundless and they were dismal.

'Why don't we just drop everything?' he asked Mozz. 'Why don't we just go? We could thumb it down to London and sleep rough.'

He suggested it bravely, knowing that Mozz would never commit himself to the idea. But they had talked vaguely of going to London. They'd talked vaguely of going over to Paris too. They were forever talking vaguely of going somewhere.

Mozz gave a cough and tapped his chest a couple of times, as he did whenever he felt under pressure and undecided.

'In the middle of winter? I think that's a bit extreme, meself, man.'

'Middle of winter?' It's nowhere near the middle of winter. We might go down a bomb in London, you with your guitar and me singing the blues. You never know,' Steve added jokingly, 'we might even make a record and become famous. The blues is gonna be the next big thing.'

He knew that neither of them would make the move. 'The trouble with us, Mozz, we do bugger all. I mean, what's to stop us? You're not stuck in any career-type job and I'm not either, if I don't go. We could thumb it down to London easy. We could ask Baz if he'd put us up for a couple of nights.'

'Baz?' Mozz looked aghast. 'I don't fancy stayin' with him. He's weird, is Baz.'

'Ah, there you go. Excuses, excuses!'

Steve shook his head, steeling himself for Monday. Where was the bad influence that Mozz was supposed to have on him? According to his mother 'that there Maurice Talbot' had been a bad influence on him since they were kids at school, and likely responsible for his 'silly daft ways', she would say, looking for someone to lay the blame on when she was being critical of her son. Both he and Mozz were 'tarred with the same brush' and 'marrer-to-bonny', she would add.

'What's "marrer-to-bonny"?' he would ask.

'It means you're "marrer-to-bonny",' was all she would tell him.

But he stuck by his friend, defending him when she spoke against him. He and Mozz had been friends a long time, since school when they discovered they were both equally as useless at PE and games. ('You have Talbot, we don't wan' 'im,' was the outcry when the sides had been picked for rugger matches during games. 'Well, we don't want Verity!' 'Well, nay, bloody hell, we don't wan' 'im either. We'll have Talbot!') Their friendship began the day they dawdled on their opposite sides at the touchline, trying to fly a kite made out of a couple of twigs and a handkerchief. Flying kites had seemed far more appealing than chasing after the ball like chickens after a piece of gristle. Though relegated to the lowest ranks for physical prowess, their one saving grace had been that they were both 'good at art'.

Of course it never helped matters when Steve shared Mozz's obsession with the Wild West and his mother saw them out in the street, for all the neighbours to see, playing cowboys with toy guns. Sixteen, going on for seventeen, and there they were, running round like a couple of idiots pretending to shoot each other.

'Eeh, a right pair of you there,' she admonished. 'Both as useless and as daft as one another. I can't understand why you don't find yourself a proper mate to knock around with, one who might help you to make something of yourself, instead of you laikin' like a kid in short trousers. Don't you ever want to grow up?'

The truth was he didn't, and neither did Mozz, but Mozz took the matter of not-growing-up far more seriously than Steve did, clinging to the brief episode which had been childhood through the many books and toys he had kept and cherished since he was little. His shelves were stacked with children's books, beautifully illustrated annuals and Buffalo Bill and Beano annuals. In amongst them was a large collection of Rupert Bear books, some of which Steve hadn't seen since he was very small. The memories and the associations of memory came flooding back. Mozz's bedroom had become a kind of sanctuary during their first year of leaving school, a place where they could retreat from the pressures and expectancies of the grown-up's world.

It was a return to an innocence of Christmas-like magic which they liked to believe they had lived through long ago.

Unable to shift Mozz towards any action, and incapable of going it alone, Steve allowed the weekend to drift by and reported on Monday morning, as requested, at Calderton Textiles.

'Hands in pockets!' Didn't I mention anything to you about hands in pockets?'

These were the first words of welcome when he entered the publicity manager's office. Mr Major was losing no time in putting his new assistant in his place.

The first duty was to clean and tidy the shelves of a tiny store-room next to the packing department. Amongst the shelves were piles of disused advert material and dusty heaps of card folders containing samples of cloth.

'You'd better do a good job of it,' Mr Major informed him. 'It's where you'll be spending most of your time.' He touched one or two of the objects on the shelves, daintily wiping the fine black dust which covered everything from his fingers. 'You'll find you're not dealing directly with me most of the time. My two secretaries will pass on the orders that need to be given as they arise, but I want you to wear this little gadget in your top pocket.'

Steve took a small grey plastic bleeper which he clipped into his top pocket as Mr Major showed him.

'You wear it at all times during working hours and when you hear its signal it means I require you to contact me immediately, wherever you are or whatever you are doing. Do you understand? You go to the nearest internal phone and ask the receptionist to put you through to my office.'

On Friday evening Steve had been to the cinema with his brother Ralph to see *Dr No*. Now, with the bleeper in the top pocket of his charcoal grey suit, he could fancy himself as some kind of James Bond.

'Do you understand?' Mr Major repeated more sharply

when he didn't answer.

The work began. Trailing after the quick-striding, tall, dignified Mr Major, then returning, via the typing-pool, carrying a bucket of soapy hot water and a dustpan and brush, he felt ridiculous and self-conscious. He never liked wearing a suit at the best of times but when he did he at least expected to pose smartly in the mock executive role. Carrying buckets of water and sorting rubbish was somewhat contradictory to the James Bond image. But not to worry, the company was a growing concern and as yet he was no more than a newly planted seed. There was to be no plush office — not for the next twenty or thirty years at least.

Within the first hour Steve and his boss had come to the mutual understanding that they hated the sight of each other. It began when Mr Major, keen on progress, returned to inspect his new recruit and found him gently dusting at the shelves, being too particular about any of the dust getting onto his clothes.

'Haven't you finished yet?' he demanded, seeing the performance with the dustpan and brush. 'Goodness me you should've washed the shelves by now, not be still dusting them.' He came forward and noticed Steve's fingernails. 'Rather grubby aren't they?'

Refusing to accept the explanation that fingernails were prone to grubbiness when coming into contact with centuries of dust, Mr Major sent him immediately to the washroom.

'The company provides plenty of soap.'

'But what's the point in washing my hands now when I'll only get 'em dirty again?'

'It doesn't take more than five minutes to wash a pair of hands. What if I was to bring a client in here and he saw how we employ staff with fingernails like yours? I don't think he'd be very impressed, do you? And another thing!

What about your hair? I told you about that at your interview. It certainly doesn't impress the management, a new employee turning up for his first day with hair as long as yours. I suggest you take far more care with personal appearance if you want to continue working here. I employ you, remember, and it doesn't reflect very well on me.'

'It's like being in the bloody army,' Steve complained to his mother when he returned home that evening after his first day at work. If it wasn't dirty fingernails, hair too long or tie not straight, then it was his hands in pockets. Mr Major couldn't abide hands in pockets. It showed slovenliness and slovenliness didn't get the job done.

Dora and Jennifer, his two secretaries, wasted no time in putting him in the picture as regards their boss. Mr Major was an absolute tyrant to work for, they told him. He was rude, impatient, needing everything to be done at the double, yet smoothly and efficiently, and when things failed to meet his standards then there was hell to pay.

Steve had seen something of this during the morning with Dora, a plump, matronly-looking woman of about twenty five. She was raved at for something she'd overlooked the previous week and was reduced nearly to tears. Then she was raved at for allowing herself to be reduced nearly to tears. Jennifer, who was a thin, quiet, mousey girl of twenty one, showed more resilience. When Mr Major tried to tear her off a strip she took it in her stride, letting the storm pass over her.

His mother showed no sympathy for his complaints. It didn't matter how much he might moan or how late he might arrive home some evenings, and without extra pay for overtime, nor did it matter how he might dirty his suit or tear the sleeve on a nail when carrying out one of the many 'important duties' of mending a broken packing crate. He was in a proper job at last and she was satisfied that he had found his station in life. When he complained she told him, 'It's about time there was some'dy to knock you into shape.'

It was only the second Friday when he received his notice. He was relieved to get the push anyway, having withstood the humiliation and slave labour for long enough. The only highlight in two weeks of dusting shelves, mending crates and sorting through some 5,000 circulars, all of which had to be folded and inserted into their pre-addressed envelopes in Mr Major's special way, was eyeing the typists and the factory girls. He grinned at them in the same way he'd seen Albert Finney grinning at the women in the film *Tom Jones*, innocently but lustily. Unfortunately the ploy hadn't seemed to work as successfully for him as it had for Tom Jones and he blamed his short back-and-sides. He hated his hair cut short, his little head looking shorn and ungainly on his thin neck while his denuded ears stuck out like a chimp's. As for Calderton Textiles, perhaps it was an expanding concern but not expanding fast enough for him.

He arrived at work that Friday morning, having run all the way from the bus station along a route that seemed longer and more impossible by each passing second. He headed straight to Mr Major's office, as he'd done every morning, to collect the key to the back room. As usual there were no smiles or exchanges of good morning.

'You're two minutes late,' observed Mr Major, not looking up from the letters he was opening at his desk.

'The bus was late,' Steve answered, gasping once or twice to show he was out of breath.

Mr Major, red-faced and appearing more well-groomed than ever in his dark suit, red silk pocket handkerchief and red silk tie, glared at him.

'Don't give me your silly excuses. You're supposed to begin work immediately on the dot of nine, not two minutes after.'

Steve felt himself wilt, totally in the wrong, the naughty pupil up before the headmaster, the criminal before the judge. He tried to rally and summon pride.

'It's all right for you, you have a car,' he managed in a voice that lacked strength.

'I haven't always had a car,' retorted his boss, affronted. 'I used to walk ten miles to work every morning when I was your age and I was never late. Not once in all those years. And why? Because I set off in good time to arrive in time, and that's what I suggest you do in future. I expect you to be here and the back room open before nine. Understand? And don't you ever answer me back like that again,' he warned, reaching for a sheet of paper from his desk on which was written a list. 'Now . . .'

He was to go over to the joinery department at the other end of the factory and check on a number of wooden sections which had been measured and cut for a display stand. The job was a top priority one intended for a clothing exhibition the following week.

'And don't take all morning over it. I want you to report back to me within the next five minutes.'

The joiner was puzzled when they checked through the list. Everything was correct apart from a six inch lat.

'He never mentioned owt to me about any six inch lat. Go back and ask him if he wants one cuttin', 'cos I can't see where we're supposed to fit one in.'

Hackles raised in advance at the thought of having to return and explain the impossible, knowing from the experience of two weeks that the simple always had to be the impossible, Steve returned.

'The bloke in the joiner's . . .'

'Don't you believe in knocking before you enter someone's office?' Mr Major interjected, busy with paperwork.

Steve waved the list concerning the 'top-priority' job. 'Sorry, but the bloke in the joiner's . . .'

'The joiner!' corrected Mr Major, needing to be precise.

'The joiner,' repeated Steve, bleary-eyed and angry, the anger mounting towards an imminent showdown. 'Would you like me to go out and start again?'

'Don't give me your cheek! What is it you want?'

Steve again waved the sheet of paper with the list. 'The joiner says you never mentioned anything about a six inch lat to him and he wants to know if . . .'

'What on earth are you talking about?' Mr Major frowned at the paper, inconvenienced by trivia and the incompetence of staff.

'This list you gave me,' said Steve, beginning to feel his lips parting from over his teeth in an uncontrollable rabid snarl. 'You've included a six inch lat and there's no . . .'

'I never mentioned anything about a six inch lat!'

'Yes you did. It's down here on the list.'

'I never wrote any such thing,' Mr Major insisted, suddenly fumbling through a pile of papers on his desk as though searching in a frenzy to prove it. Then he snatched the list out of Steve's grasp, embroiled in their clash of wills. 'I should've gone and seen to it myself. I should've gone myself. Because it's clear if I want anything doing round here that's what I have to do.'

'Then why don't yer?' Steve muttered sibilantly.

Mr Major banged his hand on the desk. 'Get out! Get out of my office and get yourself back to the joiner, and check that list again.'

Near to tears with his wrath, Steve slammed out of the office and along the corridor, past the typing pool and through the rubber fire doors into the main factory. Every time he came in here he was reminded of his brief stint at Ralstones' with Mozz, the noise, the hard slog and the labourers looking so casual in their muck and their jeans. How he longed for that period in his life when everything had seemed so simple and straightforward, and when he didn't have to wear a suit and undergo these ridiculous, nonsensical ordeals by a man who was clearly insane.

He came out of the main factory into another corridor and was making his way towards the joiner's when the gadget in his top pocket gave its high-pitched bleep.

'Ah, yes, Stephen,' came a much calmer Mr Major when he went dutifully to the nearest phone. 'I think it's plainfully obvious to us both that you're not exactly what we're looking for at Calderton Textiles. Take a week's notice as from today.'

That evening he felt like going out and celebrating. Instead he went, as he'd done the past few Friday evenings, to the cinema in town with Ralph. The week before they had watched *Tom Jones*. This week it was *The Longest Day*, a film they both fancied seeing because it had been highly recommended. That same evening he saw Rachel with Justin.

Ralph and he were making their way out at the main entrance with the crowd, having seen James Bond as a soldier and men killing each other amidst spectacular D-Day explosions when Ralph spotted her at the other side of the road.

'Ain't that your bird over there?'

She was wearing the three-quarter length brown suede coat and had changed her hairstyle from the beehive to one which was long and brushed straight, and very studentish. He couldn't help the shock of recognition, nor the jealousy which punched into him when he saw them, arms round each other, striding happily by. That day, he suddenly remembered, was her birthday. She was eighteen and full of joy. He felt severed from her completely.

It was that same evening, when he and Ralph were sitting

in the crowded, noisy upstairs of the last bus home, that Mozz came up to join them.

'Have you heard about President Kennedy?' he asked.

'What about President Kennedy?' they asked.

It was a strange, unbelievable time of reality which happened only in films or wartime documentaries, or belonged to distant periods in history, but never in the real, modern world. But it was there, the stark reality of it on radio and TV, and Lee Harvey Oswald proclaiming his innocence. Steve was round at Mozz's, having tea with the family, when the TV newsreel actually showed a man being shot dead.

Everything was so totally unreal, gratuitous and unwarranted. He'd seemed like a good bloke to have around as US President, had Kennedy.

11

It was a sad moment seeing her leave early that Sunday, the first of December. Their grandma Polly and grandpa Joe came to take her in their car to the hospital. Sharp of feature and nimble, their grandma characteristically took charge, bustling and fussing, and somehow blocking the way so that their mother became separated from them before she'd even left.

'Have you got a change of nightie, Elsa? What about your dressing gown, and your toothbrush and flannel? You have to be there to report in for ten o'clock, you know. Joseph! Go and open the car door ready for her to climb in.'

'Nay, mother,' she protested. 'I'm not an invalid yet.'

Grandpa Joe allowed his wife to fuss and natter as she liked, never letting it penetrate. Sometimes he slow-timed her when she nagged or became purposely obtuse. Old Polly was a backseat driver and when she became flustered in the car, issuing directives or yelling at him to slow down if he did anything over thirty miles an hour, he would turn calmly to her and tell her, 'It's no good telling me. I'm not driving this car. It's remote controlled, didn't you know?'

Their father accompanied them to the hospital. Steve and his two brothers watched them go, feeling it silently in the back of the throat and behind the nose as their mother waved goodbye to them through the rear window. Maybe she was a pain in the neck sometimes but hospital was suddenly a serious matter, and they didn't like to think of her being cut by the surgeon's knife.

They visited her the day after the operation and were

shocked to see how grey and ill she looked. Lying there, as though in a drugged sleep, she was almost hidden beneath the pile of blankets like a baby in a cot. At first they thought it was their grandma in the bed. She looked that old.

She was kept in hospital for a fortnight and during this time, once more without a job, Steve was able to return to his studio and the pitheads, producing three sizeable paintings: 'Pithead in Blue' I, II,and III respectively. Then on the Sunday morning, two weeks after she'd departed from them, she returned. His father announced her arrival by barging unceremoniously into his bedroom: 'Your mother's here. She wants your bed downstairs. Get up, you idle sod.'

So she was back, recuperating after having 'everything taken away', and in the days of her return she was able to observe from his bed in the living room how he slept late and how he hung about the house in a routine of idleness till midday. It started again.

'You ought to be helping your dad and our Ralph with the housekeeping while I'm off work like this. Just because you were sackless enough to get yourself kicked out of one job doesn't mean to say you can't apply for another. So don't think it does.'

'I want to paint,' he sighed, knowing he was stating the ridiculous. His mother rubbed her hand at the small of her back to ease the post-operation pains.

'Paint? You need money in this life, lad, and that means having to go out and earn it. Can't you get that through into your thick skull?'

She rubbed at her back more vigorously as if he was the cause of the pain.

He suggested working full time for his father but she wouldn't hear of it.

'Your dad earns little enough for himself as it is, never

mind him havin' to pay out wages to you plus your insurance stamp.'

There were other complications involved too, such as rigging proper toilet facilities in Ninety Four to bring things in line with the standards required by the Health and Safety Act should his father wish to officially employ anyone. But Steve wasn't too disappointed. Working with frozen blocks of stone in the middle of winter, and dipping hands into water which turned to ice as soon as it touched the stone was certainly no picnic. And the cold winds howling through the churchyards! He'd had more than one taste of the unpleasant side, waiting perished between iron-hard, frostbitten graves while his father, finger ends cracked and sore, still persisted in spirit-level perfection. He decided to try for something more temporary and better paid than so-called careers. Tired of having no money even for painting materials, he set out to look for labouring work, regardless of his mother's preferences and ideals. On New Year's Day, at seven thirty on a midnight morning, he started work as a casual labourer at Crawley and Pattersons' Engineering Works.

Everything went surprisingly well. Although he spent a sleepless New Year's Eve worrying about all the heavy lifting he'd been told he might have to do, and visualizing all the terrible things which might befall him — like great lumps of steel falling and crushing him — he found the job to be 'a piece of cake'. All he had to do was sweep out from under the lathes and various other machines, scoop the metal debris into wheelbarrows, then dump it at the swarf-tips outside the workshops.

The men were mostly friendly. They nodded in acknowledgement when he came to clean round their machines, asking him how he was liking the job.

'Not a bad number here,' they would tell him. 'Nob'dy bothers yer. All you have to do is look busy when t'bosses come.' At 5s.4d an hour, and a bit of overtime thrown in, it was 'money for jam'.

There was a novelty about it all. The world of engineering was one that he'd seen only in text books but here he was, seeing it at first hand, taking in all the things he saw around him with fresh eyes. There was the overhead crane gliding slowly like a tramcar up and down the workshop, passing beneath the crisscross girders of the roof, and there were the colours, the burnished purples, oranges and blues of the heat-affected turnings which he collected from under the lathes. He watched the hot streamers of steel as they writhed and curled like agonized worms from the cutting-tools, then fell, sizzling, into the greasy trays filled with the milk white cutting-oil. There were the machines, complex living things whirring and screeching their cries throughout the workshop, and in the roaring and pounding stood the men in their blue boilersuits, somehow dignified in their skill and confidence, controlling these wildbeast machines. Above them the overhead crane, cogs and hook-chains rattling, moved through the smoky haze.

It was a world belonging to men, the stench of hot metal and oil, and the smoke rising to the rust-stained skylights from the essential dirt.

He became familiar with his territory, learning how to handle the 'scives' from his fellow labourers who took him under their wing. From them he learned where to nip out of the way for five minutes and how to make the simplest job stretch to the longest time.

Sometimes, leaning on his broom, viewing the cathedral immensity of the workshop, he would take a leisurely stock of his life. As yet he was still only twenty, still at the crossroads and able to bask in the luxury of that knowledge. The job was temporary, a means of making money to go away somewhere, perhaps with Mozz, if Mozz could be persuaded, or perhaps he might join Baz in London. As yet he was young, not quite twenty one, with time on his hands to do all the things one wanted to do in a lifetime.

PART 3

12

Sitting in the crowded, smoke-filled upper deck, he felt the ticket machine bump against his shoulder as the beefy conductoress pushed her manly bulk down the aisle. Her bulky presence, her coldness irritated him. She was encased in her uniform, bound up in the leather thongs of her ticket machine and money bag, solid and uncompromising.

'Any more fares?'
'Sevenp'ny please.'
'Sevenp'ny? Where yer going'?'
'As far as t'White Bear.'
'That's a ninep'ny! It's gone up.'

He hated her efficiency, her brutal indifference to her unresponding half-awake passengers. He longed to trip her up and send her hippo-thighs bigness sprawling in a cascade of spilt money down the bus.

He watched her wide waddling form pushing its way between the narrow aisle of shoulders, then turned to wipe a porthole in the steamed-up window. He looked out onto the familiar route, the wet road under the grey Monday morning sky, the monotonous rows of dull terraced houses and the grey metallic slabs of their wet rooftops. From the grey haze long black fingers of mill and factory chimney stacks smoked statically against the rainswept sky.

He yawned. His eyelids burned with his tiredness. He wanted to snuggle into the relative comfort that the bus provided and go to sleep. The jerking and the rocking of the vehicle lulled him. They came to a stop outside a mill and a group of women rose from their seats reluctantly, bleary-eyed, cocooned in their fag smoke; then, once released from their confines, they became alive, cackling animatedly amongst themselves. The bus motored on, passing under a black railway bridge which carried the name of a nearby firm in large white letters across its rivetted expanse. Beneath the bridge, on either side, roadside hoardings displayed a colourful world of beans, milk chocolate, dog food and cigarettes. 'Coming soon!' At the Essaldo. *Zulu.* He must go and see that when it came.

He rose from the grudging comfort of his seat as soon as they were crossing the brown river with its pink soapy puffballs gathering like candyfloss below the weir. The river and the wide concrete bridge which conveyed them across it signalled his destination.

A couple of blokes, also from Crawley and Pattersons', got to their feet with him. He felt somehow reassured, seeing them. He wasn't alone. The three of them stood on the platform together, a small bedraggled remnant of a platoon trying to muster effort as the bus jarred to a halt. It was time to go.

The conductress, surveying her territory from the foot of the stairs, regarded them in her surly indifference. The two men, huddled in their damp, oil-stained rainmacs and gripping their canvas snapbags, managed to ring laughter at a private joke. She eyed them suspiciously, then stabbed at the bell-push, sending the bus on its way. It was grey early morning and cold. She must have had a bad night.

He followed the two men as they shuffled off through the maingate and up the drive. They disregarded the familiarity which greeted them, accepting it though they might hate it because it was a necessary part of their lives. Steve groaned. The morning was half-lit and grim and very wet, and the day stretched in front of him, endless.

'Afternoon, lads. You might make it before dinnertime, if you hurry up.'

It was one of the labourers, giving them a cheery

welcome as they passed him at the doorway into the machine shop.

'Bollocks!' came the succinct reply from one of the latecomers and stepping through into the roar of machinery, they trailed over to the time-clock.

'Looks like we didn't make it,' he said as he picked his clean new time-card for the week out of the rack.

The other man swore. He didn't give a 'monkey's' if he was an hour late. And to hell if any of the foremen should see him. They could give him his 'bladders' any time they liked.

They thrust their cards into the slot and thumped the handle of the time-clock. The bell gave a single ping.

Steve picked his new card from amongst the isolated ones which yet remained in the 'out' rack, unclaimed and unpunched by latecomers or absentees. The time-clock bell pinged. He checked the time stamped in red ink as opposed to blue ink. Seven thirty six. The firm only allowed four minutes after the seven thirty buzzer. A minute over meant a quarter of an hour docked off your time.

'Ne'er mind, owd lad,' one of the men told him, patting him on the shoulder. 'You ain't missed much. There's still rest o' 'day.'

'Roll on Friday,' said his companion.

Roll on Friday! But Friday was too remote, too impossible even to consider. Steve felt brittle, unused and unacclimatized.

Clocked-in, they separated, they to their machines and Steve to his, a large muck-encrusted thing that was basically an H-shaped framework straddling over a six-foot diameter turntable. Known in technical jargon as a vertical borer, it appeared more like an exhibit from the Science Museum. The machine was the oldest one in the works, having been installed when the workshop building was erected in 1902 — as Wilky had been proud to inform him the day it had been decided to promote him from unskilled labourer to semi-skilled engineer. In the eyes of his foreman Steve had done 'right well'.

A casting was already set and secured on the turntable, a cast-iron 'hoop' designed to fit as a disposable tyre on the rollers of a crushing-machine. All part of the heavy goods the company built for the brick manufacturing industry. Without the hoop you couldn't have the crushing-machine and without the crushing-machine you couldn't have bricks, and without bricks you couldn't have houses. Back to it again! Everything just as he'd left it, everything just as it had been the week before, the workers in their blue boilersuit uniformity, hovering obedient, enslaved to their lathes, their grinders and their milling-machines, and all around was the noise, the tortured sounds and the burning stench of cutting-oils. Another of the everydays at work.

He switched on the power and four days' accumulation of dust exploded from the pulley belt as the motor whipped into life. Satisfied that everything was running as it should, he sat down on the up-ended toolbox which he had converted into his seat. There was nothing more to do until the cutting-arm of the borer had completed its traverse. The clock above the workshop doors told him it was a quarter to eight. Only another nine and a quarter hours to go to the hometime buzzer. He groaned, a prisoner condemned to life within the dim, noise-polluted confines of these windowless factory walls. The turntable rumbled slowly in determined revolutions while the flakes of dull grey metal fell silently and steadily before the flat nose of the cutting-tool. He glanced once more at the clock. The hands had not moved.

Work! Coming to work. It was the last thing he had wanted to do this morning. Everything was the same though now there was something just that little bit different.

Circumstances had changed slightly and he was aware of it all the time like a numbness in the chest.

He tapped idly against the box with a spanner, then doodled patterns on the leg of his boilersuit with a piece of French chalk. He drew a wheel and was marking out the spokes when someone squeezed his arm. He turned sharply and guiltily, thinking it was the foreman, or worse still the works manager.

'Part-timer,' piped up the man before him above the noise.

Steve breathed a sigh of relief. 'Oh, it's you. I thought it was owd Wilky.'

'Part-timer,' repeated the man. It was Harold, on his way to the tool-stores to collect a drilling-bit. Steve knew him only as Harold-on-the-driller who worked next to Harold-on-the-grinder. While Harold-on-the-grinder was short and fat and grumpy, Harold-on-the-driller was tall and lanky and always appeared bright and happy with his lot.

Harold-on-the-driller laughed, then marched over to old Bert, the labourer, who was busy sweeping a few odd turnings together. He gave Bert a hearty slap on the back to attract his attention and almost knocked his pipe out of his mouth.

'Hey up, Bert. He's here. Part-timer's arrived.'

Bert stopped sweeping and cocked his ears towards Harold to hear what he was saying.

'Aye?' he exclaimed when Harold pointed at Steve. He leaned his small, round stocky form gainst his broom and shook his grey, short-cropped head. 'I wondered when he wa' comin' in again. These 'ere young 'uns, they just don't want the work.'

'What's wrong now?' Steve asked, seeing Harold say something into Bert's ear and knowing he was the brunt of one of his jokes. He went over to join them.

'I wa' just sayin' to Bert, tha looks miserable this mornin'. I reckon he must 'a' been on 'nest too long last night, don't tha, Bert?'

Bert decided to refill his pipe, taking out his leather tobacco pouch and groping inside with his thick grimed fingers. A few moments natter and a bit o' baccy were always a welcome break.

'He wa' late again, an' all,' Harold went on, pretending disappointment with the 'new lad'.

'Aye well, that's the trouble, Harold,' Bert told him, placing his pipe between the nicotined dentures which he usually made a point of removing when he ate his sandwiches at lunchtimes. 'All they want to do is go out and get as much pop as they can on a night, then get up to a bit o' nadgin.'

'Nadgin?' said Steve. 'What the hell's that?'

'Guzintas,' Harold answered him. 'Tha knows what nadgin' is.'

Bert puffed thoughtfully. Then he pointed with the stem of his pipe toward's Steve's machine. 'What d'yer reckon he must be earnin' on yon'?'

'Eleven quid easy,' said Harold. 'That's if he could be bothered to clock his full hours. This lad don't know when he's lucky.'

Bert puffed again on his pipe. 'Eleven quid a week, just for standin' there wi' nowt to do but watch it go round! Think of it. When I wa' his age you had to break your back for a couple o' bob.'

Bert was at his happiest when able to recall stories and relate the conditions of his early life. He'd had a hard life without much in the way of rewards, to hear him talk, and at the age of sixty four, and on the point of retirement, he still hadn't much going for him.

Steve and Harold listened while Bêrt surrounded himself and his captive audience with the acrid smell of his pipe.

Steve, wondering how long the present anecdote of hardship and lucky-to-have-shoes-on-your-feet misfortune might take, could only feel thankful that he wasn't Bert.

The anecdote didn't take long. Bert was suddenly interrupted mid-sentence by a well-known voice attempting authority.

'Come on, lads, come on. Split up. Stop tellin' 'tale.'

Bert sheepishly returned to his sweeping while Harold continued on his brisk way to the tool stores as if he'd never stopped.

'You're all right, aren't you?' the foreman complained as he followed Steve over to his machine. 'You have time off, you come in late this mornin', then you stand around natterin' when there's this job to be finished. Anyway, where d'yer think you got to last week?'

'I was ill. I had the flu again.'

The foreman nodded, embarrassed by having to assert his authority but needing to give vent to his mounting grievances against a youngster he was supposed to be in charge of. He appeared to shrink into his oversized white foreman's smock when called upon to exercise authority, especially whenever it involved some of the bigger blokes. Some of them sniggered behind his back and called him a 'creep' and a 'greaser'. Steve thought their opinions a bit unfair. Wilky was the foreman, could be a nuisance, getting in the way of idle thoughts and daydreams, but he was generally a decent sort, perhaps too soft and too polite for the rough-and-ready types who were quick to despise him.

'So you were late again this mornin', I see.' he remarked, forcing issues. Steve was one of the lesser fish in his domain.

'Bus was late,' Steve answered him bluntly, wishing the man would go away. He was in no mood for Wilky either.

'It's always the bus. You're time's half past seven, not quarter to eight. I keep tellin' yer. It's not only me notices your bad time-keepin', you know.' He passed his hand over the shining metal where the cutting was in process on the inner rim of the casting. 'Are you usin' t'proper gauge? We can't afford to have a balls-up made o' this job like you did wi' 'last 'un.'

'It's right gauge,' Steve assured him, aggravated.

Wilky, reluctant to openly imply his doubts, needed to be sure. 'Reach me 'twenty eight.'

Pouring breathless curses on the man's Monday morning head, and wishing he could turn out paintings with the same consistency as he turned out these monotonous hoops, Steve went over to the stack of javelin-like gauges by the side of his machine. They were of varying lengths. He selected one which was twenty eight inches in length.

The foreman took the length of steel rod which had points at both ends, and tried it against the inner diameter without stopping the machine. This was a practice Steve had been warned against from the very start. The turntable moved only slowly but there was enough power behind it to crush a man's body to pulp should he have the bad luck to be caught and dragged against the solid crossbeam of the H. But Wilky was deft. Testing the bore when the machine was running was all part of his expertise. He handed back the gauge, satisfied the job was still all right.

'Still a fraction to come off yet. But try and get it finished by dinner time. You've been on with it now for over a week and the darned things can be done easy within three days. It should've been finished and in 'fittin' shop by now. And don't tell me you're still learnin' how to handle this 'ere vertical borer. You've been on it long enough to know how it works inside out. Can't you set it runnin' a bit faster? It must be takin' half an hour for that cuttin'-arm to go full traverse and this is only soft metal you're cuttin'.' He shook his head wearily. 'Eeh, Stephen, lad, you're failin' me. 'You're failin' me. I thought you'd landed on your feet with a right nice steady job when we put you on here. It's better than labourin', surely, i'n't it?'

Steve gave him a blank look, saying nothing. Wilky shook his head once more, puzzled. He had recommended Steve to the management as a personable, bright young chap and a good worker, and had fixed him up on a machine. He could only feel disappointed that the 'bright young chap' was letting him down. Reluctantly he turned to leave.

'Any road, you'll have to bring a doctor's note in future when you're absent. And think on what I told you. Try and get here on time on a mornin'.'

Steve watched him go. Wilky paused halfway down the workshop to inspect a newly turned shaft which had just been taken from a lathe. He signalled to Joe in the overhead crane so that the shaft could be hoisted onto a flat-truck, then taken into the fitting-shop. All part of the day's work.

As soon as the coast was clear Steve plonked himself once more on the upturned box, returned to the vertical borer and the thoughts which lay so heavy.

The irony of it was he'd had a copy of Camus' novel, *The Outsider* with him at the time. He chose to see it as an irony at least. He'd borrowed the book from the local library, the first of many he'd planned to read as a new stage of his 'intellectual development'. He could admire the hero's detachment. Mersault, the central character, accepted all circumstances without question or reaction, or emotion, even when it came to the question of his own destruction. Mersault was a hero because nothing could reach him.

The doctor had asked him to put the book on his desk and strip to the waist.

God! How he hated being ill. How he feared it and all the circumstances which surrounded it. Regardless of whatever he might have meditated in churchyards he really had no wish to die at the age of twenty one. Yet that Saturday morning, after three more days of feeling ill, he had felt so frail as the doctor prodded him with a cold, inquisitive stethoscope.

'Breathe in. Say, "Ah".'

He'd glanced down at his own white thin, vulnerable body. It had looked like a heap of ailing skin and bone about to be dissected and diagnosed in the complex and impersonal world of medicine. Nothing had been right with him, healthwise, since the previous month and his twenty first birthday when beer, wine and whisky had rendered him not only incapable but also unable to resist every blessed ailment going. He'd spent the whole of Easter in bed, sweating out the flu, and had never fully recovered. This latest bout had hit him during the week when his chest felt clogged and tight with iron dust and the smoke from lathes.

'Again! Say, "Ah".'

Something like a pathetic moan came from him in the clinical emptiness of the doctor's surgery. The doctor folded his stethoscope and scribbled something out with a quick nonchalant hand.

'Take this three times a day.'

Steve tucked in his shirt, eyeing the prescription. He wasn't about to be rushed off into hospital with a suspected double pneumonia after all. He asked if he might collect another prescription for his mother while he was there, as she'd requested. Some more pills to ease the pains in her legs and back. Those same boring pains she'd been complaining about since the operation.

'Ah, yes, your mother.' Tall and imposing in the small room, the doctor scribbled again.

Steve knew what was coming before the doctor said anything. It was another of those unbelievable sequences, another shaker to those foundations you took so much for granted. He listened calmly, accepted it calmly, as the doctor spoke of diagnoses, X-rays, thousand-to-one chances and therapy which hadn't worked.

'It's all a question of time now, I'm afraid.' The doctor smiled briefly, professionally. 'It could be twenty years or twenty weeks. There's no way of knowing. But we felt it best not to let your father know yet. It might cause him undue stress, and we don't want that. Let me see, it'll be two years since he had the nervous breakdown, won't it?'

Yes, it would be two years, that bad winter of early 1962, his father sinking lower and lower as the freezing packed snow and ice made it impossible to work. The bills had mounted, people owing him money had failed to pay and no orders for jobs had been forthcoming. Things had become so impossible, so threatening and so blown up out of all proportion, he had finally cracked.

It was perhaps better not to tell him anything for the moment, the doctor continued. 'But we think at least one member of the family should know.'

Steve nodded calmly, intelligent, understanding, as if he and the doctor were drawn together in conspiracy within the silent privacy of the surgery. The doctor gave another smile. 'Any pain she has from now on we'll tell her is from the operation, which in effect it is, but not in the way she thinks.'

He had stepped out into the busy to-ing and fro-ing of a warm sunny Saturday morning, knowing his mother's destiny, knowing what was on the cards for her while she didn't. It was a secret the doctor had chosen to share with him alone. He was almost flattered by that and he went guarding the secret against all those who would soon no doubt shed their tears. As yet they didn't know. Only he knew and he knew it with a numbness that was like a shock.

'Mother died today. Or maybe yesterday . . .' He tried to remember the opening of Camus' novel and decided that from now on he had to be like Mersault. He would drift above his mother's illness and her death, unemotional, uninvolved, purposely deadening his responses to it. Only then could he survive. If you didn't allow yourself to become involved then nothing could reach you and hurt you, neither pain nor suffering, nor grief or love — especially love! As for his mother, her death might be now or in the next twenty years, but what difference would it make when it all came to the same thing in the end? And when it came to the day of her death and her funeral he wouldn't be around. That was definite. He was going, clearing off, either with or without Mozz. There was Baz, there was London. But one thing was certain, he wasn't going to hang about and see her die. Next week, the week after, he would hand his notice in at work. He would leave home, leave Calderton and turn his back on his family for ever, if need be. It was the only thing to do.

'Well?' she asked on his return. She was lounging on the settee, a hot water bottle and cushions at her back, and her right leg resting on a low stool. She had fastened a crepe bandage around the knee, like a rugby player's knee-support, in an attempt to ease the pain.

'Well, what?' he retorted, keeping his distance.

Her eyes smiled at him as though they shared a joke. She had been aware of his hypochondria. She knew him of old. Whenever he was feeling a bit under the weather he always made such a fuss. 'Are you dying or will you always live?'

He handed her the pills and bottle of medicine he'd collected from the chemist's on his way home.

'It's bronchial catarrh,' he told her grudgingly. 'I've got to take this black stuff three times a day.'

'Well, I knew you wouldn't be exactly bedridden, you and your double pneumonia! Did he ask owt about me?'

'Who? The doctor? Oh, he asked how you were

managing. Something like that.'

She regarded the bottle of medicine and the pills, and gave him one of her knowing looks.

'Get away with yer,' she scoffed. 'I bet he never mentioned a damned thing.'

'Why ask, then?' He kept his distance from her. She was condemned. 'He wanted to know how things were but I suppose he's got too many other things to worry about.'

Later, during the afternoon when he was reading in his bedroom, he happened to glance out of the window and see her in the back garden. Her familiar, homely figure, dressed in a crumpled polka-dot skirt and an old blue cardigan, limped a few careful steps along the garden path. He watched her as she stopped to survey the garden and the carefully pruned rose bushes showing first leaf. She turned her gaze idly to the neighbouring gardens, enjoying the mild, early spring air and the sun on her face.

He stayed to observe her from his window, knowing her destiny while she didn't. He struggled hard to think like Mersault, to be like Mersault, but saw only the bandage, the pathetic, useless crepe bandage. The tears brimmed, uncontrollable, ran down his cheeks, then bounced onto Camus' book.

13

He took another sip of his beer. It was flat and tasted vile. As flat as my lot, he thought, aching for company and wondering where the heck Mozz and Helena had got to. They'd arranged to meet him in the Horse and he was disappointed that they hadn't turned up. He needed company. Tonight was Monday night and it was dead in the Horse, dead in town, as if everyone was dead, and he needed company.

He ached in his present restlessness and boredom. It was always like that when you needed company, a bit of life round the place, someone to talk to and reinforce your belief in yourself so that you knew you still existed. He settled his gaze on the hard, cold, crystalline display of bottles and glasses on the shelves behind the bar. He was still reminded of Manet's bar, and reminded in turn of the paintings he hadn't done and would never do again. His life had become stagnant and the evening was part of the stagnation, a desert of uneventfulness which closed in on his soul.

He listened to the silence, the clock ticking loud in the silence and the chink of a glass as Paddy, the landlord, dried the few he'd decided to wash while waiting for customers. He rubbed his hand across his brow and took another sip of beer. Mozz must have taken Helena to the flicks, or another pub. Sometimes he could be forgetful like that, could Mozz.

He lit a cigarette, returned to reading the labels on bottles, and was considering all the equally unappealing alternatives to the evening when the door bounced noisily open. His hopes rose briefly as he turned, then fell when he saw the two youths who entered.

'Nar then, Verity,' came the greeting of cheery familiarity from one of them.

Steve tensed. 'Howdo, Eric,' he answered, feeling world-weary and bored as the two youths joined him at the bar.

'Gerremin!' Eric told his companion, a tall, angular, hard-looking individual in a brown suit.

'Gerramin thisen!' his companion retorted simply.

Eric made a sound in the back of his throat as if about to spit at the sawdust on the floor. He ordered two pints.

'How's tricks then, Verity?' he asked with the same familiarity, though with a slight deference for seniority.

Steve shrugged, resenting the familiarity and the intrusion on his privacy as boring as it was. Eric had been one of the first-years, a fledgling to be despised by the older generation of art students. That was last year. Now he was a firmly established second-year, grown tall and looking a bit like Baz with his curly black hair and El Greco features, and was even managing to grow a beard. He felt on a par with Steve and Steve, with an arrogance borne of easily four years' seniority, sensed it and resented this as well.

'You still go to that life class on Tuesday nights?' Eric asked.

'Nar. I haven't bothered for t'summer term.'

Eric looked at him impish. 'I thought you'd've been back to chat that bird you fancied.'

'Which bird's that, then?'

Eric grinned. 'You know which one. Don't play dumb.'

'Which bird you on about?' grunted the other youth. Hearing the mention of women had attracted him from his nonplussed contemplation of the pub.

Steve felt vaguely threatened by the youth in the suit. He was tall, big-boned and looked fierce and aggressive. He turned back to Eric.

'You mean the blond bit with the plaits?'

'Of course. Who else did you think? You used to eye her up plenty. We all did. Gorgeous bit o' stuff, she was.'

Of course, the one with the plaits! His mind went back to those dark winter Tuesday evenings which had promised like an oasis in the desert of the working week.

'Wasn't bad, was she?'

'Not bad at all.'

Not bad at all! He had watched her from his easel, the graceful way she sat, back straight and beautiful, shading carefully and gently with a pencil, then just as carefully rubbing out each wrong line.

'Does she still go there Tuesday evenings?'

Eric shook his head. 'Dunno. Our group don't have to go now like we used to. It's not compulsory so I don't bother.'

Steve returned his gaze to the shelves behind the bar, and glanced at his reflection in the mirror. Being reminded of that Pre-Raphaelite beauty with her Saxon braids gave him the same no chance sense of helplessness. He'd been even too shy to speak.

'Not that I'd bother with life drawing anyway,' Eric went on. 'I'm gettin' stalled o' that place.'

'What? You mean you don't like being an art student?'

'No, I'm gonna get a job wi' Woody here. Parks and gardens. Aren't I, Woody?'

Woody looked witheringly at his surroundings. 'What sort o' friggin' place is this you've brought me?'

'How about you?' Eric asked Steve, ignoring Woody. 'You still doin' a bit? You reckoned to be a bit of a painter, didn't yer?'

Steve sighed. 'Don't wear that little hat no more. All my chuffin' time seems to be taken up nowadays working at Crawley and Pattersons.'

'You still there?' Eric looked at him in surprise. 'You

must be settlin' down. Steady job and all that.'

'Ah well, I've been there five months, although it feels more like five years. But anyway, you can stuff art. As far as I'm concerned it's a load of bollocks.'

It gratified him to say this in front of Eric. Woody took a drink of beer and screwed his face in disgust.

'Cor! Have you tasted this? It's like piss.'

Eric laughed. 'Leave it if you can't sup it. I'll sup it for yer if it's too strong.'

'Too strong?' Woody sneered and with that downed the beer at a single draught. 'Theer!' He glared in triumph, banging his empty glass on the counter.

Eric lifted his own pint, hardly touched, studying it against the light from the window like a connoisseur of wine. 'Hmmmn! Not a bad little number. But I could've sworn I saw a tadpole in yours, Woody. It must've disappeared in t'murk afore you drank it.' He took a small sip, testing it against his palate. 'There's nowt else for it. We'll have to get over to 'Mecca and them Newcy Browns.'

He nodded his head at Paddy who was still occupied with his cleaning and sorting of glasses. Both youths sniggered because they knew he'd heard them. But Steve knew that Paddy couldn't care less., They could take his beer or leave it, and if they didn't wish to take it they could clear off.

'How about you, Verity? Fancy comin' over to 'Mecca for a bevy?' Eric asked.

'Who, me? You have to be jokin'.'

'Well, it's bloody dead here, man. What's the point of stayin' and drinkin' lousy ale with only them for company?' He indicated two old men over in the far corner who were the only other customers. 'Just think. That'll be thee in a few more years.'

Steve laughed at his youthful cheek. 'I ain't that chuffin' old.'

'Ah, come on,' Eric urged him. 'Get thisen over with

us. It's 'Under Twenty Ones, Monday nights. You'll enjoy yourself.'

The Under Twenty Ones? He was over the hill for that. Pigs had more chance of flying than him stepping foot in there.

He turned to face the bar with its shelves of glasses and bottles. Somehow there was no applying himself to anything tonight, and there was no telly at home because the tube had finally blown on the old set and he couldn't be bothered to read. Perhaps he should have taken Ralph up on his earlier invitation and gone playing snooker with him and his lot at the YMCA.

Woody stirred, impatient. 'C'mon, Eric,' he muttered. 'Let's gerrout of here.'

Eric made to leave. 'Comin' then, Verity?'

Steve cast his eyes round the empty seats, saw the two old men slumped half asleep like discarded puppets. He tried to finish his beer, gulping at it, but the bitter tasting liquid landed cold and heavy, constricting his stomach. He belched. 'Hang on a mo'. I can't sup this off so quick.'

*

The Mecca, near the town centre, was a block of pale grey, reinforced concrete with its name spread in neon lights above the glass-panelled entrance. Built four years before on the site of what had been a street of terraced houses, the dance hall had brought a certain glamour to the town and was packed most nights of the week. During those years at college Monday evenings had been a regular nightspot for students in their smartest gear. Dirty paint-stained sweaters had been replaced by bright dresses and suits and ties. The Under Twenty Ones had attracted youths from all walks of life, and from all the areas around Calderton, and with strictly no trouble — at least within the dance hall itself. The brutish looking penguins on duty at the reception, or parading watchfully inside, made sure of that. At the first sign of trouble they were there, throwing themselves into the affray and frog-marching the antagonists out.

During those years the penguins would form a watchful line at the reception, surveying the brash girl-seeking youths who waited in an eager, pushing queue to pay their half-crowns at the ticket booth. The penguins were critical of style. Suits only, strictly no jeans, and trousers had to keep to the accepted width at the turn-up. Anything under sixteen inches was labelled 'drainpipes' and drainpipes were synonymous with teds, and teds with trouble, so you were out.

Ah, but the red glow of the muted interior once you were through 'customs', the warm smell of perfume mingled with that of fried onions from the hot dog counter, and the girls in their finery eyeing the male contingent with premeditated and careful indifference.

That was how it had been the first time he came to the Mecca, full of butterflies as he'd stepped into this other make-believe world to begin a brief and chaste encounter with a slim, attractive schoolgirl. They had bopped to Johnny Kidd, 'Shakin' all Over' with his Pirates, embraced awkwardly and shyly beneath the revolving globe of mirrors during smooch-time, and afterwards, just as shyly, he had walked her home.

They bothered less about styles and widths of trouser bottoms nowadays — either because the management had become more broad-minded or, faced with a fall in profits, they had become desperate for custom. When Eric marched up to the ticket booth, followed by Woody, the penguins hardly noticed but continued to chat benignly amongst themselves. The Under Twenty Ones was open house.

Nothing had changed much apart from that. It was once

more into the soft-focus humidity of hope, perfume and hot dogs, once more becoming immersed in that muted light, full of the old expectations. Yet there, on the broad rectangle of the dance floor which commandeered the interior like a swimming pool, the dancing had certainly changed. No more bopping couples but bodies writhing in a mass.

'Now here's a lil' number I know you're gonna like,' boomed the glib Americanized voice from the loudspeakers. 'A smash hit . . . a fantastic number one . . .'

The disc jockey jigged at his post on stage, a piper to play the tune before the rippling arms and nodding heads. Spotlights circled and arms waved reedlike over a pond of highlighted faces. A crowded swim.

Steve followed after Eric and Woody, fending off his initial self-consciousness by allowing himself to feel bored at the predictable set-up of boy-meets-girl. On all sides there was the waiting, the flirting, the hesitant yet predatory glances of the eager males and the seductive, perfume-wafting movements of the females within their watchful groups. The hopeful youths gathered at the sides, attracted, unsure, summoning courage to take the plunge. He too felt drawn by the sirens in their pool but refused to admit it to himself.

'That counts thee out, Woody,' Eric joked as they made their immediate way into the bar. A sign by the door declared that no person under eighteen was allowed.

'It counts thee out an' all,' growled Woody, 'but it won't if nob'dy knows.'

He thrust his way into the bar, purposeful, raw-boned, strutting and glaring, cock of the roost. He called out to one of the barmaids for three bottled browns.

'Wait your turn,' she told him curtly, unimpressed, and he made a face.'

'Get a load of her,' he called after her, taken aback.

Eventually served, they moved away from the bar to a less crowded part of the once plush, carpeted room (the carpet was a little threadbare in patches nowadays) and stood drinking, not speaking, eyeing the talent. Eric was alert, his eyes following every female who came within sight.

'Hey! Them two over there,' he suddenly whispered in earnest and gave Woody a nudge.

They strolled casually over towards two girls who were wearing light cotton dresses and had their hair fashionably silky and long. Though appearing so haughty and sophisticated, like fashion models, they were clearly very young, perhaps in their early teens. Eric appraised them coolly, extending his personality towards them in small, easily manageable doses, while Woody tagged along as onlooker, slouching at his side. The two girls looked at each other briefly then gazed with bored indifference around them, waiting for something much better in the way of a couple of Prince Charmings to come along.

Eric persevered. He was stylishly scruffy, had the right mannerisms, was good-looking in a youthful, cumbersome way and definitely making progress. The two girls were trying hard not to smile.

Steve swigged as much of the bottled beer as he could manage and abandoned the rest, deciding to leave before Eric and Woody could rejoin him, defeated. Back to the Horse for one more, he told himself, then home — unless Mozz and Helena showed.

He came out of the bar and wandered upstairs onto the balcony before going. From here amongst the tables, each with their glowing intimacy of an orange shade table-lamp, he could look out over the dance floor and the activity which continued below like a mass fertility rite. The ballroom was a mating den, providing a small venue for the greater process of evolution, a meeting for young males and females, the genesis of courtship, marriage and children who would beget children. It was a ritual, bodies swaying and jerking to the music, all part and parcel of the game to be sealed with an embrace and a kiss or two.

He stopped to light a cigarette, choosing to observe the dancing crowd like this because it enabled him to feel aware and satisfied by his own isolation, not fooled by the game. He was free, about to leave, alone but no longer lonely, not obligated to the rite, not involved.

The jaunty, jumpy *Bits and Pieces* by the Dave Clark Five, which had been playing, was replaced by the echoing announcements of the DJ. Steve was at the top of the stairs, about to descend, when someone touched him on the arm.

They stared at each other, rooted in the midst of their passing and continuing, two ships passing in the night.

'How are you?' she enquired as they hesitated. Her voice was consciously modulated, her manner friendly but distant.

'Rough,' he responded abruptly then immediately regretted his abruptness.

'Too much to drink, no doubt,' she replied, ready to take her leave of him. She could walk away easily. She no longer cared.

'I'm not drunk,' he said, wanting to catch her interest and delay her for a few seconds longer. God! She was still as beautiful, more so without the lacquered beehive. She was wearing a pale mauve dress styled in the current Regency-revival, the neckline cut square and slightly low, the waistline lifted to below the bust. The dress was knee-high and clung to the figure, and the lightness of colour contrasted superbly with the black softness of her long hair and her dark Cleopatra eyes.

'I'm not drunk,' he repeated. 'Just going through a bad time.'

'Really?' She looked around her, preoccupied, a young

lady of breeding condescending to tolerate a churl. 'And what sort of "bad time" could you be going through?'

His heart quickened because she waited. She looked stunning, tall and elegant in her high stilettos, commanding attention. 'I'm about to suffer grief, I believe.'

'Ah, suffering a broken heart at last, are you? I knew you'd find out what it was like some day.' She gave a little laugh. 'Tell me, did you finish with her, or was it the other way round?'

He reached over to knock his ash into the ashtray of the nearest table, regarding her face glowing smooth and blemishless in the light. He smiled, shaking his head. 'It's nothing like that. That's not the sort of grief I'm on about.'

'I don't suppose it is, Steve, darling. You'd never allow yourself to fall foul of anything like that. You love yourself too much. I found that out for myself.'

He lingered on the soft smooth skin at the base of her neck while her dark eyes smiled their insolence at him. She was wary of him but interested.

'Look,' he said, hoping his confession would make her even more interested, 'I feel I've aged a thousand years since then. It's my mother. She's dying.'

At that moment Dione Warwick's new single was playing: *Walk on By*. The music, the song, caught him off guard, made the drama of confession all the more profound. As Rachel reached out to him he feared he was about to cave in. He felt sorry for himself and for all the things which had separated them. It came with the music and the shuffling, murmuring activity of the ballroom, the wafting of perfume and hot dogs, and the pop song immediacy of the evening. Back in the quiet, dull normality of home his mother still thought she was suffering recuperation pains.

The feeling passed. He got a grip. The strength to resist returned.

'There's bugger all anybody can do about it,' he said

carelessly, needing to brag some of his new philosophy of emotional detachment before her. 'My mother's had her lot and one has to accept it, I suppose.'

He looked at her carefully, confident that he still attracted her. He was Mersault again.

'That's a cold-hearted thing to say and you're a cold-hearted swine,' she told him, confused but impressed. 'Perhaps you always were but I loved you once.'

He laughed in his bravado of having nothing to lose. 'Love? What's that? Nothing but a load of sentiment and niceness designed to torment us poor mortals.' He pretended to cringe from the powers of the heavens. 'It fools us into believing we can combat our own isolation and insecurity. Insecurity! Aaagh!' He gave a show of fearful trembling. 'We're on our own, cut off like pieces of insignificant junk. It's all part of that long drawn-out game. You know the one. It comes in a neat package with little plastic counters and a dice. It's called Evolution. Evolution towards what?'

'Perhaps love's the only thing we have,' she said, turning once more to look about her.

'It's okay while it lasts,' he said quickly to maintain their conversation. 'And it can be good while it lasts, but it's all temporary.'

Dione Warwick's song faded to an end and he waited, wondering if Rachel was about to walk on by. Another record played to lend poignancy to the moment. He indicated the dance floor. 'Look there. A ritual in process. Anyway, that's not dancing,' he added more light-heartedly. 'I much preferred it when we used to bop.'

Rachel shrugged. 'Things change, don't they? All part of the "evolution". It's been nice bumping into you again, anyway. I'm sorry to hear the sad news about your mother.'

'Don't go yet,' he said.

She hesitated, glancing towards the staircase. 'I'm with someone, actually.'

'I see. Is he tall, dark and handsome?'

'And mean. I only came up here to see if I could find Gillian. He's waiting for me in the bar.'

'Who's that, then? Justin?' Mentioning the name still caused a slight tightening in the throat, even after all this time. He struggled not to show his disappointment.

'No, not Justin,' she answered. 'A bloke called Peter, as a matter of fact.'

'Another passionate romance, eh?' He was relieved to know it wasn't Justin.

'Hardly a passionate romance,' she informed him. 'I only met him ten minutes ago.'

That was even better. 'The start of a passionate romance, then.'

She regarded him haughtily. 'Who knows? It might be. He seems okay and I'm not involved with anybody.'

He moved his hand in time to the music. 'Think on. Don't throw your love away.'

'I rather think that's up to me,' she retorted, still playing haughtily, and turned as though to leave.

'I bet you're bored at the thought of having to join him,' he said, forcing the issuing when she lingered. He focused his attention at the base of her throat. It was silky, firm and fleshy, modelled smoothly into the contours of the shoulders and the gentle swell of the breasts. He longed to run his fingers lightly over the velvet softness of her skin.

She waited. He was aware that she waited.

'Peter's okay,' she said. 'He stopped to talk to me and invited me for a drink. There's nothing boring in that.'

'Come for a drink with me. Somewhere in town.'

'Why should I come for a drink with you?'

She was taunting him, he knew, holding him in suspended animation and enjoying her yes-or-no advantage. He pulled himself erect.

'It was only a suggestion, seeing as how we haven't seen each other in months. But, if you'd rather join your friend Peter . . .' He smiled, stepping aside to let her go.

*

Oh, to be out! Out in the cool evening air and away from the perfumed humidity, and the jaunty rhythms that they left behind. Rachel buttoned her coat, hesitated a moment, unsure, then linked her arm through his. He was glad of that. As they came through the reception a couple of the bouncers followed them with their eyes, perhaps wondering what a smart piece like that was doing with a scruffy weed like him. There was no justice in this life. But they were out. They had escaped without being stopped by Peter, the one thing he'd been dreading as he waited for Rachel by the ladies' cloakroom. Every bloke in the vicinity during those few tense, uncertain minutes had been called Peter. Peter, he presumed, was still waiting in the bar and would be there waiting for her till eternity. That was the way of the game. Some lost, others gained, and this time he had gained. He took care to hide his pleasure behind a sullen face.

They went to one of the up-market pubs in town. As they entered the plush upholstered world of the cocktail lounge he wilted momentarily, conscious of his shabbiness, his corduroy jacket with the torn lining and green elephant cord trousers baggy at the knees. The barman with his smart white jacket, bow tie and air of arrogance didn't help matters. When Steve ordered the barman snatched away the pound note offered for the drinks and, with the same aplomb, slapped the change on the counter as if offended by their slightest contact.

'Servile puff,' Steve muttered under his breath as he and

Rachel moved away from the bar.

Rachel produced her cigarettes as soon as they were settled in the soft leather armchairs. She took out of her handbag a neat little silver lighter.

'Oh, never mind him,' she said as Steve scowled in the direction of the bar.

'Servile puff,' he muttered again, and watched as the barman gave an oily smile to a powdered and permed lady who was perched on a stool at the bar, sipping shorts. The lady, though obviously more dignified, reminded him of the landlady of the Fleece with all the make-up and tight clinging skirt battling to contain her figure. Her plump, aging legs, which the tight skirt revealed, made him think of his mother's legs. He returned hastily to Rachel and the immediacy of her beauty and her youth.

'When my mother dies I'm gonna go to her funeral in my scruffiest clothes. I'll refuse to ride in the taxi. I'll walk in front of the hearse.'

'It's a sad thing,' Rachel said, reminded of his mother. She cupped her hand over his, wishing she could take some of his burden but not knowing how.

'What's it all been for?' he asked, wanting to take on the role of outspoken young rebel to impress her. He was enjoying her hand over his, her thumb stroking his knuckles. 'All those do's and don't's of my mother's life? All those concerns for what people might think, all that pride in home and appearances. And all those times she came home red in the face, loaded up with her shopping. What's any of it meant in the end?'

With his free hand he lifted his glass and took a drink. Compared with the stuff in the Horse the beer was far smoother and cleaner to the palette.

'What are you doing with yourself nowadays, anyway?' he asked, steering back to some kind of normality.

'Oh . . .' She shrugged. She was still without a job,

relying on her mother for money and cigs, and was now writing poetry.

'You write poetry? What about the promising career as an actress?'

She gestured a wave of dismissal, sweeping aside the past. 'It didn't work out,' she said tersely.

'What about Justin?'

'Oh him? Don't talk about him.'

'You finished with him?'

'I didn't want to go into acting anyway, and I certainly didn't want to live with him in London. He was so full of himself. Besides, I want to devote myself to poetry.'

His gaze fell to her manicured, maroon-painted nails then lingered briefly on her crossed legs in their black nylons. The roundness of her thighs was superbly outlined in the tight material of her dress.

'Where do you find your inspiration?' he asked, sensing the warmth of her nearness.

'In the countryside around our new house.'

'Your new house?'

She told him about the house they had recently moved into. It was on the other side of Lindlethorpe. 'Quite near where you live, actually. You'll have to visit me. You'll be able to accompany me on one of my country walks.'

He glanced at the roundness of her thighs. The prospect of accompanying her on country walks was rather appealing.

'It must be so much better for you than where you were.'

'Oh, yes, so much better. Now I can breathe. And it's an immense help to my poetry. So uplifting.'

He noticed a starched-looking couple, sitting nearby, turn their attention this way. Rachel's enthusiasm was becoming a little too loud.

'I wrote a poem today,' she went on. 'I have it here, in my handbag. Would you like me to read it to you?'

He saw the couple staring. 'Hmmmn. Perhaps not here.'

'Oh, darling, what are other people?' she declared with a theatrical wave, having also noticed the couple. 'I'm not bothered what other people might think. I would like you to hear my poem.'

The gesturing was overdone. It was like the early days, the naive young girl playing the sophisticated woman, yet somehow lacking the final polish.

'Listen, I'd like to hear it, but why not later? Somewhere where we can be alone. Not in here.'

He suggested it quietly. Her tendency for the melodramatic had not diminished. It threatened to overtake his rebel-against-the-world in the canned-music, muffled luxury of the cocktail lounge.

'I can't really appreciate your poem in here,' he added. Her aspirations to be 'different' drove him instantly to the steadier values of normality and dispersed the warmth he'd been feeling for her. He needed Rachel to be sensible, practical. He desired her, not her eccentricity nor her poetry. 'Not with this canned music and other people listening in, not understanding your work. Your poetry is important and if we're to give it justice you have to read it to me when we're alone.'

She leaned towards him, taking his hand and moving her face closer to his. 'You're right, of course, darling. The atmosphere in here is rather strained.'

Her warm breath wafted gently, featherlike over his cheeks. Desire stirred in him as he relaxed once more into her closeness and the gentle air of her perfume. Desire softened reason. He wanted her. The conviction came with her perfumed nearness, with the tight 'Regency' dress and the soft, lightly suntanned skin glowing and silk-like before his eyes. It came with the soft flow of her black hair, her smooth face and her dark eye-lined, brown, smiling eyes. It came too with the mellowing of beer and the quiet intimacy of the cocktail lounge.

'We ought to run away together. Down south. Find a flat in London.'

She breathed warm breath against his ear. 'Oh, darling, that would be splendid.'

He was tempted to tell her that he loved her and had never stopped loving her. He reached forward and touched her cheek. She took his fingers and held them against her lips, kissing each one.

'I need to be liberated,' he sighed. 'I need liberating from the lousy stagnation that my artist's soul's being choked to death in.'

'I too, darling. I too. We're so alike, you and I. My parents want me to get a job but I hate the thought of it. But you . . .' She kissed him on the forehead. 'What a shame that you should be subjected to such humiliation.' (He had told her all about the engineering work and his machine.) 'If only I could revive you. If only I could.'

The pot was boiling over, desire oozing juice like a ripened fruit. 'I love you, Rachel. You know I do.'

She responded with an ecstasy of kisses. 'Oh, darling, darling, you know I love you. I never stopped. Nobody else has ever meant anything. It's you I've loved all the time.' Their noses were touching. She breathed over him. 'You know, when I saw you there, standing so noble and proud on the balcony, I just had to come to you and hope against hope that you'd speak.'

They left the pub. Arms wrapped tightly around each other, their cheeks touching, they made their way through the night town of scattered people waiting in dark bus shelters, or going in search of a next port of call. There was no longer any of the grimness and emptiness. He nestled against Rachel in the love they'd both retrieved.

'I love you, darling.'

'And I love you too, darling. I do, I do.'

They left the town, embraced in each other. It was dark, silent, and they together. His heart beat within his skull. This was the thing, the substance and the meaning. To hell with the greater evolution. To hell with Mersault! Love, desire, the need for a woman, and knowing she felt the same. That was the most important thing there was. The rest was nothing.

They left the road just before Lindlethorpe and headed along a cartrack towards a grass field that he knew was there, near to the churchyard. He reached down to feel the grass. It was still damp after the morning's rain.

'Never mind, darling,' came her voice out of the darkness. 'We can use my coat.'

Throwing themselves into each other's arms, twisting, rolling, gasping, sighing, he clambered over the hillscape of her body, plunging and searching frantic with his mouth. She was there, all of her, for him, her smooth, young shapely body spreading over the grass towards the church. He enveloped her, draped himself over and around her, rampant and hungry with his wanting. He needed to crawl with his whole self into her, needed to hide himself away from everything which gnawed at his soul. He needed her to be all woman, Mother Earth embracing him and cradling him beneath her skirts.

'Hold me. Hold me!'

The words were a background pop song tuning to his urgency. He tried to free her from the constrictions of the tight dress which enshrouded her. The dress was sexy to look at but was now in the way. His hands were clumsy, fumbling in the dark. His left hand became lodged beneath her weight as he struggled with the zip at her back. The zip stuck, wouldn't budge. His fingers groped uselessly against it and he nearly sprained his wrist.

'Wait a sec,' came her voice, shattering in the darkness beyond his wheezing, thwarted passion. She got to her feet and stood, matter-of-fact, hoisting the clinging material as high as her thighs would allow.

He took her, if only to justify the preamble which had brought them to this spot. Then he stared at the blades of grass which were silhouetted in front of him against the starry sky. He stared in the irony of his awakening. Rachel wasn't Mother Earth and passion had its own limitations.

Afterwards they lit cigarettes and sat together on her coat, gazing down on the lights of the village, at the streetlamps following the undulations of the darkness like drops of luminous dew over cobwebs. He tried to imagine he was looking out towards the wide bay of a seaside town and that the lights were from fishing boats bobbing in the black hidden waters of the harbour.

'Look at the stars,' whispered Rachel in the stillness. 'How clear they are tonight. So lovely, so wonderful. It's like it used to be, isn't it? The two of us sitting like this again. I feel so happy, darling. So very happy. I feel alive inside, and it's you. You make me feel like that. It was so lonely without you there. So very, very lonely.'

He clutched his knees, watched the winking glow of the streetlamps. Then he shut his eyes against it and against Rachel, her proximity and her voice.

14

Summer! Hot, sweltering days in the machine shop and the sweating men stripping off their boilersuits to work in their vests or shirtsleeves. The heat, piercing the glass sections of the roof, shimmered over the oily black concrete beyond the opened doors and made him yearn for blue skies, and cool sea breezes to waft against his oil-grimed face. He was a prisoner, alongside his fellow prisoners, locked away in an airless boredom, pining for life.

Lunch times were a brief respite. In fine weather he wandered down by the sluggish, brown, chemical-laden river where the wild tuft grass and sparse shrubbery offered the only colour of nature in that grey, arid, man-made desert of rusty swarf-tips and foundry slag. Sometimes he sat by the bank of the river, and imagined he was by a fresh, trout-filled stream far away from the stench of industry and dull, grim factory walls. Other times he came through the foundry yard, passing the heaps of rusted scrap and stacks of rough castings, and leaned against the fence which overlooked the railway sidings. Here, gazing across at the silent rows of wagons, their wheels black and motionless above the clumps of weed-grass and wild daisies which flourished between the tracks, he thrived on the emptiness and silence, the dereliction and solitude within the mass of industry. The solitude of the railway tracks filled him with a nostalgia for the summers of childhood. He remembered those trips by train to the seaside, those happier times of naive hope and innocence. He had long ago lost naive hope and innocence, and the trains to the coast had long since departed with their hoards of ice cream and sandcastle children, almost as though they had passed this way and travelled along these same neglected lines. They had gone, leaving him to the silence, stranded like the wagons.

The afternoons seemed to go the slowest. They were like the homeward run. You were almost there, not quite in reach of your destination, but the journey continued on and on with the last few miles dragging incessantly.

His machine rattled and grinded through its revolutions, the fly-wheel spinning constant and the fly-belt whipping and slapping convulsively against it to make the turntable turn. He felt jaded, at a loss. What was the meaning of it all? What was it all for? The question hit him with an intensity he'd never really known in his student days. The game had been a simple one then, a striving for youth's identity, not the man's, but now, as he paced and ached for the end of the working day, the question became a far more desperate and frightening one. The whole conglomeration of life was a game, and he'd been picked up and thrust slap bang into the middle with no idea what the object was.

In more subdued moments, when thoughts kept pace with the rhythm of his machine, he doodled patterns in French chalk on the legs of his boilersuit, more wheels, more circles to fill with spokes. He would gaze towards the high window at the far end of the workshop, the rust stains on the panes of glass reminding him of a stained glass window in a church. He sought images in the tones of the staining — a boat beneath a bridge, clouds storming over distant hills, a couple embracing on a wide deserted beach. Fragments of music drifted through his mind, brief segments from Elgar's *Enigma Variations* which conjured images of sunlit, romantic landscapes and filled him with a longing in the pit of his stomach for some unrealized, unattainable but ideal quality of life. He visualized his mother, clean and robust in her pink nightdress with the white lace trim round the collar, sitting up in bed, laughing and chatting with her many visitors. He then contemplated the present in the perspective of twenty or thirty years when he might be married with children who were married themselves, or old and alone. His mother, now fleshy and clean in her nightdress, would have been dead and in the earth long, long ago. The thought of her being long-dead, her grave neglected and overgrown, filled him with an unfathomable sadness which, in the privacy of the surrounding din, he strangely enjoyed. Life was tragic and the tragedy was heightened by the music going through his mind, like a film.

Friday evenings he saw Rachel, enjoying the shortlived boosts to his ego that she gave. There was never any need for him to say much. She did the talking for them both and he didn't mind. She made him feel expansive, in demand, the centre of attention, and he was confident in the knowledge that if he chose to open his mouth she would be all ears to his every word. Occasionally he would respond with an understanding nod while she spoke, or show a cool enthusiasm for the things she was saying, not really listening to her many cocktail-lounge monologues but fully knowing in the muffled luxury of canned music that she was his — for the evening at least. She was no longer his 'true love' to be honoured and suffered, and they were under no obligation to each other but separate, meeting occasionally. There was a pleasurable certainty they could both share within this mutually acknowledged freedom, and in the knowing and the certainty he would act the role of misunderstood youth for her sake, enjoying the reaction it received.

Rachel took him seriously, marvelling at him. He was distant, hugging himself in an attitude of inner torture while he scowled and frowned around him. He was uncompromising, the artist and rebel, presenting that image of himself to her because she adored him and would do anything for him. She chose him before all others, willing to accept him on any terms. She was captivated still by this insipidly beautiful young man, and he had power over her in this knowledge. She was trusting, gullible, but sexy and desirable, and when the thirst was there he quenched it.

On Friday evenings her parents went out, which made it possible for them to have a quick couple of drinks in town before catching a bus to Lindlethorpe and the empty house. The distance by bus was reasonably short, but in his rearing excitement and impatience the distance would seem enormous, especially when they had to hang around waiting in the bus station. Throughout the journey to the other ends of the earth he would strive between his excitement and the fear of his impetuosity. How could he be certain that her parents weren't there? What guarantee was there that her father wouldn't return suddenly and catch them red-handed? They were the worries of old, but in the insanity of his desire the risks had to be taken.

The new house was on a brand new housing estate, about a mile beyond the village, along a recently laid tarmac road. On the first Friday evening he came back with her a gang of children, out playing, followed after them, calling out and wolf-whistling at Rachel. The children were already established in their new territory, having reduced the fresh black tarmac of the road to a dried-mud, stone-scattered playground in no time at all. A couple of them who had bikes pedalled slowly round in the road, circling predatory like sharks, ready to attack any invasion by outsiders.

'Take no notice of them,' Rachel told Steve when he expressed his annoyance. 'What are they but the offspring of peasants? The scum of human garbage.'

Yet they troubled him. They became an ordeal which

he dreaded having to face on each illicit visit to her house. Rachel already had a reputation for her eccentricity, it seemed, as well as her striking looks, and the children became troublesome like flies.

That first evening he quaked inwardly, guilty and convinced that everyone including the children, would know the purpose of his visit. Glancing around him at the shining black, vacant windows of the regimented brick dwellings, he could feel the eyes peering from behind every curtain. He tried to keep a low profile but the children, loudly hailing their arrival, denied it. He felt his intentions must be common knowledge amongst the entire neighbourhood and had visions of the estate's populace gathering outside the house, queueing at the windows to watch.

'Brats!' he fumed as he fled with Rachel down the makeshift ash path to the back door. It was sordid. He felt transparent before the whole world.

'I know, I dislike it too,' she said as she unlocked the back door. 'They're morons. Their parents must be morons, darling. It's the countryside I love around here.'

He followed her into the smells of new plaster and paintwork. This was her father's house. It was the den of that big, fearful man and his mate, a secluded place of bare, clean floorboards and wires exposed in the walls with no light sockets yet fitted to them. It was an unfurnished private retreat into which he was daring to tread.

Rachel apologized for the bareness. Her father hadn't managed to do anything about the house at present, nor the garden or the garden path. They hadn't really had time to settle in.

'Don't bore me about houses,' he replied testily, and noticed how his hands trembled as he lit a cigarette.

Surrounded by the emptiness, Rachel looked like a schoolgirl. There was no furniture, apart from the two threadbare armchairs brought from the old house. They were positioned before an empty stone fireplace and surrounded by a desert of floorboards in the large, echoing, uncarpeted lounge. She seemed vulnerable in the newness and unlived-in paucity of her home.

She tried to apologize again. Her parents were saving up to buy furniture as and when they could. It was a slow process, this moving in.

He cut her short. He wanted the woman he'd been desiring, not the embarrassed schoolgirl breaking into a monologue of self-reproach.

'It doesn't matter to me. Show me your bedroom. I want to see if it's an improvement on your last one.'

It was the same stumpy Van Gogh bed in which they had shared many short and stolen hours the previous summer. He saw with relief that there were curtains at her window, not sheets of newspaper stuck over them as there was downstairs. Peeping through them, he noted that there were no queues outside and the children had gone. He sat on the edge of the bed to finish his cigarette and staring at the unpapered walls, noticed how they had been spaced with reproductions of Dégas and Monet. Not one single tooth-shining pop star to grin down at him.

'Not a bad little pad,' he remarked as she stood waiting before him, as though expecting him to pass judgement. He stubbed out the cigarette in a small slip-cast dish he'd once made for her in pottery then went over to stand before her full-length mirror, his head held proud and hands on hips.

'Still as vain as ever, aren't you?' Rachel observed, closing the bedroom door. She came forward to take him in her arms.

'I wanted to see how shabby my clothes are,' he lied, clasping her. 'I do that when I go into clothes shops. The sight of myself makes me sick.'

'Don't lie,' she said, relaxing against him.

'Shall we undress?' he suggested, his voice thickening, knowing she'd do whatever he asked.

He tugged his shirt over his head and cursed as he struggled to kick off his trousers. God! If her mother and father should return. If her father should return! He watched as Rachel, having removed everything except her black bra and pants, dived under the covers. They were beyond the point of decency now. No going back.

The build-up was energetic. His need for her consumed him in a brief vigorous flame. He enjoyed her, sank into her in pursuit of something of her that remained for ever unattainable. Heart pounding from the burst of effort, he took her and no sooner had he penetrated her than he was spent.

He turned towards the evening light still lingering behind her bedroom curtains, listened for sounds coming from somewhere distant up the road. For a worrying moment he thought he heard a car stopping outside but the thing motored away. He felt her body pinned beneath him.

'Darling,' she murmured as he lifted himself from her 'you have the most perfect form. You remind me of Michaelangelo's David.' She reached for his hands. 'Yes, your lovely hands and long fingers. And your feet. Like the feet of Jesus.'

She touched him, stroked his body and it irritated him.

'You shouldn't say the things you do,' he told her. But she meant it. She admired and flattered him until he believed it himself.

She reached out her arms towards him as he climbed out of her bed. 'Why shouldn't I say things if I want to? I think you're beautiful and I want to tell you so.'

'Useless flattery,' he said and gave one of her breasts a gratuitous tweak. Her body, her breasts, as firm and as full as they were, no longer excited him. The electricity of desire they had inspired earlier had gone. She was simply Rachel with no clothes on, like a life-class model. He wanted to be up and dressed, and away as quickly as he could.

She pouted playfully when he resisted her, then sat naked in the bed, her hair dishevelled and her mascara smudged. 'Oh, please, lie with me, darling. Just a little while.'

He avoided her arms and reached for his trousers. 'I've got to see this bloke in the Horse. I arranged to see him there so I'd best go for the next bus.'

'What bloke?'

'Some'dy from work. He wants me to draw his wife's portrait, for her birthday, or summat. Anyway, I have to go, don't I? I don't relish having to run up the road without a stitch on and your dad after me blood. He might do nasty things to me with a kitchen knife.'

'Don't be vulgar,' she said, disconcerted as he clutched his groin. She lay back as he began to prance naked round the bedroom, holding himself. She closed her eyes, grimacing, trying not to laugh.

There was nearly half an hour before the next bus, time enough to sit downstairs and have a cigarette. Dressed, he felt less vulnerable and free to leave.

Rachel sat in the other armchair. She had put on a pair of old jeans and a crumpled shirt, going nowhere. He had refused to take her with him, giving the excuse that he'd only make it for a last rushed pint. She was happy to accept that and offered to kneel at his feet.

'Don't,' he said, irritated. 'Sit in the chair.'

He didn't want the fuss she would make, stroking his hair, interlacing her fingers through his, all those tender nonsensicals she liked to do with him.

She took the rebuff in her stride. She would wait. He would return to her.

'I'm sorry, darling. I don't mean to impose on you. It's

just that I still love you, whatever you say.'

He scoffed in a show of indifference. 'What's this love you're talking about?'

'You know what it is and you need it, though you try to make out you don't.'

'Bullshit!' he retorted, full of bravado. He didn't want love and neither did he need it.

'Ah,' she smiled as if teasing him in his indifference. 'One day you might realize different.'

'Come off it,' he sighed, and stood ready to leave. 'All this cryptic nonsense! One day never comes.' He didn't need love and didn't want it because life was full of pain and disillusionment, and love was the same. He had to deny it like a child kicking over a tower of toy bricks in anger and frustration. There was strength in being alone, even if life should become empty and lonely. Being independent of love in life's uncertainty and irony seemed the only true course to take.

As for Rachel, she failed to recognize his need to be gone from her once the physical thing was over. She desired in him far more than that. The physical part was mostly his but she was content to serve him in it, lying receptive beneath him, hugging him to her while he expended himself. She loved and honoured him with her body, offering herself to him in the quiet hope that he might return to her, loving her as he had done before. Steve, whatever way he might behave towards her, was still her prince.

15

His mother was sitting up when he arrived home from work. She was propped against a pile of pillows, browsing through the pages of a women's magazine, her arms resting over the counterpane of the neatly made bed.

'Where's me dad?' he enquired wearily, letting her see how he felt about his day.

She licked a finger to flip the page.

'Down at Ninety Four. He thought he might get on and do summat. I've been feeling a lot better this aft'.'

He came into the front room, throwing off his jacket, feeling the accumulation of grime and sweat engrained in his skin. She glanced up at him, then returned to her magazine.

'What makes you so happy, then?'

'Need you ask?'

He knew not to expect any sympathy; not that he wanted it from her. She was condemned, living out the remnants of her life. He needed to keep a distance. But he couldn't help but notice how undeniably healthy she was looking, not tired and drawn as she had been of late. Her hair was brushed and tidy, and she'd applied a little make-up. She was also wearing her pale green nightdress with the white lace collar; a clean change from the pink one she'd had on over the past few days. She was alert, rejuvenated, her air of domestic efficiency returned.

'The doctor came to see me this afternoon,' she said cheerfully. 'He says I'm doing really well.'

'Oh? Make no wonder you're looking so bonny.'

The doctor, whenever he came to the house, was like

a visiting VIP to his mother. She wilted before him like a young girl, put on her 'posh' voice and held him in awe.

'He's given me some more medicine an' all,' she added. 'It's a lot better than that last stuff he gave me. I haven't had any pains at all since I took it — touch wood.'

'Oh, aye?' He remained carefully disinterested as always when answering her about anything to do with her illness. But he was glad to see her so refreshed, her face clear and her eyes smiling and bright.

He watched her as she browzed through the magazine, cursorily glancing at each page and pausing at any item which caught her eye. He'd expected some months to go by before she'd be in bed like this, but climbing the stairs had soon become too painful and difficult for her, as had standing or walking itself, so his bed had been brought downstairs for her, the same as at Christmas. The bed had been erected in this strategic position by the wallside where she could see into the kitchen from the room, and beyond into her rose-garden when the back door was open.

He turned to go into the kitchen but she called out, pointing to the jacket he'd slung over the back of the settee. 'Don't leave that there.'

'Cor, it's good to tell you're feeling your old self,' he quipped, purposely off-hand, maintaining his distance.

'I don't care,' she retorted, 'you're forever being told about leaving your coats and jackets lying around. There's a proper place for everything in this house and the back of the settee isn't one of 'em.'

'All right. Keep your hair on.' It was a collective criticism, aimed at all of them. He took the jacket and hung it on one of the coat-hooks at the bottom of the stairs, sighing, inconvenienced.

'When your dad's spent his time hooverin' and tidyin',' she went on at him, 'you ought to try and keep it like that. For a short while at least.'

'All right. I've heard. Don't go on.'

As soon as she was anything like her normal self she was at it. He marched off into the kitchen to see about his dinner. She called after him, 'You've only need to warm a tin of peas. Your dad's left a meat and potato pie. It's on a low light in t'oven.'

Tin of peas! Meat and potato pie in t'oven! The words rolled off her tongue with a homely ring, familiar, normal with the permanence of everyday, even from her sickbed, his bed, her deathbed. He tried to block his ears against it, against her busy-housewife efficiency, dreading to let it reach him. Keeping distance, being divorced from the whole situation, that was his only armour.

'Make sure you leave enough for t'other two,' she reminded him. 'I suppose our Ralph'll be having to work over again, like last night, but where 'young 'un's got to is anybody's guess. He should've been home from school by now.'

'Him? He'll be hoverin' lovesick outside his girlfriend's with half a dozen of his mates, knowing him,' he suggested, unwilling to fathom the whereabouts of his youngest brother at this weary, hungry hour. He opened the oven door to check the pie and a hot aroma of baked pastry and meat gravy wafted into his face, normal, domestic, everyday.

'When you've got yours out leave theirs to warm,' she said in the continuum of her busy housewife's authority. 'But make sure it's on the lowest light.'

He opened the tin of processed peas which had been left out on the kitchen table for him, pouring the soupy contents into a small saucepan. While they were warming through he washed in the bathroom, still aware of the annoying tightness of grime on his face as he dried himself.

'What you doing now?' she asked when he returned into the room to switch on the stereogram.

'What? Oh . . .' He sifted through the LPs that were

slotted in cubby-holes at either side of the deck. 'A little music to dine by.'

His mother was suspicious, a prisoner of her bed. 'What d'yer think you're putting on? Not any of our Ian's stuff, I hope.'

He held out the landscape cover of Sir Malcom Sargent's recording of the *Enigma Variations*. The music had been haunting his mind all afternoon at work, the 'Nimrod' section in particular, and now he couldn't wait to hear the music at first hand.

She acquiesced reluctantly though she had no wish to share it. The Nimrod soared but failed to capture her soul. As the first notes swelled gently into the room she stirred restlessly, frowning in their direction.

'Goodness me, must we have it on that loud?'

'Loud? How d'yer mean, loud?' She was over-reacting as usual.

'I mean loud. You've got it on too loud.' The music swelled. She stirred again. 'Turn it down a bit, can't yer?'

'If I turn it down I won't be able to hear it,' he protested, immediately angry because she imposed on his involvement and enjoyment. His mother got angry in return.

'Look! I've said it's too loud. The damned thing's turned up enough to entertain the whole blinkin' neighbourhood.'

'But this is Elgar,' he yelled at her above the music.

'I don't care what it's called,' she yelled back. 'I've no wish to be subjected to it right now. I don't see why I should have to lie here all day, then have me eardrums pierced by you lot when you come home. You can turn it down or turn it off altogether.'

He tensed himself against her and against the music as each note seemed to rise all the more loud. Outraged, he rushed over to the 'gram and switched it off with a violent finality.

'There! Satisfied? Does that make you feel any happier?'

Her hand shot out to the stool which held her various pills and medicines at the side of the bed.

'I'll throw this lot at yer, bloody temperamental sod! Don't think because I'm stuck here like this you can say what you like. 'Cos I'll soon settle you your ash, m'lad, make no mistake.'

He turned his back on her, stooping to pick the record carefully from the turntable and returning it to its sleeve. She observed his offended attitude.

'I don't know, you're so damned selfish at times, Stephen,' she said, placated. 'In fact most times you don't seem to have any consideration at all. I tell you I don't want to be driven barmy with high-brow stuff like that, especially on top of everything else, but you take not the blindest bit o' notice.'

He gave a scornful laugh. 'High-brow stuff? This is music. You ought to be able to appreciate it.'

'Whatever it is, I wouldn't mind so much if you could play it a bit softer. The way you have it you want the whole street to hear. Put your record on if it means that much to yer, but not so loud.'

'I'm not playing it now,' he said aggrieved. She had spoilt everything.

She looked over at him, half smiling, half amused by his moodiness. 'No?'

'No! That's it.'

'Are you feeling tired?' she asked, attempting to smooth things over as he was about to head back into the kitchen.

He refused to look at her, not wanting her to come too close.

'Of course I'm feeling tired,' he snapped. 'You'd feel tired if you'd spent all rotten lousy day in a rotten lousy factory.'

'Nay, I wish I could spend all day in a rotten lousy factory, as you call it. I'd sooner be doing that than lying here, stuck between these 'ere four walls. Look, put your record on, if you've got to have music while you're having your dinner, but for heaven's sake not so loud. You don't seem to understand how it goes right through me the way you play it. It's enough to shatter me nerves.'

'It doesn't matter. I couldn't listen to it now.'

'Suit yourself,' she answered, willing to compromise when the intensity of clashes had subsided, but never willing to pursue a prolonged and persistent huff. 'Can you make me a cup of coffee when you're making one for yourself?'

'I suppose so,' he muttered condescendingly, then slouched off into the kitchen where he discovered the peas had been simmering too harshly, shedding their skins. He snatched them off the gas, cursing.

*

He had just eaten his dinner and was about to make the coffee, and butter a slice of bread as she'd requested, when she called out to him.

'Aye, it's comin',' he shouted back to her, still off-hand, still in his huffy mood. 'The kettle's boiled. I'm just about to make it now.'

She called out again and this time he heard the strain in her voice.

'It's your fault,' she told him peevishly when he came in to see what she wanted.

'My fault? How's it my fault? What have I done?'

'Getting me all het up and annoyed like you do.' She gasped, screwed her eyes against the pain which came then receded, then returned in force. 'It's when I went to grab that stool. I knew I'd wrenched meself. You must take great pleasure in seeing me stuck here and making things as uncomfortable for me as you can.'

'Don't talk daft.' He picked one of the bottles with a

helpless gesture off the stool. 'Here, can't you take some o' this? What about rubbing some of this ointment on your legs?'

She winced, sucking in the air through her teeth at the next wave of pain. 'Ointment's no damned good. And I've already taken me medicine.'

'Well, I don't know.' He edged away from her, knowing what she was about to suggest.

'You'll have to do it,' she insisted, seeing his reaction. He recoiled.

'But that's me dad's job. I don't want to do that!' She couldn't be serious.

'But he's not here, is he, silly fool . . .' She gave another gasp, trying in vain to massage the tops of her legs herself.

'Oh, Christ!' The idea of touching his mother's legs like that repulsed him.

She looked up at him, crying angrily. 'What's the matter with yer? Go on. You don't know how this pain shoots through me. Oh, bloody hell! Go on. They're hurting me.'

'I don't want to. I don't want to touch your bloody legs.' His voice came in a panic. He felt isolated by her, trapped and alone with a sick person in a sickroom. He grasped for the slim possibility that Ralph or Ian would return to share the isolation with him. He was helpless and afraid of her pain.

She groaned, holding herself tight as the next spasm gripped her. 'Oh, God, help me.' Then she threw her covers aside. 'I can't wait like this till your dad comes. You've seen how he does it. Rub 'em for me, for goodness' sake.'

'Oh Christ!' he tried not to look at the blue-veined white expanse of her thighs. The hem of her nightdress was bunched about her middle and he blurred his eyes to avoid seeing detail. He thought of what his father might say. 'You just can't stand around doing nothing for her. You have to get down to it and help her some time.' She waited expectantly, then twisted, gasping, as the spasms shot through her longer and more frequent.

'Go on, Stephen,' she sobbed. 'Please! Don't stand there gapin'.'

Stranded, obligated by her desperation, he turned his head aside from the warm odour of soap and sweat which rose from her, and forced his hand to touch the hot dry, wrinkled surface of her skin. He had seen how his father did it, working vigorously on each swollen limb in turn, rubbing them with a warm solution of soap and water on occasions, kneading the dough-like flesh between his fingers, coaxing them to life. When the medicines didn't work this was the only thing left to bring some small relief.

He moved both hands aggressively, going through the movements of massaging, as he had seen his father doing, shutting his mind to it and obeying his obligation. His fingers sank into the spongy bloatedness and he felt the deadweight bulk of her body rocking over the springy mattress with the pressure of his hands.

'Be a bit more gentle,' she gasped. 'Anybody 'ud think I've got the hide of an elephant the way you're goin'.'

'There's not much difference,' he answered, making light of it once he'd overcome his initial reticence.

'And there wouldn't seem to be. You must think you're helpin' your dad to rub a gravestone. I'll be full o' bruises when you've done.'

'I'm tryin' to do the best I can,' he told her, his palms and fingerends feeling hot with the friction of her skin.

He continued more slowly, less aggressively, and she rocked and sighed beneath his hands, letting go of her body to whichever direction he chose. Finally she moved from him, pushing him away.

'What's a matter now?' he asked. 'Is that still too rough for yer?'

'It's all right. Go on. I knew you wouldn't keep going for long.'

'Course I can go on. You told me to go slower. I'm only doing what you told me.'

'Never mind. It doesn't matter. Get on with your dinner, or whatever it is you were doing.'

'You okay then, or what?'

She sighed, resigned. 'I suppose so. I'll have to be whether I am or not.'

She spoke with the voice of martyrdom which meant that she was all right for the present but reluctant to admit it, even to herself. Accepting her answer with relief, he returned to the kitchen to make the coffee and butter a slice of bread.

The lull was a brief one. No sooner had he washed his hands and begun to butter the bread than he heard her restlessness again.

This time it was worse. She was inconsolable, like a distraught child, stopping him when he tried to approach her. She twisted away, rolling onto her stomach, her face pushed into the pillows.

'I thought you said you were okay,' he protested uselessly.

She didn't answer but moaned, banging at the pillows with her fists. Then the moaning became a strangled growl as she was gripped by the pain.

'What d'yer want me to do?' he asked stupidly. 'What d'yer want?'

Pinned down by her real despair, he clutched for strands of normality. He had never seen her as bad as this.

'Oh, God, please come. Please come,' she wailed and began sobbing, her sobs coming from the pillows like muffled laughter.

'Who d'yer want? Me? Me dad?' He noticed the women's magazine lying discarded on the carpet where it had fallen. He longed for those far-cry moments before when she had been browsing through its pages. Suddenly she lifted her face, red and heated and tearful, from the pillows.

'Oh, please come to me, please come to me,' she cried out in a voice strangely deep and meaningful in her despair, 'Oh, my God, please come.'

'Stop it, Mother. Don't be so bloody stupid.' He was shocked and angry in his fear of her desperation. 'Do you want my dad to come? Is that what you want?'

She continued to wail. 'Oh, my God, my God. Why has He forsaken me?'

He tried to remain calm, tried to maintain rationality. Her agony was a performance, part of the act, part of the game of being in pain and none of it was for real. Only it had run away from him, beyond his control. He rushed to get his jacket, anxious to be gone, away from his mother and her suffering.

'Okay. You want me dad. I'll go fetch him for yer.'

She turned as he was leaving.

'He's down at that hide-out of his,' she admonished through her tears, as though she held his father responsible for this. 'Go tell him he's needed up here.'

'I don't know,' he said, showing irritation at the inconvenience in his need to maintain normality. 'Just when I was looking forward to a smoke and a cup o' coffee. I'm getting' bloody sick o' this.'

His mother buried her face back into the pillows. 'Not half as sick of it as I am.'

*

His father glanced up briefly as he entered the workshop, then went on bumping with the big round wooden mallet against a claw-chisel, trimming the top edge of a long sandstone kerb.

'Now then,' he greeted, having no idea that his work was about to be interrupted. He carried on chipping at the kerb, the stone-chips flying off with each strike of the mallet like small explosions.

Steve leaned against the wall, next to the junk-table, saying nothing for the moment about his mother. In the few short seconds before he'd have to tell him he watched the claw-chisel gouging and levelling the rough hewned surface. The kerb was set on two bulky work-trestles and the teeth of the chisel left grouped indentations of powdery white in the dull ochre bumps and ridges of the stone, like furrows in a miniature ploughed field.

'Aye, well,' said his father, pausing to brush a few chips of stone away from where he was working, 'I'm trying to have this job summat like before July, if I can, but you know how things are at present.'

'Aye.' Steve pretended to yawn and stretch as though he'd called by chance. His father, wearing a blacksmith's old leather apron which he'd acquired from somewhere on his travels, checked the pencil line he'd ruled to mark his cut.

Satisfied he was still above it, he asked, 'Have you come from up yonder or straight from work?'

'From home.' Only another second or two and he would have to tell him. He felt sorry for his father because he knew his immediate destiny. The job would have to stop.

'What you doin' here, then?' his father enquired, still not knowing. 'Come to patch that lot upstairs?'

'What? That useless load of crap?' The mention of his pitheads immediately filled him with a familiar loathing and boredom.

His father said, half reproachful, 'That's not the way to go about things. It's a complete waste of time and materials. What went wrong? I thought you were doing fine with your pithead idea. It looks like you've been havin' a rare old time of it, all them drawings torn and screwed up, and your canvases torn and slashed to ribbons. You tried to set fire to some of 'em as well, by the looks of it. A wonder you didn't have the whole damned place alight.'

Steve moved away so his father could reach this side of the kerb. He thought of the previous Sunday afternoon, the hot, steamed-up, agonized atmosphere of Sunday dinner, his mother crying in pain. He had sought the retreat of his studio and his painting, only to find his efforts proving futile, a skimming of the surface which had seemed as impenetrable as granite. Filled with the sense of his own worthlessness, he had been the ruthless critic of his own meagre talents.

'There was no need for it,' his father went on. 'I've told you before, you should save everything you do regardless of whether you like it or not. That way you have something in front of you to set your standards by, surely.' He continued bumping at the stone. 'It's no use trying to rush these things. They take time. Time and patience. It's all a matter of patience. Look at me. That's all I can afford to have, is patience.'

Steve watched the chisel biting at the stone once more and blinked involuntarily as the stone chips flew. Time and patience! Time, future, patience. He listened to the rhythm of mallet on chisel thumping industriously in the coolness and stillness of the cottage. Time, future, patience. The concept was impossible to digest.

'Ah, well, I'm no artist so it doesn't matter.'

Steve watched four more strikes with the mallet. 'I'm not here for that anyway. It's me mam. She's going' off her rocker, if you ask me.'

His father nodded and stopped working. 'In pain, is she? Right, I'd best get off and see to her then.'

'It's a damned nuisance,' Steve remarked as the mallet

and chisel were put to one side and his father unfastened the leather apron. Seeing the apron draped over the unfinished kerb, he wondered how long it would have to remain there before it was picked up again. This thing was going on forever with no foreseeable end.

His father gave his clothes a quick dusting, then reached for his jacket and the flask of tea that he'd brought with him still untouched.

'It's a bad job all round, is yon', lad. A bad job all round.' He stood a moment with his back to the fireplace, as though about to deliver an official family announcement. 'I might as well tell you, your mother hasn't much longer to live.'

'I know,' Steve admitted, reflecting that this might be the cue for a highly charged melodramatic scene in a second-rate movie, agonized tearfully amongst the stone-dust and disorder. ('We can't let her die, I tell you, we just can't let her die!') Their exchange was dry-eyed, calm and realistic. 'I've known for a while,' he added, glad that his father knew and that the 'secret' was out.

His father accepted the reason why there had been the secrecy with a chuckle. 'If I had to drop dead of heart attack they'd put it down as nervous debility.' The doctor had finally consented to let him know during the visit in the afternoon. 'I'd guessed as much what was wrong with her, though, without it having to be spelt out. All we can do now is make sure she's as comfortable as possible.'

'And act as if nothing's the matter.'

'That's all we can do. She's never been one for all the soft-soapin', hasn't your mother. Do t'other two know about it?'

'Ralph does. I haven't told our Ian.' He had told Ralph. He had shared the 'secret' almost immediately with Ralph and together they had watched their parents, knowing what neither of them knew.

'We'll leave our Ian out of it for 'time being in that case. He'll get to know sooner or later, but there's no need for him to know anything yet. He's only a lad.'

'How long's it gonna go on for? That's what I keep asking,' Steve said as the cottage was locked and secured with less fuss than usual. 'Ever since I've known about it I've kept wishing it was all over and done with. I know it's heartless to say it, but I've had to accept that she's dying. What else can you do?'

His father tugged at the padlock, making sure it was fastened, then they set off walking. 'There's nothing else to do but accept it. The question I keep on asking is, why us? Why should it happen to us? Why should it happen to your mother? When I think how she's worked and slaved practically all her life, then she's got this. I get to thinking, what's the use of doing anything? All the strugglin' and messin' about, and for what? Sometimes it makes me just want to give up.'

'Maybe it's best not to think of it like that,' Steve suggested urgently to drag his father from any self-pitying he seemed likely to fall into. He needed his father to be strong, sharing the detachment he was striving for himself. 'Look on it as an intervention of fate. You're being given a second chance.'

He saw it clearly then, the past years of his father's life viewed in perspective as the breadwinning years, a mere interlude in his career as a sculptor. He wanted his father to see that, to see beyond the limitations he had imposed upon himself throughout the last twenty three or four years. The interlude was drawing to an end. The idea suddenly seemed a sound one.

'When my mother dies you'll be free to carry on where you left off when you were in Paris.'

His father gave a laugh. The reasoning was preposterously naive, carefree and amusing. 'What happens if I die before her? There's no telling how long this lot's got to go on for. But aye, I wish it could be all over and done with as well. As painless and as quickly as possible for your mother's sake. I don't like to see her suffering.'

16

'Beer's off,' he said to Mozz and Helena as they sat in the Horse one quiet Sunday evening. He spoke in a whisper so that Paddy, drying glasses behind the bar, wouldn't hear him.

He glanced at Helena. She still liked to wear the same baggy sweaters which hid her figure, and her hair was the same tangled mass hanging to her slim waist. He found her as appealing as ever.

'How's your mother?' she asked. It was the question he was being asked a lot nowadays. He shrugged, giving his usual reply.

'No change. She has a lot of pain.'

'It's sad,' said Helena, her large almond eyes full of concern.

Mozz shifted on his stool, returning conversation to the subject they'd been discussing earlier about their 'good old days'. This often absorbed them when they weren't discussing religion or the meaning of life.

'What was it all about? That's what I'd like to know,' he said, disillusionment having set in as regards his time spent at college. Like Steve, he had little to show for his wasted years as an art student. He had become despondent about the whole topic of art schools and art for art's sake. Painting, drawing, working towards the perfecting of one's talent, represented nothing more than a treadmill of disappointment. Besides, photography had replaced everything, he would argue provocatively whenever he visited Ninety Four and saw Steve doggedly carrying on. The days of the easel painter had long since gone.

'Be honest with yourself,' he would state. 'What's the use of painting in this day and age, unless you want to be patted on the back and told how clever you are? What's a painting for anyway? Something nice and colourful to hang on a wall? Something that might go nice with the curtains or the wallpaper? Everybody in the art world gets really involved like it's a life-or-death game, then they tag on a lot of clever words to make it sound even more meaningful. And what have you got in the end? Just an arrangement of shapes and colours to stick on a wall. You might as well hang a towel or something on a wall and say how wonderful and meaningful that is.'

Mozz was questioning himself, evaluating his own talents in the uncertainty of his direction. As for Steve's aspirations, he could accept 'Pithead II in Blue' as an interesting piece of work, although the blue was more a murky grey, but in his opinion it was a far better design for a book cover than a painting.

His comment had wounded taut sensitivities, pecked at the delicate foundations of Steve's belief in his own art, and seeing the effect of his words, Mozz had pecked even harder.

'Yep, I can just see the lettering spaced over your winding-gear, man. *Sons and Lovers* by D.H. Whatsisname.'

Following this, Steve could hardly bear to look at the dull surfaces of the canvases he'd been so proud to consider his retrospective work. It was partly in response to Mozz's caustic appraisal of the 'game' that he had destroyed them, taking a certain brutal pleasure in the way the canvas had ripped under the blade of a Stanley knife. A splashing of turps and a light from a match had served for their final obliteration.

'And what have we got at the end of all the theories about colour and design?' Mozz wanted to know. 'And all those notes on anatomy and the history of art?'

The only thing he'd achieved from his art education was the position of a clerk in a furniture warehouse, chasing around with a clipboard, checking orders against stocks and loading vans. 'I'm a warehouse clerk. And after a lifetime of being a warehouse clerk I'll probably become a chuffin' retired warehouse clerk.'

He spluttered, unable to get the words out fast enough, as he tended to when he became excitable on any issue.

Helena interrupted him. 'Then why don't you do something about it? What's to stop you? It's obvious you're not happy where you are, so why don't you go off somewhere? Go abroad.'

'But what would you do?'

'Don't use me as your excuse Mozz.' she told him. 'I'll manage. I'll carry on with what I'm doing.'

Helena was another of those rare successes of their college year, working at present in a graphics studio near Bradford and earning a reasonable salary. She saw the look Mozz gave her and laughed, patting his hand.

'Don't worry, love, I'd still be here.'

'I agree with Helena,' Steve said. 'I think we ought to pack our bags without giving any more thought to it.'

He turned to Helena. 'He always talks about packing in his job and heading off but he never does. Last time he didn't want to get off anywhere 'cos it was bleedin' winter.'

'Nay, don't blame me' Mozz retorted. 'I was waiting for you.'

'Waiting for me? You cheeky bugger. It's me who keeps waitin' for you.'

Helena intervened. 'If you ask me you're both as bad as one another. All this talk of waiting! If you intend doing something then do it. Now's the time. We're halfway through June. Just the right time for being impulsive. Head for the South of France, try for Devon or Cornwall.

Whatever, give it a try. Take the bull by the horns.'

It was as though salvation waited round the corner when he returned home at the end of the evening and announced his plans.

'I'm giving my notice in at work tomorrow. Me and Mozz have decided we're heading for Cornwall for the rest of summer.'

'Oh?' His father, not listening, was too absorbed in pouring away a bowl of soapy water, then fetching a tumbler of water for the assortment of painkillers and pills.

'Aye, we're thinking of heading to St Ives for a start, then we might tour round a bit, Penzance, Newlyn, you know, where all the famous artists lived.'

'You'll get no further than our front gate, you and Mozz,' put in Ralph as he spread out in one of the armchairs, reading his rugby league magazine. He was an avid fan of rugby league.

Steve whirled round on him, about to tell him to 'get lost', then thought better of it for their mother's sake. She was settling for the night and the last thing she needed was any bickering between brothers.

'I'm giving a week's notice,' he emphasized, hearing the words, yet somehow, here in the house and away from the pub, unable to believe that he meant it.

His father unscrewed the top from a bottle and emptied out a few of the pills. 'You'd better not pack in just yet,' came his calm, sensible reply.

'Why not?' Steve demanded, immediately up against the doubts which overwhelmed him in the face of real and practical matters. 'I can pack in work if I want to.' His and Mozz's plans seemed suddenly a hare-brained scheme. All thoughts of packing and leaving seemed part of a hare-brained scheme.

His father, having no wish to become involved in any heated discussion at this time of night, refused to answer.

He handed the tumbler of water and the pills to his wife, wanting to see her settled.

'Have a bit more patience,' he suggested finally.

Steve looked to Ralph, eyes lifting, mouth clamped in irritation and annoyance through his own doubting. How could you remain patient? How could you remain simply treading water while life passed by so quickly you suddenly found you'd been in charge of a vertical borer for nigh on twenty years? This was exactly what he and Mozz had talked about in the Horse. Life constantly presented ruts which it was all too easy to fall into.

'I'm giving my week's notice first thing tomorrow morning,' he repeated stubbornly, though without real conviction, 'I'm going to Cornwall with Mozz. And that's that.'

His mother took her pills, weary-eyed, preoccupied, grimacing as she swallowed. 'You're not packing in your job tomorrow, and that is that,' she said at last.

He turned to her, 'Yes, I am. Why shouldn't I? I'm over twenty one. I can leave if I want.'

Her voice took on a more forceful edge. 'And I say you can't. You're going down to no Cornwall or wherever else you think you might be going. It's up here where you're staying, never mind Cornwall. You've got to help your dad.'

'What? Stuck indoors all bloody summer amongst that noise and muck?' He groaned. 'No, no! I'll go spare.'

'I've told you, you're not packing in your job tomorrow and let that be final,' she said. 'You and that mate o'yours, Mozz, you're both as slack set-up as they come. What d'yer think folks are gonna say if they see you gaddin' off and leaving your dad to look after everything here?'

'To hell with what they'll say.' He hated this familiar slant. He looked to his father, craving his support. 'Tell her, Dad. Tell her I want to do summat else with my life, not just work a machine.'

'Never mind, "tell her, Dad!" It's what I'm telling you. It's about time you faced up to responsibilities. Where d'yer think the money's coming from to live when your dad can't work? You're needed here, at least while I'm laid up like this. You've got no sense of responsibility and you refuse to have any.'

'Oh, I see, so I'm lacking something 'cos I've got no responsibilities? Is that what you're telling me? Is that all there is? A bloke can't claim to be living his life properly unless he's bogged down, worrying himself silly about everything and worrying what the neighbours 'll think if he's not worrying?'

His mother, infuriated by his arguing, sat up and banged her fist on the stool by the side of the bed. Some of the bottles toppled over.

'Will you bloody well be told? You're not packin' your job in. You're not leavin' home and you're not goin' off with Mozz or anybody else, for that matter. I'm not havin' my name dragged down by a scruff like you.'

'What's that supposed to mean? Typical bloody stupid thing you'd say, is that?'

His father asked him to lower his voice.

'Well, what does she mean havin' her name dragged down by a scruff like me?'

'Listen,' said his father, 'don't you care a damn for anything? Really? Not even for your mother, the way she is?'

'No, I don't, I'm bleedin' sick,' he cried, feeling a certain satisfaction in his denunciation. 'I'm sick and tired of this house and sick of everything. And I'm worse than sick havin' to go out to that place every day.'

'Go to hell, Stephen.' His mother lay back and closed her eyes. 'What's the use of talking? You're nothing but a rotten selfish swine. Selfish to the end. Always was and always will be.'

'Why? Because I've got no responsibilities and refuse to have any?'

'That'll do, Stephen,' intervened his father. 'Let's have no more now. Let it rest. Your mother needs to get her sleep.'

'He's no damned use to anybody,' his mother uttered, insisting on the last word. 'No damned use at all.'

'All right, lass, all right,' his father coaxed, tucking in her bedcovers and straightening the bottles on the stool. 'He won't be leaving his job,' he added reassuringly then switched off the light so she could sleep.

'You'll have to stay here for the time being,' he said finally to Steve. 'The family's at a bit of a loose end at present and until things turn out better you'll have to stay put. I can appreciate how you feel but if Mozz wants to go down to Cornwall he'll have to find some'dy else to go with him. I'm afraid that's how it is.'

'It wasn't Mozz's idea. We both planned it.'

'Whoever planned it, it doesn't matter. It happens to be inconvenient right now and we'd like you to stay.'

Steve threw himself onto the settee, muttering his disappointment at his brother. Ralph gave an understanding nod and returned to his magazine, trying to read in the sparse light coming from the kitchen. In a while he gave up and sat contemplating in the silence.

Their father joined them. He lit a cigarette, paused on reflection, then offered the packet to his sons.

'I know you'd like to get out of this mess,' he reasoned as the relieved moment of privacy and tobacco smoke drew them together. 'I'd like to get out of it as well but obviously I can't. I have to stay, like I've had to all long.' He glanced round at his wife. Her steady deep breathing indicated she was asleep. He went on in a hushed voice. 'I had the same ideas when I was your age, visions of travelling here, there and everywhere. But things have a habit of overtaking you.'

'You've never managed to grab hold of anything, have you?' Ralph said sympathetically.

Their father brushed a hand through his hair, as if wearied by the blow that fate had chosen to deal him. His life seemed to have become one of regret for lost opportunities. Now he was losing his wife and this added to the irony.

'No,' he sighed, resolved. 'I've failed to catch on somewhere along the line. Just failed to catch on.'

'Well, I don't want that,' Steve answered, rearing against his father's pessimism and self-pity. 'Existing on boredom and being sucked into a dreary dead-end job till I'm sixty five like them silly sods at work.'

'But you have to work,' replied his father. 'How else do you get a roof over your head and food in your belly?'

'You mean poor buggers like us have to work.' He noticed one of Ian's pop magazines lying on the floor, the latest issue of *Fab*. 'I bet none o' them lucky swines'll be gettin' up at half six tomorrow morning to stick all day in a factory,' he commented, making out a black and white photo of the Rolling Stones. 'Anyway, what's the use of ought if you're supposed to do nothing but work for a living?' His father persisted in standing by the simple work ethos of his generation and the generations before him, and that was annoying and frustrating.

Aware that Steve was judging him, his father said, 'Look, your mother's on her deathbed, you might say, and it's her last wish that you stay. After she's gone you can go where you like.' He stubbed out his cigarette in the hearth and got to his feet. 'Whatever you do, in the meantime it's gone twelve and it's back to the grind tomorrow. Come on, ne'er mind the gruntin', let's have you off afore you wake your mother. Otherwise it'll be agony, like it was last night. And don't wake him up either when you go up,' he added, meaning Ian who had been in bed since half ten.

Steve turned to his brother. They were close, their mother's illness and gradual dying their shared experience. 'What would you do if you were me?'

Ralph thought it over, carefully and slowly, then reached his conclusion. 'I'd stay around a bit longer if I was you.'

17

The on-and-off affair had continued with Rachel. Each time it was love, real love, until passion slept once more, temporarily sated. During the following week, when it was hot midsummer weather, he decided to take the afternoon off work to see her. She had been in his thoughts all morning while his machine rumbled and he doodled patterns on his overalls with French chalk. Thoughts and speculations about Rachel had been an antidote to boredom, and he'd been dwelling in particular on that long-awaited walk in the countryside around her house. When the hooter signalled lunch time he rushed off for the next bus home so he could wash and change.

His father was full of moralizing and sermonizing to make him feel guilty as soon as he landed.

'But what difference does one afternoon off work make?' Steve cried, hackles rising immediately against the opposition. 'The blinking firm won't shut down 'cos I'm not there.'

'It's your idleness I'm on about, and your total lack of responsibility,' replied his father in the middle of attending to the sickroom chores.

'How am I being idle? I don't see why I should have to stick in that place, just for one afternoon, when the weather's like this.'

His father rounded on him, looking angry yet somehow comical with the polka dot apron he'd fastened on to administer a bed-bath. His face was flushed with heat and tension. He stood with a bowl full of soapy water, not knowing which way to turn.

'It's all very nice for you, isn't it? Don't you think I'd like to be outside when the weather's like this? Don't you think your mother 'ud like to be out in the sun as well, doing a bit of gardening instead of being stuck here in bed?'

'It's no use you talking to him, Percy,' his mother put in. 'You may as well save your breath.'

She was sitting propped up on the pile of pillows, ashen, tired, shattered by heat and pain. She shook her head, adding, 'No good for owt, our Stephen isn't. He cares a damn for nobody but himself.'

Steve turned to her. 'I only fancied doing summat a bit more lively, a bit o' sketching. What's all the fuss? I'm going back.'

'Yes, well, that's as maybe, but you just have no sense of responsibility.'

'That's right, Mother, and I'm just a mean, selfish, ungrateful sod. So what?'

He snatched up his jacket, duty-bound, obligated, knowing he was in the wrong. He glanced at the clock, assessing that the next bus into town would make him only five minutes late. He'd had to nip out on private business. That's what he'd tell Wilky. Amongst the workmen it was the most widely used excuse.

His mother heard his note of dejection. She said with less severity, 'Why can't you be a bit more thoughtful about what you do, eh? Why don't you try and get yourself out of your idle ways? Get a better idea of what you want out of life instead of adopting the attitudes you do? I don't know, you're twenty one years old and you still seem intent on idling.'

'There's only one thing I want to do,' he began but she answered with an urgency that surprised him.

'You don't think for a minute that I want you to stay at that engineering place, do yer? Of course I know you want to do something better. I know you have higher aims than that. All I ask is that you stay there for a while so you can help out a bit financially. Help your dad, at least till things are straightened out here. After that you can please yourself what you do. But if you want to be an artist I don't want you to be too disappointed if you never make anything of it, you know.'

She gazed up at him with her tired, sunken eyes, trying to understand him yet not quite able to. His outlook on life, his aspirations and expectations were beyond her, and all that she had been brought up to understand. She shook her head again, giving up on him. 'Eeh, lad, God knows what it is you're looking for but I hope you find it one day, whatever it is.'

18

Sunday. 'Pick of the Pops' on the old wireless below and he up aloft amongst the dust and debris of the studio. He was working on a long-awaited portrait, smudging charcoal for a soft-tone effect and using a dog-eared, black and white snapshot as a source of reference. The drawing was for Harold-on-the-driller, a portrait of 'our lass' which Harold had asked him to do ages since. 'I'll slip thee half a sheet for it when it's done,' he'd promised, handing him the photo of his wife.

'Pick of the Pops' reached its conclusion with this week's number one. He was hidden in the disorder of his sanctuary, away from the chaos of home, the palaver of suffering, the gathering of uncles and aunts, and all those other visitors-to-the-sickbed who crowded him out like a prelude to the funeral.

He sketched in the eyes and nose, decided that they bore no resemblance to those in the photo, and rubbed them off with his finger to draw them again. The sparrows twittered in the eaves for company while Roy Orbison's woebegone finale rose and ended like a forgotten dream. So too, with its uptempo, big band theme tune, did the programme. 'Until next week, pop-pickers. Allright? Stay bright.' Until next week! And what would it be next week? Would it be over, or all over now, and his mother dead and in her grave by this time next week? But next week followed with more chart-toppers to accompany Alan Freeman's bright, cheery, informative voice, and she still clung, not letting go of her stricken life.

He returned to the portrait: more charcoal, more

smudging that seemed to be going nowhere. He stared hard at the snapshot, at the slim blond with the 1940s perm and the square-shouldered silk dress. There was the long nose, the eyes almost lost in the grainy shadow, and her teeth protruding from the wide grin. He wrestled on, heart not in it, overworking the charcoal, trying to grasp a likeness, chasing himself up his own backside. He detested doing portraits but was forced to keep going. He had promised Harold and he was obligated, all for ten bob.

And so to this week's chart-toppers, pop-pickers! The Animals wailed out their four minutes' anguish about the House of the Rising Sun: 'Oh, Mother, tell your children not to do what I have done . . .'

'Oh, Mother . . .!' It gripped him with a sudden grief-wrenching of his whole being. He wanted to say, 'Oh, Mother', to declare his sorrow when all the tight-lipped, close-minded familiarity had been pushed aside. But it was useless, impossible, so out of character for them both, even to the end. They never communicated on that level. She had never encouraged it, never gone in for the shows of tenderness, the 'soft-soapin' ', as his father called it, the openness of that kind of thing. He had never seen his parents kiss and cuddle; perhaps embrace but then in fun. That aspect of her life with his father had been kept for the other side of their bedroom door.

His thoughts returned again to that Saturday lunch time a few weeks back when he'd tried to keep up the hard front towards her. It was the weekend following the one on which he'd made the visit to the doctor. They were all in the living-room together, relaxing with cups of tea after fish and chips, allowing their meal to settle. The spring sunshine had gleamed through the bay window into the room and she was in his bed, over by the wall, content after lunch and free from pain for the while. He decided on listening to some music, nothing too strident to disturb the tranquillity, and chose an EP he'd recently bought of Chopin piano pieces.

'Ah, I used to like this one,' his mother said, agreeing for once with his choice as the *Etude in E* began. 'We used to sing this when I was a girl. "So Deep the Night", it's called.'

'It's Chopin's *Etude*,' he contradicted dryly, hoping that she wasn't about to start her nattering above the music.

'It's "So Deep the Night", isn't it, Percy?' she insisted good humouredly, looking over to his father, and as if to prove her point began accompanying with the lyrics.

'Okay, okay,' Steve objected, then lifted his eyes in his irritation toward Ralph and Ian as she continued singing, her voice rising to her song. She was off, making a fool of herself, yet he felt strangely embarrassed by her singing. Suddenly it was as if she were serious about the song and the lyrics had real meaning for her. She was singing with real effort.

'Alone am I, alone am I . . .'

He mocked her to counteract his embarrassment. He had never heard her sing like that before. He sighed to show his aggravation, then noticed his father, who was leaning back in his armchair and rubbing his eyes as though sleepy, gesturing for him to be quiet and let her sing.

'Eeh, we used to love that one, our Hetty and our Miriam and me. We'd all be singing it while our Edwin played piano,' she went on, unaware that his father was weeping.

He shook himself from the memory and the hard dry solidness which formed behind his nose and down the back of his throat. There had to be no room for sentiment. That must be left for those who would gather at her grave. He returned to Sunday late afternoon in the studio, to the sparrows in the eaves and this week's edition of 'Down Your Way'. He came back to the portrait, rubbed out the entire face and started again.

*

On Monday morning, bright heatwave July already slamming its heat over the housetops by half past six, he came down expecting to be greeted by the suffering he'd grown accustomed to for so long. This morning she was unusually quiet. She was lying quite still, but chatting in a steady conversation with his father.

'. . . and they told the police to come and see about this burglary,' she was saying.

'Did they manage to make anything of it, then?' his father responded.

'Hmmn. They said if there was anything missing it had to be reported.'

'Quite a job by the sound of it,' his father acknowledged, straightening and tucking in her covers.

Steve noticed that she was talking with her eyes closed. Then she opened them, startled when she saw him gazing down at her.

'Where's that little man gone?'

'What little man?' He thought that she was joking, that she was showing a kind of exuberance for feeling better, but there was no amusement in the look she gave.

'He was sitting there, on the end of the bed. He told me he was going to help me.'

Her confusion shocked him. It was like being in a dream, her dream, and he was part of it, not real in himself. He had felt something of the same those two years before, reading the paranoid scribblings on the front of his father's desk diary the morning of a snowbound winter when the ambulance came. This time it was his father he was turning to for reassurance and support.

'Is it part of her illness or is it the drugs?' he asked him as soon as she had drifted back into sleep. He tried not to notice the tears glistening in his father's eyes.

'I don't know, it could be either,' his father answered with a shrug, attempting to maintain a rational hold on the situation himself and examine it practically.

He followed Steve into the kitchen, sitting opposite and having a cup of tea while Steve got his breakfast.

'She must've been talking in her sleep, poor lass,' he said at length.

Steve nodded, unable to speak and hardly able to swallow the mouthful of cornflakes he was trying to chew. There was a nasality in his father's voice, as though he were suffering from a cold. He looked away. He couldn't bear to think of his father breaking down in front of him, couldn't bear to see him weep. Men didn't weep.

He focused hard on the table littered with the familiar items of breakfast amongst the breadcrumbs, the butter dish, the half-used jar of marmalade with the top not replaced, the used plates from last night's supper and the remains of the loaf surrounded by the tea stains on the tablecloth. It was early Monday morning and for a second he was back once more in the once-upon-a-time washday Monday mornings that belonged to his schooldays, his mother sorting through the clothes for the weekly wash, his father cutting sandwiches for that day's snap. There was Ralph and Ian, and himself being reminded of the time, grabbing their hasty bowls of cereal before they set out for school. And in the aroma of coffee, bacon and soapsuds there came the sound beyond the open back door of fresh-laundered sheets and pillowcases billowing along the washline like sails in the breeze.

The association of memory came with the disorder on the table, but on this summer Monday morning there was only his father, bereft of hope and overalls, sitting there with tears in his eyes.

The sleep-talking, the hallucinating, signalled the end. His mother had fought and taken the punishment, not giving in, but now she was punch-drunk with all her body had taken, slipping, relaxing her hold. They were left to witness the terrible degeneration of both her body and her mind, brutalized by its regularity until there was nothing that could impress them any further. In the days which followed her voice became less coherent, her movements slower, faltering, unsure. During mealtimes she struggled to lift her food to her mouth, like an infant learning to feed itself, and when she needed to use the toilet it took two to lift her onto her makeshift latrine — an upturned cardboard box placed over a plastic bucket and a hole cut in its base. Her decline became monotonous in its harsh regularity and duration, and they longed for it to end because it had become monotonous and threatened to continue endlessly. But she was kept alive. That was the order of things. Nature had to be left to take its proper course.

One night, just before bedtime, while Steve and Ralph were sitting with their father, smoking and drinking cocoa, she seemed to rally all her flagging energies for one final effort of consciousness.

'What is it, lass? I'm here,' their father answered when she called to him in a clear voice.

She lifted her arm, reaching towards him. 'Come here,' she urged in a whisper.

Placing his mug of cocoa in the hearth, he went to her, allowing her to clasp him and pull him on top of her. They kissed, a long held kiss, on the lips. He was in her arms and oblivious of his sons.

'We'll go on holiday together, just the two of us, when this lot's over,' he promised her gently. 'Wales, eh? You've always wanted to go to Wales.'

She cradled his head, stroking his hair, curling it absently round her fingers. They were alone together, man and wife, and she cradled him to her as though he was the one needing solace because she was leaving him.

'Yes. On holiday together. In Wales. That'll be nice.'

'We'll stay in a little cottage, eh? Where we can see the mountains.'

'Yes, a little white cottage.'

'Just the two of us,' he managed, then buried his head in her, making a kind of hissing which came quietly from her breast.

*

The house continued to be crowded out with visiting relatives, friends or neighbours. Mrs Moffat and Mrs Dixon, the neighbours from either side, stayed with her most days, helping any way they could, but the most frequent visitor was their Aunty Bella. She came every day and stayed all day as soon as his mother's condition grew worse.

Bella, tall and round-shouldered thin, was the youngest of the four sisters and closer to Elsa than she was to any of the others in her family, having been practically reared by her when she was little. Elsa was already fifteen when Bella was born and, while Polly had followed Joe in a life involved with local politics, she had been left more or less in charge of the infant. Bella's appreciation of these early years was lasting. She now dedicated herself to the task of nursing, arriving as soon as her two young daughters had gone to school and staying until it was time for them to come home.

Steve felt cumbersome in her presence. He kept seeing the woeful expression that she gave when he happened to lift his voice against his brothers without thinking. She grieved for her sister, and his carelessness, his thoughtless, youthful arrogance grated on her nerves.

'Have you no consideration?' she flared against him finally late one afternoon when he decided to play an LP of Big Bill Broonzy that Mozz had lent him.

It was an afternoon when he'd dodged work to see Rachel. It was raining and he'd returned thoroughly depressed and soaked to the skin. Rachel hadn't been in.

'She's asleep, ain't she?' he retorted, crouching to turn down the volume as a compromise as soon as the record was on.

Bella stood over him, insistent like a bullying older sister with an urchin brother.

'Yes, she's asleep,' her voice hammered at him, sibilant and hushed, 'and I don't want you to wake her. Turn it off.'

'But you can hardly hear it.'

'I've told you to turn it off.' She wanted no music, especially that 'horrible wailing racket'.

She glowered at him, resenting his lack of insight and coarse indifference.

He turned his back on her abruptly, resenting the pressures and tensions she created between them in the priority she assumed over the sickroom. She was like an older sister but she was fragile and grey in her long-suffering, tragic drabness, her thin lips drooping in misery while she invaded his privacy and his home. She looked frail and brittle. He felt he could break her.

'And it's staying off,' she told him as he flicked the switch on the 'gram. 'You've absolutely no respect and not the slightest consideration for your mother.'

He spun round before she could say any more. She was aghast, eyes widening in surprise, not believing her ears.

'You what? What did you say to me?'

'You heard! Bugger off.'

Suddenly he wanted to laugh, stupefied at his own

outburst while his aunt reeled under its impact.

'You rotten swine! You rotten lousy swine,' she whimpered in fury and stormed after him as he made off for the sanctuary of his bedroom.

'You haven't one scrap of decency in you, d'yer hear?' she cried from the bottom of the stairs, and stood there, blubbering, wringing her hands, hating him, holding him responsible for everything, for all the sadness and the suffering. 'God! All I hope is that one day you suffer like your mother. You're nothing but a lousy, rotten swine.'

His father returned some time later, having been able to manage a couple of hours down at Ninety Four while Bella looked after things in the house. He came into Steve's bedroom, not angry or critical, as Steve had fully expected, but more disappointed than anything.

'You've made a bit of a mess of things,' he said, standing next to him at the window.

Steve pressed his face against the pane, staring at the waterlogged world outside. 'She upset me,' he offered lamely and scowled, displaying outrage as a front to his embarrassment.

His father gave a chuckle at his audacity. 'Upset you? I think it's you who did the upsetting. You've sent your Aunty Bella home in tears.'

'Ah, well,' Steve answered dismissively. 'I'm sick of the whole damned blasted lot of it.'

'Nay, lad,' his father said, watching the raindrops course down the glass, 'we're all sick of it, not just you. There's a woman there who's heartbroken by the whole affair, doing all she can for your mam, and you have to behave like that. You're not being fair, you know.'

'Things got a bit overbearing.'

'I'll say they did, and there's no need for it. Things are bad enough without you shouting your mouth off and being rude. You have to make allowances, especially when folk are only trying to do their best. Anyway, you'll have to apologize when she comes tomorrow, 'cos if she stops coming, I can tell you, things'll be in a right pickle.'

He dreaded having to face his aunt next day. It was on his mind all morning at work, a thing to be faced like a visit to the dentist, and he rehearsed all the different speeches of what to say and how to say it. At lunch time he went home in order to see her. As he neared the house he wondered if the curtains might be closed as a sign of his mother's death. That prospect added to the nervousness already watering his insides. But the curtains weren't closed; everything was as it had been, and he entered a hot, steamed-up smell of boiling cabbage and potatoes, to be ignored by his father who flapped around in the kitchen in a race against time. A small portion of dinner was scooped onto a side plate so his mother could be fed.

Bella was in the front room, her arm round his mother, supporting her in an upright position so she could be fed. She gave him a sour glance when she saw him, refusing to make things easy, and he found all the noble and adult words he'd planned to say gone from his mind. Hesitant, he looked on as she spoon-fed his mother, holding each spoonful of mashed food at the ready whilst the last was being slowly and laboriously chewed.

The chewing faltered, then stopped, and Bella waited but it was no use.

'We were just in time to give her something before she went off, weren't we?' she said to his father, handing back the plate still full and steaming.

'Certainly a rush,' agreed his father, then gave him a nudge, disapproving for Bella's sake and showing his allegiance to her. 'Go on, then. How about it?'

'Er . . . yes.' It was part of his guilt and there was no backing out. 'Sorry about yesterday,' he murmured humbly and clumsily.

His aunt regarded him with the same expression of woe and contempt, but nodded once, grudgingly, accepting his apology as she lowered his mother gently back into bed.

*

The other two sisters, Miriam and Hetty, were content to leave Bella to the nursing though they were amongst the more frequent visitors. Miriam, wild-eyed, wizened and grey-haired, would sit by the fireplace away from anyone else who might be visiting. Breathing heavily down her nose, she huddled in her drab cigarette ash-marked black coat, dithering, nerves taut, a cigarette pincered by nicotined fingers. If anyone chose to say anything to her she would part her bright red painted lips like a gash in the grey humourless face. A short, sharp hysterical noise resembling a laugh would follow. It was her only contribution to any social exchange.

Steve, Ralph and Ian sneaked off whenever they saw her arriving at the front gate. 'Nutty as a fruitcake!' was one of their appraisals of her, yet she had been quite beautiful in her earlier years. Old photographs of her reminded Steve of Rachel with her black hair and large, dark, sloe-berry eyes. Two years younger than their mother, she had been the most attractive of the sisters but two broken marriages and several nervous breakdowns had taken their toll. For years she had lived alone, pouring out her troubles and her upsets always to their mother, always convinced that people were talking behind her back. They had heard all about it many times over and much more besides. Now when she came she remained in silent vigil by the unlit fire, chain-smoking and coughing her ash over the carpet and her black shapeless coat.

Hetty, the most hearty and fun-loving of their aunts, usually visited on Sundays, arriving around tea time with

Arthur and staying a couple of hours or so. She was a big, blustering, though kind-hearted and generous woman with a large pear-shaped face and double chin. She also had a raucous, infectious laugh which rose from her middle to escape from the back of her throat with a resounding staccato, 'Ha ha haaagh!'

She had lost her first husband, Alfie, shortly after the war, and though she fussed and pampered Arthur she still remembered Alfie with affection. She would give way to her loud gushing laughter as she recalled fond anecdotes of her times with him, then break midstream into weeping at his memory, lifting a handkerchief to wipe the tears.

'Eeh, I miss the bugger, I do that,' she would declare, dabbing at her eyes beneath her specs; then she would put the hanky to her wide, fleshy nose, giving a great trumpetting blow.

Nowadays when she landed with quiet Uncle Arthur, both of them appearing like the classical seaside couple in humourous postcards, everyone knew what was in store. The moment she entered by the back door out came the handkerchief.

'Eeh, it shouldn't happen to such a good woman,' she blubbered, gazing on their sleeping mother. 'Bless her, it didn't ought to have happened to her.'

Her weeping was as infectious as her laughter. Bella and the other women wept and sniffled together, Miriam continued to dither and chain-smoke, while the men in the room looked away embarrassed or quietly talked. Then Aunty Hetty blew her nose once more and took a grip.

'When you thinkin' of gettin' that hair cut, or d'yer intend growin' it down to your arse?' she demanded of Steve in her renewed bluff, friendly manner. It brought murmurs of shy laughter from the others.

Steve, having just returned from the studio, found himself suddenly at the centre of an audience of uncles and aunts from both sides of the family. It was a dress rehearsal for the funeral. They had come to watch the dying of his mother while they talked of other things.

'And where's t'other long-haired beatnik an' all?' Aunty Hetty joked banally for the benefit of the audience.

'Who? Our Ralph?' he said, trying to think of something witty.

'Aye, Ralph,' she said breezily. 'That little sod ought to get hisself off to a barber. Pair on yer go about like a couple o' lost sheep.'

'At least Ralph's heart's in the right place,' put in Bella without humour. She'd accepted his apology on the surface but still smarted against his insult.

'Oh, I know Ralph's heart's in the right place,' remarked Hetty seriously, having more than likely heard of the incident with her sister, yet making no mention of it as a point of delicacy. A thing like that could only be hinted at and criticism hurled from other directions.

'Your mother's dying, you know,' she threw at him like a challenge.

'I know that,' he scoffed, feeling the eyes of his uncles and aunts upon him. He sat rigid and cornered, wondering why the hell he'd not stayed longer wrestling with the portrait.

'Then you ought to be more thoughtful and helpful,' Hetty told him. 'Your mam's been good to you, she has. Good to all three of yer.'

Her words nearly dissolved. She choked back the sobs and out came the handkerchief.

'Help your dad as well, poor bloke,' she added in appeal, knowing how his father, upstairs and out of earshot, had not been to bed for the past few nights and was catching up on sleep.

'I do my best,' he answered, thinking it all as predictable as he'd known it would be.

His aunt assented, 'Aye, I suppose you do,' and gave a stiff blow into her handkerchief, deciding to ease the tension.

'What about thee, little 'un?' She turned to Ian who had been sitting over by the window all this while, stroking his cat. 'What are you gettin' up to with yourself?'

Ian replied with a grin, saying nothing, giving away nothing of his thoughts and feelings. Hetty regarded him in her maternal fashion.

'Ah, but you're not so little, are yer? What's the matter? Has t'cat got your tongue?'

Ian gave another laugh, the small boy having no part in these adult gatherings and therefore not expected to respond to them, or their disasters. He continued to stroke the cat, curled comfortably in his lap.

But he was no longer the small boy, the 'little 'un' to be indulged by aunties and uncles. He followed his own pattern, independent of his brothers, soon to be entering into his final year at school. Steve had been astonished recently to realize how much taller and really grown up he had become. One Saturday afternoon he'd joined Ian waiting at the bus stop in town. Away from the environment of home and in the busy town they had been nearly like strangers with each other, Ian with his shy laughter and his voice beginning to break. Like a fledgling in the nest he had laughed wholeheartedly at Steve's banter while Steve had marvelled at the transition which had come so soon and unnoticed. Ian was almost an adult.

'What are you doin' at school?' Hetty still pursued in her brusque and breezy fashion.

'Nowt,' Ian said, not looking at her but inspecting the cat's ears.

'Nowt?' she bellowed. 'How d'yer mean, nowt?'

She gave vent to one of her laughs. Sometimes dim, sometimes downright aggravating with his silences, Ian 'tickled her pink' with his reticence.

She pointed at the cat. 'See, look at it. See how it's looking at him.'

The staccato laugh came from her middle. 'Ha ha haaagh!' and all the visitors-to-the-sick-bed laughed with her, happy for the light relief.

19

Friday night in the Horse, Manet's bar and the crowds. Tonight was as packed as ever, and Paddy and his wife were sweating before the clamouring mass.

'Cor! Like a chuffin' oven in here.'

Steve wiped a hand across his wet brow. The evening was grey and close after the day's heat, and the windows open as wide as possible made no impression on the sticky, clinging airlessness. They were in for a storm.

Rachel tried to link his arm.

'Pardon, darling.'

'Nothing.'

He snatched his arm away, hating her to address him as 'darling' in front of others like this. He remained waiting, hovering at the periphery, ignoring her as she stood right up next to him. Around him suntanned, sunburnt young men posed before posing suntanned girls. They were packed together in the narrow sawdust aisle before the bar or squashed in around the glass-laden, beer-soaked tables, faces aglow from a day of burning sun. Their tans were the trophies of the heatwave, proudly displayed in the dim, humid confines of the pub. He touched his own damp forehead, knowing how pasty white it must be, not golden, not ruddy and healthy like those of the strutting peacocks.

'Don't!' he told Rachel when again she tried to link his arm. The heat and the crowd oppressed him, and he was in no mood for her tonight.

He returned to Jeremy, straining his ears to catch the snatches of discussion in the general hubbub — mainly repartee, it seemed, between Jeremy and his two closest associates, Paul and Daniel. No one had acknowledged his arrival so far, except Mozz. The rest, Helena included, were drawn towards a single point of interest, namely Jeremy. Everything that was said or happened within the group appeared to revolve round Jeremy.

He watched the long, manicured fingers ballet-dance in gesticulation about the firm, cleanshaven chin. They sifted once through the soft, downy, dark wavy hair. Now they extended forward, fluttering affectedly to add emphasis to words.

Jeremy had presence. Above all others he commanded attention and people gravitated towards him. He was tall, fine-boned and graceful in movement, his eyes, bright blue, laughing, intelligent and mocking. He was witty, blatantly arrogant, nor did he care if anyone accused him of being arrogant. 'Of course I am,' he would laugh merrily, indulgently. 'That's because I'm beautiful, and so witty and intelligent.'

Steve watched him and struggled to shake off the sense of inadequacy which manifested itself whenever he came into Jeremy's presence. He, like many of the others who hung in with this 'intellectual set', was guilty of a certain sycophancy, a certain deference towards this gracefully 'arty' and cosmopolitan twenty-six-year-old. He too had sought friendship and recognition of friendship in the hope of being included and accepted into the privileged inner circle of Jeremy's friends. They were all so knowledgeable, so confident, so articulate, their clever wit, their love of art and literature firing him as much as Baz's philosophizing had done in those earlier years. He had yearned to know, to understand, to be on an equal footing, but their erudite exchanges, their talk, so important and full of meaning, left him benumbed and feeling totally ignorant. He could only drift with ineffectual voice to the sidelines, another overawed spectator watching the tennis ball of debate bouncing between the intellectual-haves.

He caught Sarah's eye and nodded. She and Humph were on another of their frequent weekend visits from London. Humph had succeeded in landing a job as a layout artist with a magazine. He was immediately wary when he saw Humph sitting there in the Horse.

'Give up!' he hissed at Rachel. 'I don't want to hold hands or link arms. It's too warm. All right?'

'Good evening, Stephen.' It was Paul, sitting next to Jeremy who was the first, apart from Mozz, to openly acknowledge him. 'We all know Steve, don't we?' he declared with pretended formality, playing host before the gathering. 'And, of course, his girlfriend.'

Steve was inclined to contradict him about Rachel being his girlfriend but remained silent, appreciating the welcome.

Paul made some light remark as backsides edged up and stools were shifted to allow room. Steve, knowing it must be something witty, though he'd failed to hear, gave a polite and appreciative laugh as he squeezed himself in. Paul was far more amenable, less snobbish than Jeremy.

'All right, then, are you, Steve? Not too exhausted by this heat, I hope.'

'No, not so bad, you know,' Steve responded, his voice self-consciously modulated. He dreaded sounding clumsy.

Paul smiled, reassuringly. He was a tall, broad-shouldered individual, well over six feet and well-groomed in appearance. With his short, slightly greying hair and small, black goatee beard he looked very distinguished, a mature, almost middle-aged adult towering over a clutter of ex-art students whose infancy was hardly behind them. He was older than most of the group anyway, being twenty eight.

'I see you've brought your delectable young lady with you,' he said in his suave manner, nodding at Rachel.

'And she does look rather ravishing, I must say,' interrupted Daniel, regarding her distantly with his small, twinkling, mischievous eyes.

Daniel was an artist, taking time off from creating his universe to down his whisky chasers on these Friday night sessions in the Horse. He gazed at Rachel, ever the gallant.

'Rachel, my dear, you look delicious. Absolutely delicious.'

Rachel gave a little hiccup of a giggle, basking in the attention.

'Absolutely,' Paul agreed. 'Though God knows what she sees in Stephen here.'

'A classic example of pearls before swine, perhaps,' commented Jeremy, smiling sweetly at Steve. 'How nice to see you,' he added, not meaning it and making it obvious that he didn't. This was part of his charade, his act before his public, the bored intellectual surrounded by apes.

Daniel gave one of his characteristic horsy laughs, loving these put-downs by Jeremy. The laugh reverberated through the room: 'Haw! Haw! Haw!'

Such outbursts were frequent and deafening.

He breathed towards Rachel, eyes twinkling. He was nearly forty, far the oldest of the group, a real old beatnik, though he would claim to any of the girls he chatted up that he was in his late twenties. He was short, round in stature, and with his round, wrinkled face full of merriment he reminded Steve of a gnome.

'My dear,' he implored, placing a hand over his heart to signify his intoxication with Rachel's beauty, 'When are you going to pose for me? You could bring inspiration to me where others have failed.'

'Oh, Daniel, how could you?' Helena cried, making out she was jealous and offended. 'That's just what you told me.'

'And me,' chipped in Sarah. 'He told me exactly the

same thing.'

Helena shook her head, disappointed. 'Daniel, I think you're a pig.'

Daniel lifted up his hands in submission, innocent. 'Ladies. Ladies!' Then gave another of his reverberating drunken colonel laughs.

'You pinchin' Verity's bird?' Humph called across to Daniel, intending to provoke Steve. 'You'll be makin' him jealous. He's mean when he's jealous and blokes pinch his women, is Verity.'

The taunt had the desired effect, as did the louder than necessary guffaw which followed. All the negative responses he thought well behind him, regarding Humph, filled him with the same impotent rage.

'Not to worry,' Daniel chortled, disregarding any tension, and looked to Rachel. 'I wouldn't dream of pinching her, as you put it. But she's delightful. Quite delightful.'

The disruptions of new arrivals over, things settled once more into general repartee and conversation. Steve, trying to avoid further contact with Humph, turned once again to Jeremy, waiting for a pause in the conversation he was having with a youth with thick horn-rimmed glasses. The youth had only joined them the previous week and was clearly an intellectual type. Jeremy found his company and his talk inspiring.

'How's your mother, lad?' Mozz asked him, leaning forward from the opposite stool.

'Still much the same,' Steve answered, not wishing to dwell on the subject. All that was part of the tedium of home and he didn't want to be reminded of it.

'Bit depressing really,' said Mozz, also willing not to delve too deeply. It was so awful he could hardly bear to contemplate it.

'I don't think she can last much longer,' Steve added,

then noticed the lull in Jeremy's conversation.

'I say, Jeremy, did you manage to find that copy of Henri Barbusse's *Le Feu?*' he ventured, taking great care over his French pronunciation.

Jeremy had a great love of French literature, in fact a great love for everything that was French in style or design. A discussion about Rimbaud had been their first common ground — or rather Jeremy had listened patiently while Steve waffled on without any real idea what he was talking about.

'Oh, er, sorry,' Steve was quick to say when he saw the puzzled expression. 'I was just asking if you'd managed to find a copy of *Le Feu*. You know, Henri Barbusse. You suggested I should read it. A while ago now. You said you might be able to get one from your friend who has the bookstall.'

'Ah, yes, Henri Barbusse,' Jeremy reflected, tightening up on Steve's pronunciation. 'Which did you mean exactly? Was it *L'Enfer* or *Le Feu?*'

'*Le Feu*, I think,' answered Steve, suddenly not sure.

'That's right,' Jeremy remembered, 'Lar Few.'

Steve cringed. Was that the way he'd pronounced it, the way Jeremy had exaggerated it? It was another calculated put-down. Jeremy was making it clear that he was being pestered, being distracted from those whom he considered on his own level. Things were like that at times with him. Only when he was feeling expansive, extra benevolent and in command of his own destiny did Jeremy gladly suffer fools.

'You must mean the one in the Everyman edition,' he went on. 'Under Fire. *L'Enfer* seems to be out of print. I've not seen my friend yet but I'll certainly ask for you.'

He turned back to the youth with the horn-rimmed glasses, abuptly halting any further exchange. Steve retreated, hating Jeremy for his arrogance and evident snobbishness, and hating his own sense of inadequacy which he was powerless to override.

'Did you find any likely addresses?' Mozz enquired, intruding on his moment of frustration and grinding humiliation.

'What?' Steve couldn't stop himself from showing his resentment of the intrusion. He felt impatient with Mozz.

'Jobs, lad! Jobs,' Mozz retaliated, hearing the tone of his voice. Steve was annoyed at something, letting his shirt-tails hang out. Mozz smiled, ready to aggravate him in his mood. 'Have you found any addresses for outdoor jobs?'

'No, not yet, Mozz.' Mozz wasn't part of the privileged inner circle either and had really no wish to be. He was aware of his limitations within these Friday night gatherings and was content to leave 'all that intellectual claptrap' to others.

'They're always on the look-out for labourers at the gas-board,' Steve added to make amends for his abruptness. 'Maybe we could give them a try, digging trenches for pipe layers.'

'We could go and ask, I suppose,' said Mozz, whose idea of finding outdoor work locally for the summer was an alternative to heading south. He'd also met with opposition from his parents concerning the plans for Cornwall.

'Aye, perhaps we could.' Steve shuffled on his stool, the sweat making his trousers stick uncomfortably against his buttocks. 'It's as warm as hell in here.'

'Must be the monsoon that's comin'.'

'It must be. What about going somewhere less packed? Ask Helena if she fancies another pub.'

Mozz glanced round the crowded bar. More people were entering, crushing in through the door. Most of them were youths with really long shoulder-length hair, art students from Batley or Wakefield. Rumour had got around. The Horse was the place to be.

'I don't know,' he said, giving a little cough and a gentle pat of his chest. 'She was saying something about a party after this place closes. Jeremy's, I think.'

He reached over to ask Helena even so and was met by a gleam of intolerance.

'What did we arrange when we came out, Mozz?' She sounded patient but annoyed.

'We'd be going to this thing at Jeremy's.'

'And now you don't want to go, is that it?'

Mozz opened his mouth in a lingering yawn. 'Nay, I'm not bothered one way or t'other meself.'

'So what do you suggest we do?' Helena demanded, forcing the issue. Mozz never allowed himself to be bothered by anything one way or another. It could so annoy her at times.

Mozz gave another half yawn and patted his chest, as he did when he found himself under pressure in making decisions. 'I don't know. I feel shattered meself.'

'Oh, you would, wouldn't you, when we're going anywhere. You agreed. We were going to Jeremy's. Why do you have to change your mind?'

'I haven't changed me mind. All I asked was if you fancied another blinkin' pub.'

'Not when Sarah and Humph are here, love. We haven't seen 'em in ages.'

'Right. We'll stay here.'

'We don't have to if you don't want,' Helena said, knowing she was having it her way. 'We can easily go to another pub, if you really need to.'

'What do you think, then?' Stretching, half yawning. Shrugs. 'I take it we're staying here.'

Steve wiped the sweat from his palms. Mozz, faced with Helena, became lost to him. Helena, faced with the distractions of so many people, became lost to him. Yet that was all part of Mozz and Helena together, agreements and disagreements, their life as a firmly established and steady couple.

He watched their mouths opening and forming words beyond the rim of his beer glass, watched the smoke from their cigarettes drifting in the humidity to the blackened oak beams of the nicotined ceiling. Mozz and Helena together! Sometimes, as a couple, they could be so exasperatingly boring.

Taking another drink, he surveyed the packed-out room. At the far end of the bar, standing jammed together in a tiny area away from the main concentration of bodies, two girls with their boyfriends talked animatedly, laughing at a private joke. They were smartly dressed, shades of the tennis club. One of the girls was dark-haired, attractive. The other was blond, slim and rather shapely in a light summer frock.

It came with a jolt like fear, shooting from his ankles to his windpipe, as soon as he focused on her and recognized her. Hardly able to believe what he saw, like seeing her out of context in the familiarity of the pub, he sprang away in a bid to compensate the shock and regain control.

Someone asked Jeremy for his views on Sartre and existentialism. Jeremy gave some typically aloof and witty reply: Sartre had made him 'bourgeois' while his philosophy had almost succeeded in sending him 'screaming back to God'. It was the continuation of a discussion inspired by the earlier query about 'Barbewse' and 'Lar Few'.

Steve simulated interest in what they were saying in a struggle to be amongst them, but remained separated, cast adrift from his moorings. In those first few seconds of recognition he felt transparent, exposed, convinced that all around him were about to pounce on his transparency, his sense of exposure, and ridicule him in front of the girl. He shifted on his stool, fidgeting, gave a cough and lowered his head, ostrich-like, his concentration fixed on peeling a beer mat. No one seemed to notice. They continued with their chatter, unaware of his exposure or the significance of the moment, Helena arguing over something with Mozz, Jeremy elaborating on his views, Rachel being teased and flattered by Daniel. He re-emerged gradually, like a snail from its shell, and focused on the girl.

She was about seventeen or eighteen, still with the peaches-and-cream innocence and freshness which had so infected his soul, still with that luxuriously long blond hair fastened in Pre-Raphaelite braids. She smiled for the tall youth in the white sports shirt who was with her. The youth returned her smile, indulgently, adoringly. She was his.

Steve fixed his gaze across the crowded distance, eyes lingering, retreating, returning, bobbing subtly round her like a midge. For an instant she appeared to glance this way and immediately he shot away in case their eyes should actually meet. One look and he would be smitten, reduced to a grovelling, love-lorn, blushing little schoolboy.

He cast once more. He recalled what Baz had once told him. You had to work hard and play hard, and regret nothing that you did. Life was only life, simply that, and there was nothing to stop you from doing anything you really wanted to do. He wondered if he could ever dare to act on that, to walk blatantly over to her, devil-may-care. 'Excuse me for intruding. I know we never spoke but do you remember me? I'm the one who did the life-sized life drawings at the classes on Tuesday nights . . .'

It was beyond contemplation, one Bazism he'd never bring himself to work on in a million years, even if it was only life. That was the way it had been during the life classes. She was beautiful, but forever distant and unattainable. He could only go dry-fly fishing with his eyes, the rest had to rely on dreams.

He reeled in, about to cast again, when Rachel's arms came snaking over his shoulders. He tried to shrug her off, feeling her strength as she resisted.

'Get off. What d'yer think you're doing?'

Her kiss enveloped his words. It was a wet and sticky kiss, and the wetness, the stickiness, clung to his mouth like drying fruit juice. He pushed her away, wiping his hand over his mouth to rid himself of the viscous aftertaste of the cherry brandy she was drinking.

He glared at her. She wasn't fresh, mysterious, goddesslike, but familiar like old clothes, like a well-worn boot, caked with her make-up and dowdy in comparison with the girl with the braids.

'What the hell's the matter with you?'

She purred, her warm breath wafting against his face. There was a hard glint in her eye.

'I thought I'd like to squeeze you and see if you are real, darling.'

He heaved her aside as she leaned obstinately against him. 'Push off, and don't call me that. I don't want you calling me "darling".'

'Oh, what a misery guts you are.' She pouted her pale mauve lips, threatening him with another kiss. 'I like to call you "darling", darling. You're so lovely and adorable. Don't you think so, Daniel? Isn't he lovely and adorable?'

Daniel responded with one of his reverberating laughs. 'Far be it for me to answer that, my dear.'

'Tell me something,' Rachel said eagerly, nearly falling sideways as Steve moved suddenly away from her. 'Did you finish with her, or did she finish with you?'

'What d'yer mean? Did I finish with who? I don't know what you're talking about.' He felt his neck and his cheeks in flames.

Rachel eyed him carefully. There was a smirk on her

face, a look of defiance.

'Don't you? I thought you were looking quite love-sick, sitting there.'

'With who? For Godsake. I was just sitting here.'

'Who's that? Who's love-sick?' Humph butted in, overhearing them. 'C'mon, Verity,' he demanded, always ready for any leg-pulling, especially if it was against Verity. 'You can tell me. I promise I won't tell. Who's this bird who's finished with yer?'

'No bird's finished with me,' Steve uttered lamely, unable to counteract the follow-up of Humph's bellowing, ridiculing laughter. The blush rose from his neck to behind his eyes, blazing and suffusing.

'Cor, he's gone red,' laughed Humph. 'She must be somebody important.'

Daniel beamed at him. 'Don't get so upset over it, old boy. Always remember. Unrequited love has a habit of kicking you in the goolies. I ought to know. I've been kicked there a few times myself.'

Steve turned to Rachel, hating her for the humiliation she was causing him. 'What's the matter? Are you drunk, or what?'

'Or what, darling. But I intend to get steaming, if you really want to know.'

'No, I don't want to know. You can get steaming, rank-arsed pissed to your heart's content for all I care.'

Paul gave a loud clearing of the throat.

'How's the sculpture coming on?' he asked Daniel in order to remove the spotlight from quarrelsome lovers. Steve was a decent sort of lad, sometimes got in the way of the flow of debate, thinking he had something to say when he had nothing to say, but these adolescent tiffs in public were positively distasteful.

Daniel, distracted from the entertainment being provided by Steve and his girlfriend, made little effort to answer.

The pieces of sculpture, lumps of concrete and plastic tubes extending in all directions throughout his garden, had been dragging on for months.

'Ought to give more serious thought to it than I do,' he said, 'and break the bloody thing to pieces.'

He returned to Rachel, having no desire to be roped into lengthy discussions and analyses of his work. He was in with a chance.

Steve downed the remainder of his pint as Paul's question was taken up by Jeremy. Sparked off on another brilliance of words, Jeremy drew gracefully on his cigarette and proceded to assess and criticize Daniel's work, comparing it to that of Caro's. Just then the girl and her party were leaving. Steve followed her surreptitiously with his eyes. Her escort held the door open for her, clicking his heels in salute like a gallant German officer. She smiled, curtsying with a pretty gesture as she passed beneath his arm. Then she was gone.

'I say, I say, I say,' Daniel murmured, forgetting all about Rachel. 'Did you see that?'

'See what, see what?' Humph butted in with a voice that was an affront to the ears.

'The girl who just left,' Daniel told him quietly, pretending to be startled. 'The one with the braids.'

Paul said, 'The one with the braids? Yes, she was quite nice actually.'

Daniel gulped off his whisky appreciatively. 'My word she was absolutely gorgeous.'

Steve felt his chances all the more remote, the girl more unattainable than ever because they had seen her and were enthusing over her.

'Which girl was that?' he asked.

'You didn't see her?' Paul raised eyebrows in surprise.

'Me? No, I never noticed,' Steve said with a shrug as he contemplated the almost impossible trek to the bar.

20

The bedroom smelled faintly of camphor and aftershave, a musky sort of perfumed smell which hung over everything and got up his nose. He had made for the bedroom with Rachel as soon as they arrived at Jeremy's, locking the door quickly and barricading himself against the activity and noise.

'. . . Could 'a' been a good man, yeah, a good man and not a jerk . . .'

Manfred Mann reached from the buzz and commotion beyond the bedroom door. Humph had just been in a fight. Someone had given Sarah the eye and come too close. The fracas had been a brief one, settled by Paul and Daniel. Things were sorted now.

Steve moved his hands over the cool silk surface of the eiderdown. The coolness was welcoming in the humidity of the night. He lay against it, competing against the head-filled dizziness which sent the room in a continual capsizing before his eyes. He gave a soft belch and breathed in steadily through his nose, balancing himself against the dizziness and the full uncertainty of his stomach. He dreaded being sick.

Slowly he pushed himself from the bed, staggered over to the window, worrying that he was about to succumb to the throat-weakening pressure within his stomach. God! Never again.

He waited until the wave of nausea passed, resting his elbows on the window ledge, clinging to the churning contents of his stomach, not daring to let go.

'So life means nothing.' Her words echoed inside his

brain.

He swayed before the window. Out over the townscape horizon a faint afterglow of daylight lingered above a black-grey mountain range of dispersing storm clouds. The wet road below reflected the lights of the streetlamps. It was a last pause before the brief total dark.

'I know you only go out with me for one thing,' her voice came again, slightly slurred. 'You treat me like a whore. Someone's just told me that. But it doesn't matter. Nothing matters.'

Footsteps ran up and down the stairs to the accompaniment of laughter. He came back to sit on the edge of the bed, noticing a silk dressing-gown belonging to Jeremy. He thought vaguely of puking in one of the pockets. Things were easily destroyed, relationships with girls and even respect for someone like Jeremy. Especially someone like Jeremy. Iconoclastic. He owed Jeremy no favours, him with his 'Lar Few'.

'Life is meaningless and it's not worth living anyway.' Rachel sniffled as she swayed before the mirror of a large dressing table. She looked ashen and her mascara was smudged like coaldust around her eyes.

He held himself tense against the next wave of nausea, belching gently. When he thought involuntarily about the beer he'd supped he felt worse. He stared at the dancing patterns of the carpet, another possible venue for relinquishing the struggle. The sweat felt cold on his forehead. The wave diminished. Oh dear, never again.

'What is it, really?' she mumbled, examining her face in the mirror and dabbing gently at her eyes. 'And what is love, when all's said and done?'

He watched her through his fingers, objectively as if from another room. She was beyond his vision, nothing to do with this incapsulated existence of dizziness and feeling sick.

'Life is meaningless,' she said again out loud.

Someone tried the door and gave it a kick when they found it locked.

'Who's in there?' came a girl's voice.

'God knows,' came the reply. A hefty thumping on the door was followed by a jovial yell. 'Get your clobber back on and come out here.'

'Is that the bog?' another asked and more pounding followed as a side event to the euphoria.

Rachel wiped at her mascara with a handkerchief. He gazed around the bedroom, making out the details in the soft white glow of the bedside lamp. There were a few large abstract paintings by some budding genius that Jeremy knew and more shelves of books spread along the walls. Over in one corner a life-sized wood carving of a primitive masculine form stood guard next to a bookcase crammed with dog-eared paperbacks. A piece done by Daniel in a more representational period.

'Just as well you feel like that,' he said, 'if you've downed a bottle full of aspirins on top of half a bottle of vodka. I suppose any minute we can expect you to drop dead.' Things were easily destroyed.

'If only I had,' she replied. 'If only I had the courage. If only I could curl up and forget about everything, and go to sleep forever. Perhaps that is the answer. I should kill myself, then you'd be rid of me for good. Perhaps the bedroom window. We're quite high up here, aren't we? Perhaps if I had to open it just a little wider for fresh air I might lean out too far. Think of it, my darling. To be released from the cell of my weary existence. I'd be happy for ever.'

She had moved over to the window and was reaching slowly towards it as though it beckoned.

He leaned forward, contemplating the pattern of the carpet. Watching Rachel and listening to her was like watching a second-rate actress out of yesteryear. She read from her own scripts, even now, then performed in the badly rehearsed play. Even worse when she was this drunk.

'If you're thinking of throwing yourself out close the window behind you. There might be a draught.'

He shut himself from her and turned his thoughts once more to the girl with the Saxon braids. She was out there somewhere beyond his horizon, and beyond his own drunkenness, a vision to be savoured in the privacy of his disrupted mind. Seeing her in the pub like that had certainly disturbed the equilibrium again.

Rachel mumbled on, something to do with wishing she could swap places with his mother. He thought about the girl and saw her in the shuttered confines of the life room, moving with that shy yet graceful way of hers between the easels and the donkeys. She had been his vision, Dante's Beatrice, Modigliani's Jeanne, and he had sought her attention through his drawing, throwing his black ink and chalk at huge sheets of paper in the hope of appearing great before her, unique for her in all the world.

'The mad artist,' That's what Eric and the others had called him as they observed 'that Swedish looking piece with the plaits'.

The mad artist indeed! More than likely she'd never noticed him, or how he performed with the chalk and ink. Probably she had never been aware of him, nor had their eyes held, as he liked to believe, for that brief but timeless moment during the last class before the Easter break. It was all pie-in-the-sky and he could only torment himself, as he had throughout those evenings of life drawing, his mind reeling through dream-only notions while he never mustered the nerve to exchange a smile or a word. Faint heart had not won fair game.

'You wouldn't try to stop me if I had to throw myself out,' Rachel said, coming to sit with him on the edge of the bed.

She was the has-been, the yesterday's papers. Her defeat was a play-act and it provoked him. 'Do it and find out.'

'Do you hate me all that much?'

He shook his head. 'I don't hate you.'

'You don't hate me? You mean you love me? Oh, darling, I'm so happy that you love me.' She threw her arms round him, kissing him fervently, shamming her delight in the bitterness of rejection.

He resisted her, wiping a hand across his mouth.

'Ah, well, at least I don't have to pretend any longer,' she told him with sudden determination and leapt to her feet. 'I've found out the truth now and that's all I needed to know.'

'What truth is that?' he taunted, deciding to enter with her into the drama of their final parting.

'The real truth.'

'Oh, the real truth.'

'Yes, the real truth. You don't give a damn for me at all. And the only reason you dragged me in here was to satisfy your own selfish lust.'

'What about you? You followed me. I didn't make you.'

'I don't know why I followed you up here. You're just a conceited, self-centred bastard and you've treated me like a whore.'

'How do you spell it? Would that be iron ore?'

'Would you like to know what I've been told by someone tonight? Would you?'

'No,'

'I've been told I have a lively, enquiring mind.'

'Is that so? Sounds like they've been shooting you the same kind of stuff you've got between your ears. Eeh, the things some blokes say to get into your knickers.'

'Who cares? I need to be shown some attention. I need to be appreciated. I need to be able to give love and have love given to me in return. But you, you're so high and mighty in your own eyes.'

'That's because I'm young and beautiful.'

She scoffed. 'Young and beautiful?' She reached to unlock the door, waving one arm in a dreamy gesture of going onward to wherever her destiny lay.

He let her go. She was the vulnerable and tragic heroine of her own comedy, and he had neither the energy nor experience to reach or understand her.

'See you around,' he called after her as she opened to an inrush of people waving bottles of beer.

*

The party had overspilled up the stairs. Couples, locked in a passion of embraces, spread themselves in oblivion. It made it difficult for anyone trying to pass. Down in Jeremy's kitchen, which was a carefully arranged clutter of studio pottery and various objects d'art amongst hanging bunches of garlic and onions, a crowd flocked around a large food-laden table. A glass fell to the floor and broke. Nobody bothered to pick it up as the turkey-gobble continued amongst a fare of salads, meats, French bread and delicacies on cocktail sticks.

Humph was at the centre, piling all he could manage onto an already piled-high plate.

'Outa me way, Verity,' he growled, playfully aggressive, as he pushed himself away from the trough.

It grated on the nerves, set the hackles rising. Tall, angular Humph barging his way through to find a quiet corner where he could devour his grub. There had been no happy reunion between them, none of the 'how's it going?' bonhomie. Humph was in full swing, had the world at his fingertips and was ready to thrust aside all those who held no importance for him.

Steve allowed him to pass, turning to where a few

hopefuls foraged among the empty 'party five' cans and bottles. His stomach was definitely in no mood for food and drink. The mere thought of it still caused him to swallow with uncertainty. He followed instead the subdued wailing of a clarinet which reached him from the lounge. It came above the soft heartbeat of a double bass and piano notes which sounded distant and ethereal. The music was Jeremy's choice: Mezz Mezzrow wailin' with Maxime Saury. Steve liked it and was familiar with it. It always brought an atmosphere of the Left Bank of his imagination, the intimacy of subdued light in a 1950s Parisian jazz club. It reminded him too of his art student days, of candles in waxy Chianti bottles, of Russian tea and frothy coffee in the Flame.

But that atmosphere was soon dispelled.

'Ne'er mind this crap, Jeremy. Put summat else on,' Humph bellowed out.

He was sitting in a flickering glow of candlelight, alongside the demure, petite Sarah, munching from his plate. Jeremy, at the other side of the room with Paul and the youth with the horn-rimmed glasses, called in response to Humph, 'Shut up, you horrible man.'

Humph held up two fingers. 'That to you, Jeremy, old bean.'

Jeremy was highly amused. Humph was incorrigible.

'A young man of Rabelaisian wit and a certain bucolic charm,' he observed while his audience chuckled in appreciation.

'Enjoying yourself?' Helena said to Steve and asked, 'Where's Rachel?'

'I think she's gone looking for fresh inspiration for her poetry,' he answered and noticed Daniel sitting cross-legged by the record player with Mozz. They were browsing through Jeremy's record collection, discussing folk and blues. She wasn't with him, which is what he'd been assuming.'

Helena gave a sigh. 'Oh dear, I thought you two were back together again.'

'Whatever gave you that idea?' He held out his arms in readiness. 'Shall we dance?'

She accepted and he guided her slowly, holding her small waist as they joined the swaying couples to Humph's choice of records. Brass-necked as ever, Humph had managed to have his way. Yet the music was immediate and romantic, full of the fun and the drama of parties.

Someone swayed too far. Bodies went sprawling amidst gales of helpless mirth. He steered Helena clear of the debris, shuffling his feet and holding on slightly and gently a little tighter. She felt light in his arms.

Mozz frowned short-sightedly at the record sleeve he was trying to read in the candlelight. Alongside him the neglected, overlooked, middle-aged and balding youth called Daniel remained cross-legged. Steve brought his face in closer and his lips gradually forward for the kiss which never came. Helena anticipated his move and turned her head away. At the same moment he caught sight of Rachel. She was with a tall youth with shoulder-length black curly hair, one of the Batley Art College mob, and as she staggered her entry she waved her arms in that affected way, admiring the young man's face and his cavalier's beard as if they were part of a beautiful carving. Then the disorientated movie star of the silent screen stumbled, weaving herself round her escort's neck for support. The young man was highly flattered but amused. He swept her up, grasping her, and attached his mouth over hers.

'Gettin' off with my woman, lad?' Mozz said, interrupting the dancing.

'We were planning to elope,' Steve answered him jokingly, acutely aware of the emptiness in his arms as soon as Helena broke away.

Mozz tried to catch her as she wandered off. 'Where you going? I've come for a dance.'

'Oh, not now, love. My feet are aching to blazes. I'd just like to sit for a while.'

'Well, blimey, I wish you'd make your mind up. You were pestering me for a dance not ten minutes ago.'

'That was when the jazz was on. I want to sit now.'

Steve glanced over at Rachel necking with the black-haired youth. She was swamped by him, engulfed. It was part of the drama of parties, part of the fun and the music. He felt severed, shut off. Never again. Like the ale, never again. Though the ghost of jealousy might niggle that was his choice.

'I'm taking a stroll,' he said to Mozz and Helena. Neither heard him. They were too wrapped in the early stages of a quarrel.

'I think you're the one who ought to make your mind up, Mozz. You didn't want to dance in the first place. You told me you'd rather sit down and listen to the music.'

'But I've hardly seen yer. You've been talking to Paul most of the night. He must have summat over you.'

'Surely I can circulate and talk to different people. I don't have to stay rigidly with you the entire night.'

'Christ all blitherin' mighty! Who's wantin' you to? I only came over 'cos I thought you might fancy a dance.'

'All right, I know. But not just for the moment, love. Let my feet rest.'

After the downpour the air was much fresher. He breathed in deep against the persistent heaviness of his guts. He hadn't been sick, he'd overcome it, but the sensation was still with him like a constant presence. No more boozing ever again!

A few drops of water splashed from the eaves and landed on his head. Behind him, in Jeremy's terraced house, the noise he'd left seemed set to continue till morning. There came a flash, a bright bluish pink one, then another followed by a long pause which gave ear to the dying nightsounds of distant traffic. Then the rumbling came, low and assertive from a far point in the heavens, rolling and fading in the tail-end reminder of a brief storm.

21

He kept his face to the window, looking out over the stillness of the Sunday evening. Dusk was falling and though the sky was still a bright orange pink where the sun had settled behind the rooftops, the garden and the houses facing were subdued in a cool heavy shadow. He gazed down on the garden where his mother's roses were still a showpiece of colour, and where the lawn was trimmed and abandoned to the evening. In Mrs Dixon's, next door, a rubber ball and a skipping rope remained as remnants of a day now silenced after children's games. The children, bereft of play, of their noise and screams of laughter from a warm afternoon, were tucked out of earshot, asleep in their beds. At the other side, in Moffat's, a grass-heaped bonfire smouldered, sending wisps of white smoke curling through the top of the green pile.

A few minutes before he had watched Mr Moffat raking up the grass cuttings, the residue of his afternoon in the garden, piling them over a fire which for a time had been a healthy blaze. Then Mr Moffat had leaned on the rake, contemplating the quenched steaming heap, contemplating his achievements in what was left of the light.

He lifted his eyes to the clouds. How many times, how many years had he stood here giving breathing space to the polarities of optimism and defeat? How often had he watched the progression through the garden? Hands on the window ledge, forehead resting against the glass, he imagined he had grown and expanded upwards and outwards, from childhood to adulthood, like a fruit or a flower in a speeding time-sequence film. The flower had bloomed, the fruit had glowed and ripened, and now, at any second in the time-sequence shot, they could expect to wilt and rot.

He focused his attention on the dying day, not on the dying that was going on in the living room below. Behind him his room cocooned him with its clutter of clothes, bedding and books. On a table lay the book he'd been reading: Dostoevsky's thick tome filled with grim poverty and nerve-wracked Raskolnikov having a hard time. The clouds were solid and solitary in the quiet dusk, spreading outwards across the sky like long outcrops of red and purple rock. The impression of the evening touched him, bringing the same anticipation and memories of summer evenings long ago.

He smiled to himself, gave a brief laugh that was no more than a short exhalation through the nose. Those summer evenings of childhood! Childhood remembering. He had attended the threnody of his youth. Those light summer evenings, when he was a child, he had tiptoed out of bed, peering through the black-out curtains. He had not slept in the false dark. He had sneaked to the window, gazing from behind the impenetrable blackness onto sunsets, gazing onto the silent aerial landscapes of hills and valleys, seascapes with mythical coastlines, and shores washed by the hint of waves that were lit by the sinking sun. The sky had extended like a beautiful canopy over a day that was done.

It had been there for him, all of it, the nymphs in their storm-caves, the settled grandeur of sea-hewn cliffs, and beyond, in the brighter light, he had seen where the sea birds had once wheeled to the constant silence of sky's hidden tides.

Seeing it now filled him with that same longing the *Enigma Variations* had brought in him. He was unable to grasp exactly what it was. The feeling was a sad but intangible one which he could only evoke as he gazed and concentrated on the vision through his window. But no sooner did he strive to maintain it than it evaded him and left him feeling restless, irritated because it evaded him and always would.

His restlessness made him fidget. What was the use of dreaming, or dwelling on all those visions and impressions? Drift along like a cork on water, he repeated to himself, don't allow anything to touch the soul because what did it prove in the end? Love, romance and marriage, even with the girl with the Saxon braids, then hassle and children, more mouths to feed, more mouths to voice their protest, like a wheel revolving, the cycle of life returning. Hatch, match, dispatch! Everything. The sunset vision. He turned his back on the twilight, choosing the 'not-playing-so-there' pessimism, though he could never deny the glow of hope that he felt inside.

He picked up the present reading for 'improving the mind' but had barely started on Raskolnikov's dispatching of the old moneylender and her daughter when his father shouted up to him from the bottom of the stairs.

'Come on, get yourself down here.' He sounded impatient, annoyed.

Steve placed his bookmark back in the pages. God! What now?

'She's wantin' to get on her bucket. I can't manage her on me own,' his father told him peevishly when he came down. His mother was sitting on the edge of the bed, supported by him, and looking like a fat repugnant child. 'Come and take hold of her arm, and don't be so rough with her. Steady her underneath the armpit, like your Aunty Bella showed you.'

Steve did as he was told, the way Bella had patiently demonstrated while he'd felt like a bungling fool in front of her, a raw, uncouth youth being taught how to handle a new-born baby correctly. He held his mother and lifted her at the same time as his father, feeling the warmth of her body and the soft bulkiness beneath the nightdress. She was a bulk of a thing, a bloated, white, dimpled bulk to be coaxed and cajoled, and shifted in gradual stages away from the bed. Her eyes, remaining closed, screwed up in painful protest as they tried to lift her and she resisted their attempts.

'Come on, lass,' his father prompted gently, 'afore you settle down for the night. You don't want to wet the bed, do yer?'

Steve tugged at her arm, nudging her, reminding her. Her belly had become swollen, hanging between her short white thighs like a liquid-filled skin bladder from her wasted shoulders. Her thighs too had swollen to gross proportions while her arms, like her shoulders, had become painfully thin. She was heavy, bloated, useless, finished and heavy. He turned his face from her stench.

'Come on, woman,' he urged abruptly. 'Gerron your bucket.'

His father cut him short. 'Don't call her "woman" like that! She's still your mother, so call her "Mother".'

The reaction caught him by surprise, and he felt ridiculous and guilty. He counteracted it with anger. 'I just want her to get on with it so we can get her back into bed.'

'You mean so we can be rid of her and you can get off back upstairs. I know what you mean, lad. There's no need to explain. It's a burden on us all. Not least your mother.' He returned to the rag-doll lolling drunkenly between them. 'Come on, love, you're getting cold being out of bed like this.'

She mumbled something, hardly opening her mouth so that the sounds came down her nose. She began to shiver and she clamped her toothless mouth shut tight, as if in an attempt to combat the shivering. Steve and his father looked at each other, wondering what it was she had said.

'You feel wobbly?' his father asked her.

Steve put his ear close to her mouth in case she said anything more. 'I think that's what she said. It sounded like that.'

They tried to lift her again and again she held them from her, resisting with what little strength remained to her.

'Her eyes are all bunged up,' his father remarked. 'It could be that what's troubling her. She can't open 'em. Hold onto her. I'll go get some warm water and bathe 'em.'

Leaving Steve to support her where they'd managed to move her, he went into the kitchen to fetch a basin of warm water and a lump of cotton wool. Her lashes were stuck together as though with dried adhesive paste, and the warm water softened them until the eyelids could be gradually forced apart.

'There, that's better for you,' his father told her, dabbing gingerly at her eyelids with the soaked cotton wool. He wiped away the water as it dripped down her chin.

For a moment they were dead, unseeing, then the sticky lashes parted to reveal a glassy hazel eye. She looked at Steve's father as he gave a few final dabs, trusting, like an injured animal accepting treatment at the hands of rescuers for its pain. Slowly she tried to lift one hand towards her face but couldn't quite make it. She let it fall to her lap, still shivering, still clamping her mouth in a kind of determination. Then she gave a few short breaths, making effort, and said in a croaking voice, 'This won't do.'

His father humoured her. 'No, it won't, will it? Shall we have you on your bucket now?'

There came more sounds through her blocked-up nose, like someone trying to breathe through a heavy catarrh. 'I'll need my handbag,' she said.

'Nay, you'll be all right as you are, Elsa,' his father assured her. 'You won't need your handbag.'

She became more insistent, more concerned. 'I know. I've felt like this before. All wobbly. I shall have to go to school. Tell 'em I'm poorly.'

His father placed his arm round her. 'It's all right. You've got no need to worry. You don't have to go to school tomorrow. I'll tell 'em about it. You can have the day off.'

She made a move, trying to get to her feet. 'Shall have to get dressed. I'll be better if I get dressed.'

'I can't let you get dressed, love,' his father said, holding onto her.

'Let me get dressed,' she pleaded.

'No, lass. You're poorly. You need to rest.'

'I know,' she answered. 'I shall have to go to school and tell 'em I'm poorly.' She tried to lift herself once more. Her predicament was a torment and it was becoming annoying to her. She sank, frustrated in her efforts, and cried in a louder voice, 'Help me, Percy!'

'Nay, I wish I could,' his father murmered quietly, then spoke up cheerfully. 'Don't you worry about it. We can easily let 'em know you won't be in school tomorrow, can't we, Stephen? We'll let 'em know how you're having to stay in bed.'

'Course we will,' Steve answered, joining in humouring her.

His mother turned her head slightly in his direction, hearing the voice. She reached out to touch him and he lowered his head towards her so she could feel his face and hair.

'I know who that is,' she said. 'It's Edwin.'

'That's right. That's who it is,' humoured his father, and Steve deepened his voice in an attempt to sound like his uncle.

'Yes, it's me, Elsa. Thought I'd just drop in and see how things are. Give Percy a hand here to lift you out.'

She sat rolling the hem of her nightdress between her fingers, trembling, giving no indication of what she felt about her brother being there, or whether she believed he was there.

'Are you going to sit on your bucket, Elsa?' Steve asked again in the same imitative voice.

She remained a few seconds, considering.

'Go on,' he added. 'For me. I can help Percy to lift you while I'm here.'

She came to her decision then, allowing them to heave her onto her feet. Leaning forward between them like a drunk, she shuffled her legs in a feeble imitation of a walk as they moved over to the bucket.

'Right, Stephen, if you can take her weight a bit more I'll try and edge it under her.' His father gasped with the exertion of lifting.

'Hang on,' Steve exclaimed. His father was moving too quickly for him and he wasn't sure if he had her balanced correctly. He wrapped both arms around her middle, leaning her bulk this way.

'Now, if we can lower her we'll get this lot over and done with.' His father reached for the bucket with one foot and eased it nearer towards them. 'Time and patience, lad. Time and patience.'

The 'seat' of the upturned box was bulged in round the hole and the cardboard shiny from use. They held her poised, like a child over a potty, and waited for the obedient trickle. Steve fixed his eyes on the nape of her neck as they held her there, on the smooth skin and wispy curls of brown hair. It looked so vulnerable as she squatted between them, her head forward in that drunk and incapable way.

Ian arrived home as they were hoisting her back into bed. He watched as his father nearly toppled over her in the lifting. What he thought about his mother, or her illness, no one had any way of knowing. He kept it to himself, though he had laughed on one occasion when, in her drugged state, she had sworn at the vicar. The vicar had called to give her Holy Communion but it had been without success. 'Trust you to do things arse first,' she had declared suddenly as the vicar placed his hands on her. What she said, and the nonsense of it before the startled vicar, had struck Ian as funny and he'd laughed.

'Where d'yer think you've been till this time o'night, mop-head?' his father asked as he settled the covers. Ian was the youngest and still the child.

'Round at me mates,' was all he volunteered as he picked up one of his pop magazines.

'Round at your mates till this time? You ought to be in sooner than this. It's way after ten and time you were in bed.'

'Sherrep!' Ian replied aggravated, like being aggravated by a fly.

'I'm tellin' yer,' his father said ineffectually. 'It's school in 'mornin' and you're not gonna be late even if it is your last week. I don't know, I suppose you'll be gettin' up at dinner-time after Friday. What with you and our Ralph, and him here, I'm blessed really good and proper.'

'Listen, Dad,' Steve interrupted, 'why don't you get off upstairs to bed yourself?'

'What's that?' his father joked, not believing his ears and making light of the suggestion.

'Well, why don't you? I don't think you've been to bed in over a week. Go on. I'll stay down here. I'll call you if you're needed.'

*

Later, lying alone in the dark when everyone else was

in bed, he listened to her breathing. Ralph had kept him company for a while but, around two o'clock in the morning, had given up on the all-night vigil and taken off upstairs. Now her breathing came disembodied in the darkness, encroaching on his mind and on his drifting into sleep. He lay on the settee, arms behind his head, gazing at the light from the street lamp through the chink in the curtain. He listened to her breathing. It came with a deep rhythm from the back of her throat, a drawn-out rhythm punctuated by a long pause sustained between each breath. He wondered if she had at last reached the time of her dying and he was about to hear the seconds of her death. Would it be with that great final rattle he had often heard about, that noise at the very end of things? He tuned in to her breathing, hearing without seeing, suspended in his own darkness while his imagination prolonged the silences between each breath.

He closed his eyes, listening to the pauses, expecting each release of air to be the last. The air was taken in, slowly, graspingly, then held until all vital nourishment to life had been scavenged from it. Another gasp, then another, and now a silence that was louder than the breathing itself. His heart pounded in the silence, seeming to come from within his head. There was another gasp, another deep, groping for air, another silence followed by a long, sighing letting-go.

'Go on, mother, go on, for Godsake,' he urged her, rigid and dizzy with his tension. 'Just let go of it. Just die!'

But she continued to torture him with her breathing and her silences, teasing him with her promises to give up finally on the struggle. A gasp. A silence. And yet one more yearning, groping intake of breath.

He waited. This time the breath was expelled from the back of her tightened throat like an escaping of high-pressure gas. Then there was nothing more.

He opened his eyes, peering through the darkness, making out the vague shape of her body in the dim grey mound of the blankets. He sat up, focused his eyes on the grey mound and wondered if he should go tell his father. Then he saw the body and realized it was moving, struggling to lift itself up from the bed.

'Don't say she's starting again already,' he groaned. He was reluctant to disturb his father but not sure if he'd be able to cope with her on his own.

He got up off the settee, ready to see to her, expecting the usual bouts of her fevered restlessness, but after a few short gasps of discomfort she settled back into a more peaceful sleep.

It was light when he woke next to her agitated movements. She was a baby in its cot, wide awake in the first light of morning and needing attention. Her eyes were closed, caked and stuck together again at the lashes, and she was frowning, making muffled noises of sobbing as she twisted and turned in the tangled disorder of the bed.

It was no use. She would never settle now. She needed to be seen to, needed the bucket, needed her pills and yet another dose of that liquorice black potent stuff.

Oh Gawd! Half five! He dragged himself from the settee, feeling cold, light-headed, his back and neck stiff and aching from lying awkward.

'All right, we've heard you. We're coming,' he told his mother and went upstairs to wake his father.

'Right, lad. Off again, are we?' His father got up immediately. He had slept in his clothes.

'Aye, off again,' said Steve, drawing back the curtains.

22

The end when it came was rather like an anti-climax. His father called him up for work in the usual way, barging into his bedroom and flinging back the curtains to shock him with the daylight.

'C'mon here, Stephen. It's nearly quarter to seven. Time you were off.' Almost as an afterthought, he added, 'Your mother's dead.'

Lifting himself up off the mattress, Steve blinked against the sudden awakening but felt strangely wide awake: 'Dead, is she?' It was as easy as saying, 'The goldfish is dead, the budgie has died.' It was that casual.

'Aye,' his father said, pausing a moment at the window. 'It's all over for her, thank the Lord.'

'What time did she die?' Somehow it seemed important to know.

'Half five. Therabouts. Don't take so long in getting up. You'll have to go to work. It's pay-day today. I'll go now and see if I can wake yon' lad without too much fuss and palaver, then I best get downstairs. The undertaker's here.'

'What? Already? He's quick. Who is it?'

'Alec Watkins.'

Steve grimaced. 'Thought it might be. What's he doin'? Measuring her up?'

His father ignored the sarcasm. 'Think on, here. Don't lie down again. I don't want Alec to see what sort of a performance I have to go through wi' you lot on a mornin'.'

'What's it got to do with Alec?' Steve retorted, but his father marched off into the next bedroom to issue his gruff, half-serious commands.

Ralph grunted the token remonstrance against the intrusion on his sleep, then fell into reflective silence as soon as he heard that his mother was dead.

Steve listened as his father descended the stairs then flung aside his covers. Pay-day! Friday was pay-day and another day when he was called upon to mind that infernal machine. Yet there ought to be something different, he reasoned, something to signify a slight hiccup in routine, a flavour of difference like on a birthday. But there was nothing different about this morning. The birds were twittering, the weather was silently sunny as it had been the day before and he was dressing for work.

He pulled on his grey corduroy work-trousers. They stank of oil and metal, and felt damp and uncomfortable when he put them on. There was nothing different about today. He had watched the process of dying like a ringside spectator, sometimes wondering what the actual day of her death would be like, wondering whether it would sweep down on them with that sudden colossal changing of their lives. He examined the moment, conscious of it. From downstairs came muffled voices in a new quietness which now replaced the hectic activity of the sickroom. It was like the cooling down and sweating free after the ordeal of fever. Up here in his bedroom everything was the same — the crack on the ceiling which looked like a map of Africa, the pink delicate flowers of his mother's choice of wallpaper. It was all there, the same as it had been the day before, the weeks before, the months before, and today was just another day for heading off to work.

'What d'yer think about it?' he asked Ralph, wandering into the next bedroom, and stood in the aisle between the two single beds, tucking in his shirt.

Ralph, fully awake, which was unusual for him at that hour of the morning, lay with his hands clasped behind his head. The experience was one they were sharing, her suffering an experience that they had had to share over so many weeks. He explored his mind for his own reaction.

'Relief, I suppose,' he answered.

'Same here. We've had to wait too long. I'll tell you something, though, I feel a bit nervous about going down.'

'Why. What is there to feel nervous about?'

'I don't know. I've never seen anybody dead before. She might be lying there with her eyes boring into me, her mean, selfish, ungrateful son.'

Ralph laughed and shifted into another more comfortable position. 'Don't be so daft. Pretend she's a piece of furniture. She'll be covered up anyway.'

'Aye, you're right. I'm being stupid.' Steve turned his attention to the other bed and its sleeping occupant. 'Look at this idle swine. D'yer think I ought to pull his pillow out from under him and beat him round the head with it?'

Ralph smiled hopefully then shook his head. 'Nar, don't be so rotten. Leave him to it.'

Steve looked down at the pale, smooth face with its Beatles mop snuggling, half hidden, beneath the bedclothes. Today was Ian's last day of term before the long summer break. 'Lucky sod, and he don't have to get up till eight.' He sighed. 'Such is life.'

Ralph commiserated with him. 'Yeah, it's a pity we can't have the day off.'

Downstairs the sun made bright patterns and shadows from the bay window. The brightness of the room surprised him. He was fully expecting the curtains to be closed and everything cast in gloom. The only gloomy thing appeared to be Alec in his provisional uniform of shabby black blazer and black tie. He lifted his pink scraped face from a file of notes balanced on his knee when Steve entered.

'Good morning, Stephen,' he greeted sombrely. He had taken over from where the doctor had left off.

Steve gave a cheery response, ready to show him that

there was no need for the solemnity. He glanced quickly at the bed as he went by into the kitchen. Apart from a slight hump where the feet were the bed looked empty and freshly made.

'I reckon we'll need only two taxis, Percy,' Alec continued. 'If you need any more just leave it to us.'

Steve put the kettle on for a quick cup of coffee then went into the bathroom. Along the window ledge were boxes of pills and bottles of medicine — parts of the scenery no longer required after the play. One of her soiled nightdresses had been slung in the bottom of the bath. The soiling on it was black, like tar.

'Now, I don't want you to concern yourself with anything whatsoever,' Alec was saying. 'We'll see to it all. We'll be here at ten o'clock, as I say, to take Mrs Verity to the chapel of rest. But if you need any advice between now and next Tuesday don't hesitate to ask.'

'I think everything's okay, Alec. I don't see that there'll be any problems.'

'Righto, then, Percy. I'd better get off. I've got to go now and call on a house in Lindlethorpe. It's an old bloke who dropped dead of heart attack last night.'

'A busy man, our Mr Watkins,' Steve remarked when his father had returned from seeing him out by the front door.

'What you goin' on about now?' his father said as they heard the van drive away.

Steve took a sip of the coffee he'd just made. 'He sounded as miserable when he spoke to me as if he'd just lost on the hosses.'

'You don't expect him to do a merry jig in front of you, do yer, you dope?' His father sat down on the settee, opening his tobacco tin which was full of his dockers and tab-ends. 'It's his job, man. He has to be like that when folks have just lost someone.'

Steve watched as he pulled strands of tobacco from the tin and pushed them into his Rizla machine. This was a standby whenever he ran out of cigarettes.

'Did you see her die?'

'Yes, I saw her go.'

'What did you do?'

His father carefully licked the gummed edge of the cigarette paper. 'There wasn't much I could do, apart from dabbing her lips with water 'cos they were getting too dry. I knew she was going, the way she was struggling for breath. It sounded just like two dogs havin' a fight.'

Sipping his coffee, Steve stood by the bed. It was strange to know she was there when he could no longer sense her presence or hear the sound of her breathing. On her stool was a glass and a bottle of the black stuff for drugging her to oblivion. Out of necessity she'd had the wool pulled over her eyes.

'Is she gonna be buried or cremated?'

'Buried. Lindlethorpe churchyard. I think she'd've wanted it like that.'

Steve thought of reminding him how she had always joked about being cremated rather than 'eaten by t'worms'. It made no difference either way now. He stared at the top edge of the bedspread, where the pillows disappeared underneath. She was in there somewhere, no longer able to sit upright but still occupying his bed.

His father finished off rolling his cigarette. When he lit it the thing flared up momentarily at the end. 'I suppose I'd better phone your Aunty Bella and let her know. There's no point in her bothering this mornin'.'

'Yeah, better let her know. There's nowt much she can do here now.' He reached down to touch the mound where the feet were, pushing at it gently, feeling the weight of her body attached to the toe, how it threatened to move with the springiness of the bed. He was aware of his growing unease. He knew he must take advantage of present opportunity and have curiosity satisfied.

'Is it all right if I have a look?'

'Help yourself,' said his father. He could relax for the minute, enjoying his smoke. His long demanding role of male nurse was over.

Outside the people in the neighbourhood were stirring. A nearby neighbour was having trouble starting his car, probably a flat battery. Steve gripped one corner of the blankets and slowly pulled them aside.

The first, most striking thing about her was the whiteness of her face, and the whiteness of the tongue which hung out a little from the side of her mouth. There was a translucency about her, as though she were modelled in wax, the whiteness almost shining against the dark of her eyebrows and damp-looking matted hair.

He pulled back the blankets further to reveal the upper half of her body. She was in the same sleeping position he'd seen her in last night before he'd gone to bed, her hands tucked against her stomach while she lay on her side. She had not moved since that last moment he'd seen her but had simply expired.

He noticed the hands, how white they were and the skin wrinkled and set as if it had been pickled. An absorbent sheet was spread under her, and he saw how her pale green nightdress with the white lace collar had been hacked off at the waist when it had been no longer possible to sit her on the bucket. The nightie looked damp and was bunched around her middle, exposing her bloated purplish pink belly with its operation scar.

He turned back to the face and its closed-for-ever eyes, sunken and blue around the sockets. He reflected how horrible this might have been had it been a sudden death, but his mother had died long before she stopped breathing, slopping about the bed totally gaga while his father administered the all-important medicine up her backside. She was dead, really and finally dead, as if her bedsore-covered flesh had never been alive.

'Has our Ralph gone back to sleep up there, or what?' his father asked. 'I can't hear him yet.'

'Dunno,' said Steve. 'He was awake all right when I came down.' He half expected his mother to respond to his voice but she remained inanimate, like a piece of sculpture, a waxen image of herself.

His father sighed. 'That lad, he takes more gettin' out on a mornin' than I don't know what.' He shouted to him from the bottom of the stairs. 'Hey! Do yer intend stayin' there all day?'

Ralph made a few thumping noises on the floor to show he was out of bed.

'Suppose I'd best draw these,' he said, stopping by the curtains, noticing they were open.

'Why bother? There's no need for all that just yet,' Steve told him.

His father considered a moment, then drew them closed. 'Ah, sod it, might as well. As a sign of respect.'

Steve shrugged as the curtains cast the room in an orange half-light. He was glad that his father treated it so casually. They were together, sharing the early quiet before the funeral madness should descend on the house. He took a quick glance at the clock on the mantlepiece, cursed when he saw the time and gulped off his coffee.

'Aye, on your way, son. Keep the wheels of industry turning,' his father told him in parting and laughed at the withering backward glance he received.

*

The day of the funeral was like another new day of her death, only more final, and more public, an event that was like a holiday, like a wedding with the morning of it filled with the same disruption and expectancy. It was sunny, breezy, and the wind blew the rose trees, merrily twisting their leaves.

The coffin arrived about half past ten, its chrome and polished elm gleaming incongruously against the greenery of the front garden. Alec and his assistant struggled with it from the hearse to the door.

'She was rather a heavy woman, Mrs Verity, wasn't she?' Alec gasped diplomatically as they tried to manoeuvre their mute burden through the narrow hallway and into the living room.

He suggested removing the coat and jackets from their pegs so that the door could be opened wider.

'Steve, Ralph, Ian!' their father called. 'Take this lot away upstairs. Dump 'em in your bedrooms for now.'

They did as they were told, grabbing the bundles of coats and throwing them in a jumbled heap onto the nearest bed which happened to be Ian's. But Alec and his assistant were still having trouble. These houses weren't designed for funerals and they were obliged to stand the coffin upright so it could be lifted into the room.

It was like a brand-new piece of furniture, there in the house, placed on two polished chrome biers where the bed had been, and giving off a faint smell of new wood and beeswax. Alec, still in his black blazer and not attired as yet for the big finale, unscrewed the lid. Aided by his assistant, he lifted off the lid and it was placed upright against the wall, behind the coffin. Her name and the date of her death shone out from the engraved chrome plaque on the lid: 'In Loving Memory of Elsa Verity. Died July 24th. 1964. Aged 50 years.' The official seal to corrode beneath the earth.

'You pull these two folds back like this, Percy,' Alec was explaining, 'and this veil fits over her face like that.'

He lifted a square of gauze-like material edged with silk like a ladies' handkerchief. They strained to look. Something pink and slightly suntanned snuggled deep in the crib of rich cream linen and delicate silver ribbons of silk.

'Excuse me, Percy. If I can just straighten her head a bit.' His handiwork had flopped slightly when they stood the coffin upright to get it through the door. There! It was all right now. 'If anyone wants to look at her they can lift the veil. Or you can leave it off till we close the coffin. It's up to you. Now, are there any questions you'd like to ask before we leave?' he added quietly, confidentially.

'No, I don't think so. Alec.' Their father had no wish to make a big issue out of it. 'I reckon we're about ready to get the show on the road.'

'Okay, well, as I say, don't concern yourself at all with any of the arranging. We'll see to all that, and we'll be back just before half past two.'

'Ooh, she looks lovely, doesn't she, Mr Verity?' said Mrs Moffat from next door when she saw her. She had volunteered to be their help for the day, answering the door when wreaths and bouquets arrived — as they had been doing in abundance throughout the morning — and preparing the funeral tea.

She was a small, round woman with a round face, and wore spectacles that were too large for her and made her look like an owl. She came in from buttering bread in the kichen to take a peek, the butter knife in her hand.

Steve and his two brothers gathered with her to see the proud, firm-jawed countenance of their mother in death.

'Yes, she looks lovely,' said Mrs Moffat.

'She certainly looks better than she did on Sunday afternoon when I saw her at 'chapel o' rest,' their father acknowledged. 'Otherwise I wouldn't have let 'em take the lid off.'

'Eeh, well, I think they've made her look really grand,' Mrs Moffat repeated, then returned to the kitchen and the making of sandwiches.

Steve and his brothers stayed to admire the occupant of the coffin. The face appeared youthful, handsome even, the smooth forehead devoid of wrinkles and the high cheeks touched with rouge. The neckline of the shroud, edged with silk, made Steve think of a priestess's garment. His mother, no longer the practical, down-to-earth domesticated woman, seemed transcended to the loftier plane of some form of holy order.

He made a sketch of the face, enshrouded in its rich linen folds, peering closer, objectively, at the subject in order to study its contours. There was the merest hint of a sickly sweet smell about her mixed with the beeswax smell of new wood. Moisture glistened lightly over the forehead and the eyelids. He studied the face closer, becoming familiar with its detail. This was his mother. She resembled his mother, had all the features he had known for a lifetime, yet she wasn't exactly the same one who had lived. She was a still-life version, neatly packaged and part of a mortician's display, complete with the chrome biers and purple velvet floor covering, and set with flowers like an altar. She was part of an exhibit tastefully put together where the bed had stood. And she might have been alive and simply sleeping were it not for her eyes and cheeks being slightly sunken, and the pieces of cotton wool he could see wedged up both her nostrils.

'Look, stop messing about,' said his father when he saw him touch the cold-storage dampness of her forehead. 'No damned respect to the last, you haven't. Come away and leave things alone.'

'Sorry, Dad. Nothing seems worth taking serious, that's all.'

'Aye, well, that's as may be, but try doing something

more useful like moving them shoes and taking the rest o' them coats out o' the way.'

Steve showed him the sketch he'd just done in ball-pen on lined paper. His father nodded without approval or disapproval, though at some stage during the following weeks he was, for some reason, to quietly destroy the sketch.

The remainder of the morning was spent carrying out the odd chores, waiting for the event of the afternoon like waiting for the wedding to begin. Steve joked with his brothers, Ralph and Ian allowing him to lead them in the joking and laughter out of a need for the release of tension. They would be glad when it was over and the curtains could be opened. They were bored now with being blanketed in the half-light.

'Why all this?' Steve stated philosophically. 'The owd lass has gone and kicked the bucket.'

Ralph and Ian grinned at his bravado. He wanted all of them, his father especially, to treat it as a game, a farcical and obligatory game which they were forced to play before they could return to normality with the house to themselves. He wanted them to be a team, the four of them ready to face the opposition which would be arriving soon to play the game for real.

The first member of the opposition to land was Grandma Polly. She strode in at the back door, followed by Grandpa Joe, while they were in the middle of washing and changing, and trying to polish shoes.

'You're early,' their father remarked, fastening his tie in the mirror above the mantlepiece.

Grandma Polly didn't answer but went over to the coffin. She gave a single strangled cry as soon as she saw her daughter actually dead and prepared for burial, then took a grip of herself and blew her nose.

'Our Edwin's comin',' she announced, recovered, throwing down the gauntlet before their father. Her voice was sharp and challenging.

His father chuckled and continued to fasten his tie.

'Don't pick on him,' she cried. 'He never came to see our Elsa because he was worried she might think her number was up if he'd come all that way to visit her.'

'Oh aye, it would've been a long way for him all right. It's a long way, is Durham.'

'Well, he's been up to his neck in it, what wi' not bein' well himself then havin' to look after his Doreen when she's not been well.'

'He could've paid her a visit. She was always wonderin' why he never came to see her. He's all right comin' now, ain't he? He's too late. She's dead.'

'If he'd been able to he'd've come. Both him and Doreen. And they'd've helped out just as much so there's no need for our Bella to think herself so high and mighty, tryin' to make out nobody's done ought to help. We've all helped best way we could.'

Steve moved up behind her, standing head and shoulders above her and looking down on the new-for-the-funeral black straw hat. He felt he could lift her up by her narrow shoulders and carry her out of the house. She reminded him of a cackling hen with her beak-like nose and fierce beady eyes. He turned, grinning to Ralph and Ian, but they were skiving off upstairs, away from these internal upsets and family politics.

She wasn't finished. She went on with what bothered her about Edwin and her youngest daughter. Grandpa Joe stood mutely by her side, hands clasped in front of him, allowing her to have her say, then interrupting when he considered she'd said enough.

'Now come on, Polly, I think this is getting us nowhere.' The excitement and anticipation of meeting all those people she was going to meet was getting too much for her.

Polly stopped herself, gave a sniff, then changed the

subject. 'What's for the tea afterwards, bread rolls or ordinary bread?' She popped into the kitchen to look at the sandwiches which had been cut. 'I think bread rolls might've been better,' was her opinion.

'Mrs Moffat from next door has been seeing to that side of things,' Steve's father answered patiently, but Grandma Polly was fussy, authoritative in a last-minute urgency, just the way she was at weddings.

'What about plates and cups? And knives and forks? Have you got enough of them?'

His father moved away from the mirror, his tie complete. 'I should think so. Mrs Moffat's brought in a load of her plates and Mrs Dixon's lent plenty of her stuff.'

'Well, what about servin'? Is it going to be a sit down do or will folks just help themselves?'

'Percy's told you already,' Grandpa Joe put in, pulling the reins on his wife. 'Mrs Moffat's seeing to it.'

'I'm just makin' sure, that's all,' Grandma Polly insisted, as if doubting that things could be managed without her.

Not long after that the entire gathering of relatives and friends arrived, seeming to land at once. Steve was crouched on the kitchen floor, giving his shoes a final polish, when a great assortment of aunts and uncles barged through the door. Not seeing him, they went to view the contents of the crib then drifted into their various groups to chat amongst themselves. He nipped into the bathroom to comb his hair as they were landing, finished off dressing, then prepared himself to meet them.

The hum of crowded conversation swelled the room. He checked the knot in his tie, checked his turn-ups and fly buttons, feeling self-consciously overdressed after lazing round in jeans the entire morning. On the kitchen table, which was covered with a clean, starched white cloth, two large plates were piled with Mrs Moffat's sandwiches —

thin knife-slits of boiled ham or salmon paste in thinly sliced white bread all sheltered beneath sheets of greaseproof paper. Next to the sandwiches his mother's best china remained ready to be set for the tea party afterwards.

'Eeh, I never knew she was so ill until Mrs Dixon told me.'

'I'm Percy's sister, Clara. We've met before, I believe.'

'Now let me see. Last time I saw you must've been at Dora's wedding.'

Never had he known the house so full. Most of them were women, aunts from both sides of the family, and the various ramifications, their men having preferred to stay outside. All of them were too engrossed in each other to notice him and he was thankful for that. He had no time for any of the questions they'd be sure to fire at him, nor for any of their small talk. He was the artist as a young man, the rebel of the family, and this was a day of significance. Death held the theme of romanticism before grief. His mother's suffering was over and this was the new day of her death. There was novelty in it after all, like the novelty of a recent birth.

He inched his way through, making for the staircase door. His father had long since done the disappearing act through there, together with Ralph and Ian, and he intended doing the same. He moved as hastily as the throng would allow. There was Aunty Miriam alone in the corner, huddled in her cigarette-ash marked coat, but without a cigarette in her mouth for once. There was Aunty Bella in one of the armchairs, leaning against husband Lionel and as pale as death. Grandma Polly, seated like the guest of honour before her audience, smiled and nodded at many aquaintances. Edwin, her eldest, was with her. Small, semi-bald and dapper in a dark suit, he stayed close to Polly, alienated by the crowd. He had come without his wife. Doreen could never cope with a thing like this.

'Oi! Where's your dad?' Aunty Hetty thrust her big face-powdered face towards him, grabbing his arm.

Steve brushed her off.

'Upstairs,' he replied tersely, trying to make his escape. Hetty stopped him.

'Upstairs? What's he doin' up there? Is he all right?'

'Of course he's all right. Why shouldn't he be?'

'He should be down here meeting everybody,' Grandma Polly butted in, and hasty whispers of agreement echoed from some of the women round about.

'It's not right, you know, Stephen,' Aunty Hetty appealed. 'He should be here.'

Steve shrugged and smiled. His father was breaking the rules. A confidential voice behind him asked the same question. It was Uncle George, his father's youngest brother, a miner who had bony, sinewy features and stood well over six foot. Although he towered above them, he was made shy by the women and looked awkward, out of place, in his ill-fitting baggy suit. He liked to keep his distance of them at these family gatherings, preferring the atmosphere of the pub and the company of men.

'He's gone upstairs out o' 'road,' Steve told him, relieved to see an ally.

'That's where I'm bound then,' George muttered under his breath, 'if I can get through this lot.'

Managing to join the evasive host, George was breezy with his brother, humouring him though uncertain of the depths of his grief.

'Sithee, t'house is jam-packed and they're all gunnin' for thee, them women, aren't they, Steve?'

Steve's father chuckled at the consternation his absence was evidently providing. He was sitting between Ralph and Ian, on Ralph's bed, having a smoke, and accidentally knocked ash down his suit as he coughed on his cigarette.

'Ah, but you're okay where you are for a minute, Percy,'

George said, and shifted coats to sit on the other bed. He spread his large collier's hands on his knees. 'You don't want to be bothered with'em, do yer?' he suggested as a leveller to any drama.

The other winked. 'A smoke first, and a bit o' peace. Then we'll see what's what.'

The smoke and the 'bit o' peace' lasted no more than a minute before the bedroom became swamped with most of the women who, led by Hetty, had decided to seek out and pull their host out of hiding. As soon as they saw him they burst into tears at once.

'She's been a good 'un to you, 'as Elsa . . .'

'She was a good mother to the lads . . .'

'You did all you could for her, Percy . . .'

'You've no call to reproach yourself for anything . . .'

Their bobbing hats of different styles in black crowded into the bedroom.

'Aye, she was a good wife to me,' he told them to pacify them.

'A good wife. Yes she was . . .'

'You'll look after your dad, won't you, Stephen?' Aunty Hetty urged him, taking him to one side.

He glanced out at most of the menfolk who had been content to congregate in the back garden. A few more tears persisted amongst the ladies, then the funeral excitement gradually subsided to conversation pace. Recovered, they stood talking amongst themselves around the bedroom door.

'Help him all you can, d'yer hear me?' his Aunty Hetty said, slightly more belligerently. 'He's all the three of you have now, so look after him. Help him all you can.'

He looked at the tears still wet in her eyes. 'Of course we'll help him.'

'Think on, then, love, what I'm tellin' yer. I'm sure your mother would've said the same thing.'

He smiled. It was part of the ritual, the niceties of the game, the sort of thing a bereaved son should expect to be told, caught in the ritual.

Someone shouted from the bottom of the stairs, 'Tell Mr Verity the undertaker's here.'

There came a buzz of renewed excitement, a gathering of momentum. The thing was about to commence.

'We'll stick by him,' he promised his aunt as they returned downstairs.

Now they were at the final seconds of waiting. He was alert to every one of them, the crowding together, the whispered conversations, Alec, dressed for the part at last and with top hat in one hand, making polite exchanges with one or two of the ladies. Careful not to tread on the many floral tributes which were spread over the floor around the area of the coffin, Steve took up his position by the hearth with Ralph and Ian. He glanced over at his mother. The veil had been left off for the sake of convenience. She slept on, undisturbed, unconcerned for the crowding, the whispered tail-ends of conversations. She had far better things to dream about. He kept his eyes on the familiar profile, the familiar bridge of her nose and the high forehead he would never see again. He tensed against his thoughts, against the churning nervousness which suddenly filled him. It was a game, it was a ritual, and he ached for it to be over with and done with.

'Where's Mr Verity?' Alec wanted to know, looking at his watch and worrying about the time.

Grandma Polly, standing between Grandpa Joe and Edwin, sighed with mounting despair. 'If he i'n't in the garden now! Doesn't he know when he's keepin' everyone waitin'?'

Alec looked at his watch again and coughed to clear his throat. 'I would like us all to be present when I close the coffin, especially Mr Verity.'

Aunty Hetty, her arm now firmly linked through Uncle Arthur's, gave Steve a nudge. 'Stephen! Go and fetch your dad.' She gave him an aggrieved expression when he refused to budge. 'But we're all waiting for him, love.'

But much to everyone's relief his father returned, unruffled, unhurried. He chuckled at something George was saying to him. They had been out in the garden together.

'We're closing the coffin now, Percy,' Alec prompted.

'Righto, I'll be with you,' he said, reminded, and leaving a pair of scissors he had in his hand on the kitchen table, he went over to the coffin and placed inside it a small red rose. It was a parting gesture to his wife, done in his typically careless and off-the-cuff way.

Now it was happening, it was really happening, but so fast there was hardly time to grasp and believe it. Events moved like a speeded-up film, like a rapid rotation of snapshots or colour slides, fleeting detail, fleeting impressions: Grandma Polly bent double as though winded and heaving a heartbreaking sob, and, as though this were a signal given by the chief mourner, the other women all raised their handkerchiefs in one. Heartless, unheeding their tears, Alec and one of the bearers set down the lid and screwed it tight. There was the same trouble at the front door but they managed her out more easily this time round. Meanwhile, Grandma Polly, having decided that protocol allowed her, together with Grandpa Joe and Edwin, to share first taxi as part of the immediate family, offered round a bag of toffees as soon as she was in.

'Where's Bella and Miriam going? In Lionel's car? They ought to have gone in t'other taxi with Hetty and Arthur.'

She was nervous, craving normality, clinging to the mundane, full of aimless comment and shocked by her own grief.

'Eeh, I wish I'd brought a thicker coat with me. It'll

be blowin' a draught up there on top o' yon' church hill.'

Steve chewed on the toffee she had given him, feeling it stick between his teeth. They were moving, they were on their way, two big black Humbers and a long line of cars heading down Willow Avenue, passing its once familiar childhood landmarks of hopscotch pavements and neighbours' houses with closed curtains, his mother in the lead in a carnival of flowers. As they turned out into the lane the hearse advanced too quickly, leaving the rest of the procession. It irritated him. Overtaking cars disrupted the order. They became intermingled with the cortège while the hearse seemed to speed along with an urgency to get there, leaving the leading taxi two cars behind.

'There's Percy's workshop,' Grandma Polly pointed out to Edwin as they went by Ninety Four.

'So, that's the workshop, is it, Percy?' he asked, seeing the dereliction among the weeds. He had never been down here before.

'It's a bomb site,' Percy gave out bluntly, refusing to elaborate further, and they passed squat Ninety Four, and the post office and the Fleece where the landlady stood watching from the doorway, knowing whose funeral it was.

Like the rotation of snapshots, like the rotation of colour slides, they followed that familiar route. There was the railway bridge and the tall chimney of Ralstones' mill, then they were out onto the village high street, passing the butcher's shop, and soon hastening up the final ascent towards the iron gates and the church bell's mournful toll.

A bunch of white chrysanthemums, caught in the breeze, blew off the top of the coffin as it was being lifted from the hearse. One of the taxi drivers rushed to retrieve it. Disembarking in the courtyard before the church, as if for a wedding, they gathered and followed the white-frocked vicar whose voice echoed between the grey stone pillars to the organ pipes in this marriage to the earth.

'I am the resurrection and the life . . .'

The service passed in a dreamlike scenario of polished wood and chrome and flowers set before them like a mini-altar in the central aisle. Afterwards, after the praying and the kneeling on prayer mats, the artist as a young man walked proudly by his father's side as she was borne aloft before them. Feet crunched the ash path, the church bell tolled. He was conscious of acting the part, of acting through the romantic and tragic scene. There was the sunlight and the breeze blowing and rustling the grass between black tombstones and forgotten graves. There was the lion who spewed water and here the red granite memorial with its carved Grecian urn. It was Alec, walking at the other side of his father, who knocked the edge off the solemnity.

'Is that your sister I was chatting with earlier, Percy?'

'Aye, that's Vera. The other's Dora. They're twins.'

'Oh? Twins, are they?' He turned round briefly to look. 'And you say there's four of you brothers. What about that elderly lady who was in the taxi with you. Who's she?'

Steve tried to concentrate on the drama of the moment but Alec persisted, spoiling it for him. This was a regular run. They were out on a job, searching for the next cleaner and refixer. It continued like that until the vicar brought the procession to heel and the bearers lowered their load, fumbling quickly and adjusting straps before lifting the coffin over and swinging it into the hole.

The vicar, standing stately at the head of the grave, held prayer book at the ready. Harold, in his gravedigger's workclothes, assisted Bella onto his makeshift platform. She allowed him to, then huddled against Lionel as though frozen to the core. They were on the lawn cemetery. There was something vaguely disappointing about it, like receiving a wrong present at Christmas. There'd be no kerb sets for his mother's grave, only the modern, uniform deskhead design to join the others which stretched in a neat mute line. He noticed that they were near the end of the first completed row.

Harold turned next to help Ralph and Ian, but Steve resented the strong hand offered to him. He felt clean and frail against the man's ruddy healthiness. Harold, bareheaded, serious and silent, gave no hint of recognition. He was the funeral's servant.

'Take unto you, we beseech thee, this our beloved sister, Elsa . . .'

His mother bloated and poorly! He thought it strange to have her referred to as his 'sister'. Opposite was his grandmother, standing at the lip of the dark cavity. She too was huddled, eyes closed in pain, no longer able to offer toffees or cling to the mundane. Below them, surrounded by the neatly cut sides of the grave, the clean polished piece of furniture nestled with a perfect fit.

'Ashes to ashes . . .' Almost unnoticed, Harold let fall a few dried peas of earth in the hope of resurrection and eternal life. They peppered with a hollow sound.

'Right, that's it. Come on, lads.' Their father set off back to the taxis with Alec as soon as it was over, avoiding the hovering.

They should have done the same as most of the others were doing, dispersing to their cars or pausing to read the cards on wreaths and flowers. But the three of them remained, gazing down on the gleaming chrome nameplate which bore their mother's name.

'Come on, Stephen,' Hetty beckoned, indicating he should bring his brothers with him. He looked at her, then looked away.

'It's a shame for 'em,' she murmured to those who were standing near her, then reached out to Ian as he came towards her, crying like an abandoned child.

23

He stared at the white void, ignoring the heap of scorched and ripped canvases, the dust, the rubble and pieces of broken glass scattered over the floor by the back window. It was no good asking if it was worth it or what the point of it all might be.

'If you have any belief in what you're doing you'll get on with it, never mind what anybody else might be doing or what beliefs they have. You get nowhere in this life if you don't try, lad.'

His father had told him that, adding, 'But don't expect everything to happen at once. Rome wasn't built in a day.'

Outside it was bright sunshine and fresh, like midsummer again, a warm last day and the end of another brief pause in the long sequence of the working weeks. The weekends seemed to pass so quickly. As for the workdays, summer-at-work had merged into autumn-at-work without any significant break, except for the bank holiday week at the beginning of August when the works had been closed. But there had been no changes, no movement of groups or new arrivals in September for the start of a new academic year. One or two school-leavers after July perhaps, but the men had stayed at their machines, constant, static, buttoning up their boilersuits once the weather turned cooler. Everything had remained in the workshop at this level, undivided by term times, Monday morning blues and wage-packet Friday afternoons, the years rolling on and following on in a monotonous straight line.

The long sequence of the days at work! He had hoped to be in Cornwall by now, or maybe even further, in the

South of France, but Mozz still couldn't be shifted, nor was he himself above making his excuses. Perhaps next spring or next summer. So much for heading off this side of '64.

He stepped back from the two-by-three foot sheet of white emulsioned hardboard, concentrating on the brushmarks of the priming. Rocks on a shoreline, water cascading over escarpments. He turned the hardboard upright on the easel for variation, seeking more images within the void, seas crashing and plunging, swirling like his life, uncertain and caught in the eddying and churning of its uncertainties.

He took another step back and felt a piece of glass crunching underfoot. Catapult marksmen, under the guise of angling, had had a field day in his father's absence, but apart from nailing the usual pieces of planking over the worst of the damage he was refusing to do much about it. Why bother? The cottage was still 'a rum shop' and he looked to the day when he could sell up and move, lock, stock and barrel, to some other place.

His father was downstairs at present, clearing himself an area in which to work. This Sunday morning, as with the previous Sunday morning, he was taking time off from carving and lettering memorials to continue on a more personal effort: 'The Theme of Man', as he had chosen to call it. Constructed out of reinforced concrete, three life-sized caryatid figures, man, woman and child, were set on a curiously arched base which looked like a bridge. The central figure of the man had been given a small compact torso and colossal upstretched arms.

'Mankind bound to the earth, trying to find unity with his fellow men and reaching for the heavens,' had been the tongue-in-cheek explanation.

Whatever the concept behind it, Steve liked to believe that the inspiration for this renewed creative urge had emerged from a Saturday evening's drink they'd had together in the Fleece shortly after his mother died. During that evening, with the impressions of the recent months scorched indelibly on their minds, they had opened themselves to each other, sharing the drama and the frankness of their conversation against the busy murmur of the pub and the ballads of the jukebox which the landlady liked. His father had returned again briefly to that period he would always regard as 'the best years', those years in South Kensington and Chelsea, and in particular the one on the Left Bank of Paris with its various crowded moments and evenings of drinking wine or vodka on café terraces.

London and Paris! He had shaken his head, remembering. They were as remote from the Fleece and its environs as you could get, and they had passed in the blinking of an eye.

'But now you're a free man again,' Steve reminded him, encouraging him, as he'd done before, to view it from this perspective. A part of his life might be over but not his career as a sculptor.

'Ah, sculpture.' His father had chuckled, sceptical. 'Who wants to know about sculpture in these parts?'

'What do these parts matter?' Steve had argued, his father's reluctance to shed the blinkers frustrating him as ever. 'It's you that matters, you as artist and sculptor. You're no longer under any obligations, not to your marriage and definitely not to the folks round here.'

He had so wanted to reach his father, for them to become like close friends doing things together, travelling off to somewhere like Cornwall or sharing a flat in London. He'd even had the crazy notion of his packing in the business and becoming a labourer at Crawley and Pattersons for the novelty of experience, earning money so they could travel.

Of course he never expected that they should ever forget the past months, or disregard the memory of his mother and the loss they inevitably felt. That feeling of emptiness, of loss, came upon them in quiet moments of reflection when she was no longer there in the house. There had been an unaccustomed feel, a sudden starkness when the place where the bed had stood, and finally the coffin, had been taken over by a bookcase and the tidy addition of a chair. The flat surface of the hoovered carpet spreading across the vacant space had been like a slab over her tomb. Sorting through her belongings afterwards, her few pieces of jewellery, her brooches, buttons, keepsakes and her clothing, had intensified the realization that she was gone, yet that evening in the Fleece, enthused by their talk, he had needed to focus on her death as the element which had granted a second chance. Everything had seemed plausible in the crowded immediacy of the pub.

His father knew, however, that things could never be as clean cut and simple as Steve would have liked them. There were still so many obligations and considerations, still 'that lad there' not left school and in need of looking after, and Ralph too wasn't quite as independent as he tried to make out. Those were his restrictions and commitments, though he understood and appreciated what Steve was saying. It offered a gleam of hope for the future, a glimmer in the loneliness which sometimes faced him and which he chose to hide from his sons.

Steve moved over to the table where he kept his materials, the tubes of oil paint with their tops dried and sealed, the brushes stiffened and the rags for cleaning them starched with dust and dry paint. He could hear his father whistling as something heavy was dragged along the floor below. Work was in progress. Soon he would be twisting wire and bending metal rods to shape for armature before mixing and building on with concrete. Around half past one they would hopefully be nipping over the road for 'a quick 'un' before he returned to extend his talents to 'a bit o' bakin' ' and seeing to the dinner back home. His father had had no wish to give up on the family routine and tradition of the Sunday dinner.

Steve hoped they might call in at the Fleece. He looked forward to the familiar lunch-time bustle, the blokes with their darts or dominoes, their beery before-dinner joviality and the landlady's repartee, and her choices on the jukebox giving it all a sense of belonging and permanence. But until then there were things to do.

He picked up one of the tubes of paint, a Prussian blue, and managing with some difficulty to twist the cap off, squeezed some of the colour onto his palette. As he did so he noticed a small hardboard panel, warped and forgotten, and lodged in behind the table. It was one of his old paintings, the dull surface practically obliterated by grime but showing the vague shape of his one and only formalized nude.

He smiled ruefully. Another of his thwarted ambitions! Another abandoned step-on-the-way. No doubt there'd be many others. He took the cleanest of his brushes, then returned to the void, the battered rocks, the swirling sea, the plunging of circumstances, the rocks washed by the waves, washed by the experience of life.